"DIDN'T YOU ADORE THOSE PEACE DOVES, AND THE FLYING FISH?"

"What doves is she talking about?" Martin asked Ellen.

Barry grumbled, "I never saw any fish, just those really annoying screaming meemies."

"What about the flowers? They were incredible."

No one said anything until Ellen laughed. "That's why we teach science and you write books. You always did have the best imagination of anyone I ever knew. You'd look at a cloud and see a rhinoceros with a butterfly on its ear."

No birds, no fish, no flowers? I kept my mouth shut for the rest of the ride home. I dropped my passengers off at Martin's house. He invited us all in for drinks and dessert, but I said I needed to check on the dogs. And my sanity. I'd print out the camera pictures to prove I wasn't crazy or delusional. Ten minutes later I drove up Garland Drive. The road had no lights, but it was well lit by the moon tonight, I thought. Until I got to my own front yard.

Flowers were blooming. That was nothing unusual for late August, but these were incandescent roses seven feet off the ground, on the lawn, where no rosebushes were planted. They waved and bobbed, as if welcoming me home. Then they separated into individual flames that danced close enough for me to see they were the same oversized fireflies that stung Barry. I kept my hands at my sides. My heart was in my throat.

"Hello. You don't really belong here, do you?"

They didn't answer. They didn't show up on my digital camera, either.

"The world-building is the best part . . . The people and places come alive; the fantastical back-story is unusual and fascinating; and the whole of it is definitely something new and extraordinary, and a welcome break from vampires and were-creatures."
—*Errant Dreams*

Fire Works

IN THE

HAMPTONS

A Willow Tate Novel

CELIA JEROME

DAW BOOKS, INC.

DONALD A. WOLLHEIM, FOUNDER

375 Hudson Street, New York, NY 10014

ELIZABETH R. WOLLHEIM
SHEILA E. GILBERT
PUBLISHERS

www.dawbooks.com

First Printing, November 2011
1 2 3 4 5 6 7 8 9

To Anne Bohner, agent extraordinaire

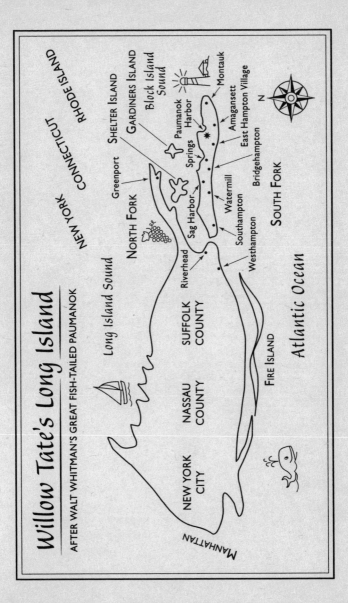

Willow Tate's Long Island

AFTER WALT WHITMAN'S GREAT FISH-TAILED PAUMANOK

Celia Jerome lives in Paumanok Harbor toward the east end of Long Island. She believes in magic, True Love, small dogs, and yard sales.

You can visit Celia at www.celiajerome.com

PROLOGUE

WHERE DO YOU GET YOUR IDEAS? That's the most common question people ask authors at book signings, writers' conventions, and library talks. The stock answers are: the idea fairy, dreams, newspapers, in the shower, or the idea mall, where an author would shop all the time if she had better directions or a GPIS (Global Idea Positioning System.)

But what if the writer's ideas, especially those fantastical, off-the-wall ideas, actually come from another universe where magic abounds? Where trolls and elves and night mares and mental telepathy really exist? What if an author's brilliant visions were nothing but presentiments of forbidden visitors from that unknown, alien universe trespassing on Earth?

Then the world as we know it is going to hell in a handcart, and the author is getting walloped by the wagon as it races past.

Chapter I

I NEEDED A MAN.

Last time I had a girl, then a boy and a troll. Now I wanted a man, a strong, heroic type. For my new book, of course. I'd sworn off real men for life, or until I finished my next book, whichever came first. After all, I'd known and loved two of the most wonderful, talented, intelligent, adventurous, gorgeous, and sexy men—who weren't right for me. What was left? A dull-as-dirt accountant? Been there, done that. And so what if I was thirty-five? If I ever decided to make my mother ecstatic by giving her a grandkid or two, I could always adopt. That's what she did, with dogs. I petted Mom's crippled Pomeranian, who now appeared to be mine. He sniffed my hand for a biscuit. Dogs were a lot easier than men.

Don't get me wrong, I like having a man in my life. What I didn't like was them taking over my life, or them leaving. Picking up the pieces was too painful, so now my career comes first.

I write books, illustrated graphic novels for the young fantasy reader, under the pen name of Willy Tate instead of my too girly-sounding Willow Tate. Kids love them, reviewers love them, my publisher loves them. How cool is that, getting paid to do what I like best?

I write better in my Manhattan apartment without the distractions of the beach and the relatives and the small-town calamities that seem to occur regularly in Paumanok Harbor at the edge of Long Island's posh Hamptons. I might—just might—be responsible for some of the recent chaos, so the sooner I get back to the big city, the better for all of us. I'll leave the week after Labor Day, when my houseguest goes back to teaching middle-level science at a private school in Greenwich, Connecticut. I am happy to have my old college roommate here for the week, but I can't write with Ellen in the house. I have to show her around, see that she's entertained and fed, keep her company on beach walks and bar hops. That's what old friends are for, isn't it?

A few more days and we'll both be back at our jobs and the real world. My cousin Susan can look after my mother's other rescued shelter dogs if Mom doesn't get back from saving a pack of greyhounds in the South, if she can't shut down the tracks altogether. Susan is already living at my mother's house, avoiding her own family's disapproval of her wild ways. I don't exactly approve of all the men she drags home either, but I am less than ten years older than Susan, and definitely not my cousin's keeper.

So nothing is going to keep me in this tiny, ingrown, backwater town past the end of the tourist season. I'll take Ellen to the last big fireworks display in East Hampton on Labor Day weekend, then start packing. I want to see the fireworks, too, for the new story I am working on, or would be working on soon.

The idea for the new book came from all the idiots setting off firecrackers on the beach near my mother's house all summer long. Some were pretty, but most were just loud enough to wake the neighbors and scare the dogs. Inevitably, some kid burned his hand or lost a finger or set the dune grasses on fire. Just as inevitably, the slobs left beer bottles and trash and still-burning coals on the bay-side beaches. Paumanok Harbor's small police force tried to stop them—the bigger, more dangerous ones at least—but the shore was long and dark, and no one wanted to ruin the Hamptons' summer economy by chasing down and arresting tourists. Or their own neighbors' kids.

Illegal firecrackers were easy to come by. I'd seen them sold on street corners in Pennsylvania and Florida. Fools bought them—and recklessly transported them in their own cars!—even though everyone knew only a licensed pyrotechnician, a Grucci-type, could safely set off the really spectacular displays.

That's what I wanted. Not some gunpowder geek, or once-a-summer sparkler setter, but a fire wizard, a pyromage, a red-hot superhero. He'd shoot flames from his fingertips, encircle bad guys in blazes, fight evil with fire. He'd start backfires for forest rangers, and warm stranded mountain climbers until help arrived. A regular Lassie with a flare. Literally.

And there he was, right in my living room when Ellen and I got back from breakfast in Amagansett, the next town over. A man I'd never seen before was fast asleep on the sofa. Tall enough that his feet hung over the end. Dark and handsome, he had an unshaved shadow on his strong jaw, a thick lock of sable hair fallen on his forehead, another sticking up in a boyish cowlick. He was nicely built from what I could see under Mom's patchwork quilt and the black T-shirt he wore. Yup, my hero, except his mouth hung open, an empty beer bottle sat on the coffee table, and one of Mom's old dogs whined next to the couch. The white-muzzled retriever wanted his quilt back.

Ellen took a seat near the sofa and sighed at the stranger. "Oh, my. That's better than the raspberry muffin I just ate. And not half as fattening."

The guy might be a good model for me to sketch, but he sure as hell wasn't an invited guest. I stayed standing up, ready to reach for the fireplace poker or the heavy dog-breed book on the coffee table.

"Quiet," I whispered to Ellen, not ready to defend us from a waking trespasser. "I bet he's one of Susan's strays." My mother brought home old, injured, or abandoned dogs. My cousin brought home men. With abandon.

"Can I keep him?" Ellen asked. "Please."

"He belongs to Susan."

"He's too old for Susan."

He did look more late thirties than mid-twenties, but age didn't count, according to Susan. If a man was breathing, he was fair game. Everyone figured that my cousin's collision with cancer changed her attitude. I never heard of chemo killing a person's scruples, but I made allowances for her, which was why she lived in my house. Besides, she was a great cook.

"He has dimples!"

"Come on, El, we don't even know if he's house-broken."

"Any man this gorgeous has to be."

"Okay. We'll get him a collar and you can take him back to Connecticut with you. Maybe you should buy a six-pack to win his loyalty away from Susan."

As if the name conjured her up, Susan shuffled into the room from the kitchen, a blue pottery mug—mine from one of the craft shows—in her hand. She was wearing an oversize Snoopy T-shirt—mine, too, damn it!— and her hair, pink this week, was in pigtails. She looked about sixteen instead of twenty-six. No one would guess she was head chef at our uncle's restaurant. She was definitely too young for the Romeo in repose.

At least she hadn't put in all the eyebrow hoops. And the nose stud must have been too uncomfortable because I hadn't seen it this week. Not that I missed it.

"He's not too old, and he's not mine," she said now, sitting on the edge of the coffee table sipping her tea. "But he does look cute sleeping like that."

"Yeah, as cuddly as a teddy bear. Get rid of him. You know I draw the line at finding your lovers in my living room."

"I told you, he's not my lover. He stopped by the Breakaway for a late meal last night on his way back to the city from Montauk, but his car died in the parking lot. No one answered at Kelvin's garage to come tow the car, and all the motels were booked with the Labor Day crowd. When the restaurant closed, I offered a ride and the couch. That's all. What was I supposed to do, make him sleep in his car? We stopped off to admire the sunrise."

I'm sorry to admit I snorted at the unlikely tale. The sound wasn't ladylike or mature, and showed a big lack of faith in my own cousin. Little Red, the three-legged Pomeranian, started barking at the sudden noise or when he finally realized yet another stranger had invaded his territory. The bark turned to a snarl when I tried to shush him. Red weighed six pounds but had a seven-pound mean streak. He'd been abused before he came to Paumanok Harbor, so we all made allowances for him, too.

The stranger jerked awake. His eyes, a nice soft brown with yellow flecks, focused on the angry dog, the other dogs, Ellen, me, then finally Susan. You could see his relief at recognizing someone in the room. He gave her a tentative smile.

"Barry, this is my cousin Willow and her friend Ellen. Ladies, this is Barry Jensen." Susan sipped her tea again while the man blinked and brushed his hair back from his eyes. He was definitely cute, but now that he was sitting up I could tell he was older than I thought. The lack of sleep didn't help, but the lines and wrinkles added character to his face, without taking away from the good looks. Clark Kent with a dash of maturity. I could go for that. For my book, of course.

He looked at me. Not at Susan who every male found adorable, and not at Ellen, who was pretty in a whole-some, unfussy way and whose lush figure still made heads swivel when we walked through the village. I made myself pet Little Red instead of trying to hide the coffee drips on my ancient T-shirt, or finger-combing my windblown blonde hair, trying to cover the darker roots, wishing I'd had it colored last week. Wishing I hadn't had a million-calorie muffin for breakfast, too.

"I am so glad to meet you," Barry said. "I've heard great things about you."

"Me?" Okay, I wasn't great at conversation, either.

"When Susan told me who lived here, I was floored."

"You must mean my mother. She's famous. Too bad she's still in Florida."

"Your mother's the dog-lady, isn't she?"

I nodded, gesturing toward the canine collection. "That's my mom, all right. She can do anything with a four-legged stray. Three legs if you count Little Red."

Barry ignored the animals. "But you, you're Willy Tate! I've admired your work for years. I was at that convention where you won the YA graphic novel award. I've followed your career ever since."

So maybe he was a hero after all, instead of a ma-rauder or a mooch. Darn few people outside of friends and family knew my name. "Thanks."

"I've met a bunch of authors in my day. I work free-lance for a small-town news syndicate and website. I do the book page. And I've sold a couple of reviews and articles here and there. But to write and illustrate, both. Wow. And now here I am, on your couch. How's that for luck?"

Luckier than sleeping in a broken-down car, I supposed, or on the beach. "Would you like a cup of coffee? I could put some on. Or tea? I think we have orange juice."

"Nothing, thanks. I don't want to impose."

Ellen went to get the coffee anyway and came back with a bowl of cereal, a creamer of milk, and a glass of OJ.

Barry smiled his appreciation, but kept looking at me. "Damn, I wish I'd met you last week when I didn't have to worry about getting back to Manhattan, or finding a place to stay until the car is repaired. I'd love to write an article about you. You know the kind of thing, how the author lives, a personal glimpse into the real world of a fantasy writer. I can see the picture now, you on the beach, dogs romping in the waves. It could be a winner."

Ellen leaned forward from her chair next to the sofa. "It would be great publicity, Willy."

"I bet Barry could sell an article like that to a bigger audience," Susan added. "Or get it all over the web. I know you're a big fish now, but your pond is kind of small. With the right PR, you could sell a lot more books. Maybe get a bigger advance on your next contract. At least you could get your expenses paid for the next ComicCon."

I refused to think of having to speak at another of those huge conventions. Instead, I admired Barry's dimples and nice white teeth.

The idea of free publicity won me over, not the dimples or the smile, I swear. "Why don't I give you a ride to the garage? We could talk along the way. Then, if Kelvin says your car needs a lot of time for parts or whatever, maybe I could ask around town for a place where you can stay."

"That would be great! Maybe some of your talent will rub off by proximity. Or maybe I'll learn enough just listening to you to start the novel I always wanted to write. You"—he politely gestured toward Susan and

Ellen, after me—"can be my inspiration. Three beautiful women."

Red snapped at his moving hand. "And a ferocious watchdog." He tossed Cheerios at all three dogs.

Yeah, cute. And Mom always said you could judge a man by how he treats a dog. Besides, I needed to see more of him to develop a feel for my fire wizard, facial expressions, musculature, the way his body moved. Character development, you know, research. So I invited him to come watch the fireworks with us.

CHAPTER 2

B ARRY JENSEN WAS NICE. Almost too nice, if that makes sense. He was too pleasant, too complimentary, too interested in me and the village. Or maybe I simply hadn't gotten over the idea of him being one of Susan's leftovers. On the other hand, I was flattered that he'd preferred my company to hers this morning. No one ever accused me of an abundance of logic.

"I've never been to Paumanok Harbor, barely heard of the place," he said when we stopped to get him an egg sandwich on the town's main street.

He didn't seem to notice how Joanne at the deli had the sandwich ready and waiting for him. She winked at me while he looked around at the shops on either side of the wide village green that divided the town, New England style.

"I used to come out to Sag Harbor, but this time I was visiting friends in Montauk. I only stopped off at the Breakaway because I'd read a rave review of your cousin's cooking and wanted to try it for myself. The review didn't do the place justice. Susan is an amazing cook."

Susan was generally a pain in the ass, but she was my baby cousin and I was proud of her. "She uses only the freshest local ingredients, a lot from my grandmother's farm." I didn't say that Grandma Eve's herbs and spices were exotic and possibly ensorcelled, or that Susan's cooking was known to affect a diner's mood. No way was I going to tell a stranger, no matter how nice he was, that I suspected my family of being witches. Actually, I firmly believed my grandmother could cast spells; the jury was still out on Susan.

"It's a cozy little town, isn't it?" he was saying as we decided to walk the few blocks to Kelvin's garage. The weather was perfect for a summer morning, not too hot yet, with a soft breeze and no humidity. "Sweet."

Sweet was one word for it. Bizarre was another, but I wouldn't let that ruin my enjoyment of the day or the company.

"While I was waiting for Susan at the bar last night, some guys were laughing about how Paumanok Harbor had more than its share of harmless characters and kooks, but bad stuff, too. Drug busts, kidnappings, murder, and mass—"

"Hysteria." I quickly interrupted him. "I know. Don't you know better than to believe a bunch of drunks?" Who were telling the truth.

He laughed. "Yeah, and so far I don't see anything out of the ordinary." He turned to smile at me. "Except a lot of sweetness."

I was too old to blush, wasn't I? I pretended to help Little Red up a high curb—and almost got my fingers bitten. Barry's flirting was as refreshing as the gentle breeze with the hint of honeysuckle in the air, but I couldn't let him continue. That is, my ego could have listened to his silly flattery all day, but my rational mind couldn't let him get too curious about Paumanok Harbor. We were part of the whole clandestine Royce-Harmon Institute for Psionic Research, with psychic Royce descendants settling the place centuries ago and inbreeding with witches, shamans, mystics, and nut jobs ever since. I knew our locale was a forbidden gateway between worlds. And I knew better than to discuss the Harbor or its inhabitants with anyone else. I changed the subject. "I bet the same people at the bar still believe mad scientists are conducting mind control experiments in the tunnels under Montauk."

He laughed again. "Yeah, I read some of those books about it. I even looked into the oddball theories about Montauk while I was there, and got lost in the retired air force base near the lighthouse. They've got bunkers and underground artillery batteries, but no tunnels as far as I could find out."

I murmured something about urban legends in the boondocks while I waved to old Mrs. Grissom, hoping she wouldn't give me the latest insights from her husband Vern, who'd been dead for decades. Instead, I pointed out our new arts and recreation center, and the school where Susan's mother was assistant principal. She'd made my friend Ellen a courtesy appointment with the science teacher there for ten o'clock, which is why I had Barry to myself this morning.

Which the entire town noticed. Once again I'd be the topic of the day at the beauty salon and the supermarket and the bowling alley. My mother in Florida would hear I was parading around with a strange man in about an hour, I figured. I turned my cell phone off before she could call.

Barry needed a few things at the drugstore. I waited outside with Little Red, praying the pharmacist wouldn't stuff a few condoms in with Barry's purchases the way Walter always did when he sensed they'd come in handy. I also hoped Bill at the hardware store didn't set the loose nails to jingling an embarrassing tune like "Going to the Chapel." And that no one spoke to Barry about the weather; Paumanok Harbor predictions were always accurate.

"We better hurry," I told him when he came back out to the sidewalk. "Uh, Kelvin might get too busy to look at your car if we wait too long." I picked up Little Red so we could make better time before someone proved just how peculiar Paumanok Harbor could be.

I wasn't that fast, or that lucky, except the cranky Pomeranian was too tired to nip.

Vinnie stood outside his barbershop. He smiled, but shook his head, no.

Big Eddie, with his K-9 police dog, stopped marking tires in the two-hour parking zone to look at us and shake his head.

Micky from the Fire Department shrugged and shook his head.

"They're all shaking their heads. Does that mean I'm trespassing?"

I almost choked. Vinnie's gesture meant Barry had no aura, no paranormal talent. He wasn't one of us. The cop's head shake meant he hadn't smelled anything suspicious on Barry, no drugs, no weapons. Micky's meant Barry wasn't gay. Oh, boy.

"Just the opposite. They're most likely warning me not to mess up. They're friendly, I promise." I walked faster, cutting across the green to avoid as many people as I could. I rushed Barry past the tourists taking pictures in the bandstand and the kids playing ball on their last days before school. I couldn't ignore the locals waving at me to stop and chat, though.

"Have you heard when your mother's coming back?"

"Thanks for teaching my son at that free-your-mind workshop the arts center held. It got him away from his video games for a change."

"When do you think Bayview Ranch will be ready to move horses in, and when will they be hiring? With the crowds leaving, there'll be a lot of folks without jobs."

Barry whistled. "Wow, you know everyone."

I didn't want to tell him they were all checking out the new man in town. Did I mention how everyone in the Harbor agreed with my mother—my divorced mother—that it was high time I got married? Skewed logic ran in the family, as well as eccentricity.

Mom wanted grandchildren. The psychic crew wanted to find out what kind of kid I could produce, to propagate the species of paranormal oddities. That was another reason I was eager to go back to the city. No one there cared whether a woman was single or not, pregnant or not. Well, no one knew me that well, either. Maybe they didn't care, but at least they didn't nag.

Barry didn't pick up on the unspoken interest in him as a sperm donor. Thank goodness.

"No wonder you like this place. It's clean and open and the people are friendly. I bet you and your neighbors started those rumors about mad cow disease and magic tricks just so you wouldn't be overrun like the rest of the Hamptons. I can see why you've kept your little corner of heaven a well-kept secret."

See? He didn't see anything, not the sly looks, not the small-time surrealism. Which didn't say much for a would-be writer's powers of observation. Paumanok Harbor held more secrets than the CIA. If the CIA knew what we could do here, they'd have us flown to Guantanamo, or declare Paumanok Harbor a quarantine area and condemn it, with the inhabitants held captive inside barricades for experiments and government work. Talk about captive breeding programs, we'd belong to Uncle Sam. If we weren't all burned at the stake.

We? Funny how I couldn't wait to leave, but still thought of myself as one of them, the oddball espers. I have almost come to accept that I am one of them, no matter how hard I've tried to avoid the fact.

Kelvin reminded me.

When Barry instantly agreed to the semi-exorbitant

price he charged just for the tow, the mechanic grinned in approval. He liked the new guy. His eleven-year-old son, Kelvin Junior, also known as K2 for his size and appetite, liked the baby blue Mercedes convertible. He liked it so well he stepped back so his ice cream cone didn't drip on the shiny paint job.

Barry didn't pay any attention to the kid or Little Red, who was licking the drips off K2's bare toes. Yeck. "What do you think is wrong?" Barry asked Kelvin Senior.

"Won't start," was all Kelvin said, wiping his hands on a rag. He thought he might have time to take a better look at it this afternoon. If he couldn't get it going today, though, Barry might have to wait until Tuesday. This was Friday and no one delivered parts over Labor Day weekend.

"Of course I could tow the car to the Mercedes dealer in Southampton, not that they'll look at it until Tuesday either, by the time I can get it to them."

"That's okay," I said. "Barry's staying for the weekend. He wants to see the fireworks in East Hampton Sunday night. And he thinks I can help him with the novel he wants to write."

Kelvin bent down to scratch his big toe. K2 wiped his runny nose on his sleeve.

Uh-oh. The supernatural strikes again. Kelvin was from the founders' clan of human lie detectors. His itchy toe and K2's congestion signaled that what I just said was a lie. I repeated my words in my head. Barry didn't want to see the fireworks in East Hampton? He seemed excited when Ellen mentioned it, offering to bring marshmallows to the beach. He wasn't going to write a novel? Almost everyone I met wanted to write one. He didn't think I could help? Of course I could; I was a professional. So the two Kelvins must have reacted to my lie. Barry wasn't staying for any of those reasons. He was staying for me, because I wanted him to, even if I didn't want another man in my life. I wanted to do some sketches of him for my book, take some photos of him at the fireworks to paint later. Research, perfectly legitimate research. And a good thing neither Kelvin could read minds.

We met Ellen at the school and listened to her rave about Mr. Martin Armbruster, the seventh grade science teacher she'd just met. He was smart and funny and the kids adored him. He had students go on to win science fairs and get scholarships to MIT. He was well-read and well-conditioned for a middle-aged bachelor. He had a new honors project he was willing to share with Ellen. And he was coming with us to see the fireworks Sunday night. So now I didn't have to feel bad about monopolizing Barry.

While we were at the school, I stopped in to see my aunt Jasmine, Susan's mother. She was willing to let Barry sleep in Susan's old room for a couple of nights, if he'd come back for Career Day to tell the kids about book reviewing and writing for the Internet.

So now my reputation was pulled out of the gossip muck, and Barry was still across the road from my mother's house on the private drive leading to Grandma Eve's home, farm, and produce stand.

In return, he treated all of us—Ellen, Aunt Jas, and me—to lunch at the clam bar at Rick's Marina. Susan met us there and he put the whole meal on his credit card. Nice, huh?

By the time we got home, Susan had to leave for work. The restaurant was facing its busiest weekend of the summer and she had to prepare. Barry took his suitcase over to Aunt Jasmine's, and Ellen went up to study Mr. Armbruster's syllabus for seventh grade honors science.

Knowing I couldn't put it off any longer, I checked

my phone messages. Yup, two from my mother on the landline, one on my cell. My father had called, too.

I called him first. He was a half-assed clairvoyant, not a hard-wired matchmaker. He'd recently had a heart attack, so I didn't want him to worry. "How are you feeling, Dad?"

"All recovered from the bypass surgery," he told me. "Not quite recovered from your mother's visit."

"She worries about you." That was my job, mediating. I'd had a lot of practice at it before they finally separated, to the relief of all of us. "You needed someone to take care of you when you got out of the hospital."

"I didn't need her lecturing the condo board about allowing pets in the building. Or shouting at my neighbors for going to the dog track. Or—"

"She's on her way back north, isn't she? I bet you miss having someone to fight with."

"Not as much as I miss you, baby girl. I don't know what I ever saw in that woman, but I wouldn't do anything different because I got you out of the deal."

"Aw, Dad, cut it out before I get weepy. I miss you, too."

"I don't mean to make you cry, Willy. I just wanted to warn you about something."

Here it comes, another of my father's inscrutable alerts. It wasn't his fault, I knew. He got feelings of doom connected to those he loved, but the feelings didn't come with names, times, or places, only vague clouds of foreboding. "What is it, Dad?"

"Old tables. Don't know what or why. Just watch out, baby girl."

If that was the worst of it, nothing would ruin my nice weekend. I wouldn't lean on the rickety wicker table on the porch, or sit under the dining room table in an earthquake. "Got it, Dad. Thanks."

I took a deep breath and called my mother. "Yes, he's

handsome. Likes books. Must have money to judge by his car and buying lunch. Yes, he's single. No, he's not talented."

I hadn't seen his writing yet, but we both knew those weren't the kinds of talents I meant.

Mother sniffed her disappointment. After all, I'd almost been engaged to a wealthy English lord who half ran the Department of Unexplained Events. "Does he like dogs?"

"Little Red hasn't bitten him yet." He tried and missed, so that doesn't count.

"That's a good sign. Put him on the phone."

Let my mother talk to a man I'd just met this morning? In her dreams. "Barry's staying with Aunt Jas for the weekend. He's over there now, unpacking."

"Not the newcomer. I want to talk to the dog."

I tried to be subtle, without being insulting. "Uh, Mom, Ellen is here."

Even my mother had her limits. "Oh. Well, be careful."

"I know. Old tables."

"Huh?"

"Dad mentioned that. Danger in old tables."

"He's an old patoot, your father. Don't listen to him. He never makes any sense anyway. Have a good time. And ask your young man if he'll adopt a retired greyhound."

"He's not my—"

She hung up. I should have let Little Red talk to her.

Chapter 3

THE SCIENCE TEACHER CALLED on Saturday and invited us to go out on his boat. Ellen was thrilled and begged me to come. I was not thrilled. Boats and I didn't do well together. Some of my worst experiences have been on board something too flimsy to float. Hell, the one I was on a few months ago—not by my choice, either—caught on fire and sank. How could I admit to one of my oldest friends that I was uncomfortable, if not terrified, any time my feet were not on solid ground? That included boats, planes, skis, and elevators.

"I get seasick."

"There's not a breeze in the air, not a whitecap in sight. Not even you could get sick on a day like today. Besides, Martin said we're following the shoreline, not going out into the Sound. You have no excuse except you're still the same chickenshit you always were."

That was the trouble with longtime friends. They had long memories. "Don't you want to spend time alone with your new friend?" They had a lot in common, chief of which was they were both single, living in areas without many opportunities to meet like-minded adults of the opposite sex. "Yes, but I don't want to be so obvious about it. He said you could invite Barry, too. And Susan."

Susan refused. "Spend the day with my old science teacher? Ee-uw. 'Sides, I'd worry about calling him Farty Marty to his face."

Ellen gasped. "You didn't call him that, did you?"

"Of course. Everyone did."

Ellen called to invite Barry before I could tell her not to. I didn't want him to see me wretched, or retching.

He agreed instantly, of course. "Perfect day for a sail."

A sailboat was ten times worse! They always rocked or got becalmed or heeled over or whatever you call the step before capsizing. "I need to work."

"I thought you said we were going to the beach today." Ellen started packing a bag with sunscreen, bottled water, and binoculars. "You weren't going to get a lot done anyway. The only difference is we'll be on the water instead of in it."

I prayed we stayed that way.

Martin had a converted lobster boat, not a sail in sight but only a single sputtering engine. The boat's name, hand-painted on the back, was the *She Crab*. I wondered if that was the original name, or if Martin was a misogynist. The tub smelled like a dead fish anyway.

It was low and narrow, with a shallow draft, according to Martin's lecture about its history. *Her* history, he corrected me. The craft was a she. That's what he thought. No female would tolerate a boat without a bathroom, only a bucket. A *head*, he said. There was a tiny three-sided protected cabin for the driver. *The captain*, Martin preferred. And benches installed along the low sides. *Gunwales*. There was a tiny deck up front. *Fore*. Where Martin thought I should sit to be lookout. *Jackass*.

The *She Crab* contained one other furnishing: a stained and scarred wooden table bolted to the deck. An old table, like my father warned me about. I eyed it warily.

Barry was so damn cheerful about leaving the dock I

wanted to throw something at him, but I wasn't about to touch the bucket. Okay, so he wasn't a sensitive, but couldn't he see my hands shaking, my knees knocking? I was wearing shorts, for Pete's sake.

I relaxed some when we got underway with no problem. Barry went forward for a better view, so I took out my sketch pad to capture him looking heroic in a black T-shirt and surfer baggies with the sea and the sky as background. If I concentrated on him enough, I wouldn't notice the distance from shore, or the doom-laden table.

About twenty minutes later, Marty announced we had to collect water and seaweed samples and whatever else we found in the shallows, for his students' experiments. He turned the engine off, having more confidence than I did that it would start again. We were close enough to shore that I figured I could swim.

The boat drifted while he leaned over the side with a long net, directing a suddenly giggly Ellen to lean next to him with a pail.

Barry came back and started asking Martin about the shore and the village and the events of the summer.

"Can you point out where the drugs were stored? How many people came to watch? Where did that yacht blow up, and how did they rescue the kid?"

The *She Crab* was drifting sideways, rolling with the tide, roiling my stomach. Memories of those awful events weren't helping. Nor were Martin's answers. He wasn't there, wasn't a sensitive, wasn't aware of the otherworldly actions. What he was doing was feeding Barry's curiosity.

"Isn't it time for lunch?" I chirped, although food was the last thing I wanted. They ate the sandwiches Martin had packed. I ate some crackers. Then they went back to filling bottles and plastic bags for the science lab while I sketched some more.

"Hey, look at that," Martin said, calling Ellen and Barry to where he leaned over the rail.

Three passengers on one side? Were they crazy or just plain stupid? I held onto that old table as if my life depended on it. Maybe it did. They caught an eel.

If there is anything in the world worse than a writhing snake with slime, it's knowing what Barry wanted to do with it.

"Why don't we skin it, then slice it up for sushi?" While it was alive.

I lost my lunch—and my hero. Barry Jensen looked a lot better on paper than he did in person.

Being sick excused me from cleaning the boat and going out for beers and burgers after. What I did instead was go home, get the dogs, and head for a secluded, residents-only beach. The rocky shoreline kept it pretty empty, the way I liked it. We walked some, the big dogs played in the warm shallow water for a while, and Little Red barked at the seagulls. Then I spread an old blanket, set up an umbrella so the dogs didn't get hot, and contemplated the waves and life.

That's what writers did: consider plots, characters, and the human condition.

That's what fearful introverted idiots did: retreat and worry. All my efforts led to one conclusion. Maybe I could never be as comfortable with any man as I was with my dogs.

I still had to get through all day Sunday and the fireworks after dark.

Barry moved in with his new best friend Martin, having found Aunt Jasmine and Uncle Roger not as welcoming as he wished, and not as forthcoming with information for his story. Martin had no problem telling everything he knew, which, as seemed usual, wasn't as much as he thought he knew. Ellen thought I was being overcritical and old-maidish. I thought she was too eager.

Either way, Barry learned more about Paumanok

Harbor and me than was healthy. He tried to be attentive and caring, bringing coffee and buns for breakfast, telling me how amazing everyone thought I was, what joy he heard the town took in having a successful writer, a brave heroine as one of their own, how lucky he was to know me. What a great story he'd get out of this visit.

My eyes saw his wide smile. My head saw that wriggling eel on the old table. I told him I changed my mind. I didn't want that kind of publicity. Reviews of my books were one thing, excursions into my private life—and Paumanok Harbor's—were another. He wouldn't listen. Modesty, he told me, couldn't help anyone climb the ladder of fame. So I gave up a little privacy. Every celebrity did.

I replied that I had to help my grandmother at the farm.

No matter what anyone told him about me or Paumanok Harbor, they had to mention my grandmother and the genital warts. No one messed with Eve Garland.

Explaining the fireworks was safe. Ragging on East Hampton Village was always fun for those of us who belonged to East Hampton Township but couldn't use the village beaches, although they could use ours. We also had to pay sky-high school taxes to the village for our high schoolers, without any say in how our kids were educated. And their tourists were snobs, their main street stores were snooty. So we were glad when their Fourth of July celebration got screwed up.

In what might be its most ordinary ritual, Paumanok Harbor always held its festivities on the Fourth, whatever day of the week it happened to be. We had a concert on the village green, then fireworks over the bay beaches. The weather always cooperated. With our resident weather dowsers, it had no choice.

As for our other near neighbors? Southampton had a

big parade on the Fourth. Sag Harbor's fire department ran a carnival and a light show for three nights on the nearest weekend. Montauk, as ornery as a wild Western steer, to use my Texan friend Ty Farraday's expression, had to postpone their fireworks two years in a row due to rain, wind, or fog. So they moved July Fourth to Columbus Day weekend when the weather was still more uncertain and a lot colder, but the fireworks companies charged less. And their Chamber of Commerce, we all figured, decided the last town on the South Fork had enough tourists in early July, but not enough in mid-October. The Montauk Library did hold a huge book fair in the center of town on the Saturday of the long Independence weekend, which clogged up the roads back to Amagansett.

But East Hampton, that beautiful elm-shaded village with its swan pond and windmills and proud colonial history, could not hold a traditional holiday celebration until Labor Day. A certain shore bird nested on the only beach deemed suitable, big enough for the masses of viewers, far enough away from the mansions. Any crowds at Main Beach could step on the hatchling piping plovers; the noise could frighten the parents into abandoning the chicks. And the endangered species regulations forbade endangering the small gray sandpipers until they were hatched, fledged, and on their way.

It wasn't the Boston Pops or a Macy's Manhattan extravaganza, but East Hampton usually put on a nice show for the end of summer if you liked firecrackers, smoky beach fires, burned marshmallows, and parking miles away.

On our way there, stuck in traffic, Barry wanted to chat about this summer's horse show at the school's playing field. Paumanok Harbor had hosted Ty Farraday, his Lipizzaner mare, and some other entertainers in a huge fund-raiser to purchase an abandoned ranch.

"Martin said it was spectacular, but he couldn't remember how it ended."

The equestrian show had ended with the mayor telling the audience of thousands to forget they'd seen a prancing line of riderless, iridescent white horses rise up in majestic synchronicity, then disappear into the night sky. It was awesome. And impossible.

Mayor Applebaum often forgot to attend the board meetings and his lunch and his trousers, but when he ordered ordinary, un-para people to forget, a haze settled over their memories. The mayor's real job was keeping Paumanok Harbor out of the news and off the Close Encounter radar.

"The last act was classic dressage from the Spanish Riding School ending in Airs above the Ground," I told Barry and Ellen.

Martin nodded. He remembered that much. "It was amazing. But what about after?"

"Afterward, the mayor asked everyone to leave quickly but in an orderly fashion because an electric storm threatened."

Martin said he didn't remember Mayor Applebaum's speech or the storm either.

"I don't think it ever materialized, but the police didn't want to take a chance, not with such a big crowd and so many cars on the narrow roads."

Barry seemed to accept the explanation. Then he asked, "What about you and the rodeo rider?"

I gave Martin a dirty look for gossiping about me. Then I gave Barry a dirty look for prying. "We're friends, and it's none of your—"

"Oh, look." Ellen tapped me on the shoulder. "There's a parking space."

CHAPTER 4

MY COUSIN HAD TO WORK at the restaurant. My grandmother said she'd seen enough fireworks to last through the winter.

I'd rather have more company, but we were on our own. I drove Mom's Outback because it could hold the most.

Ellen and I brought a blanket, two low beach chairs, sweaters, and a bag of Oreos.

Barry brought a bottle of wine and four plastic glasses.

Martin brought a large cooler, a shovel, one of those little shrink-wrapped bundles of firewood and kindling, a plastic garbage bag and a metal bucket for water to douse the fire and then carry home the hot embers. No absentminded professor, Mr. Armbruster. No muscle man either. By the time we got all his stuff from the car to the beach, he was breathing so hard Ellen made him sit in her chair while she fussed about unpacking the heavy cooler. Barry spread the blanket and made a big show of opening the wine bottle.

So it had a cork. Big deal. I didn't drink wine; it gave me a headache whether it cost five dollars or fifty. I started digging the hole for the fire, figuring one of the men would relieve me shortly.

"Deeper," Martin ordered.

Barry was going from group to group nearest us in the sand. He needed to borrow a corkscrew because the cheap one from the liquor store broke.

I kept digging.

Ellen cooed over the food she unpacked, enough for all the families Barry was chatting up. You'd think we'd skipped dinner a couple of hours ago the way she was exclaiming over hot dogs and potato salad and cheese and crackers and—

If there was sushi in that ice chest, I was going home.

Martin recovered his wind in time to stand over me and direct the placing of each freaking split log. He used a battery-operated lighter to catch the newspapers he wadded up. No super firepower for him, either.

My chair, naturally, was downwind of our blaze so I couldn't see anything past the tears in my eyes. If I moved across the pit I'd dug, my back would be to the fireworks, which was what I came to see. Not a cloud of smoke or a shrimp on a skewer.

I moved to sit sideways on the blanket. Barry took my chair.

Someone had a boom box going loud with patriotic tunes, so it almost felt like July Fourth, right down to the whiny "When is it going to start?" from a little boy on a nearby blanket.

"Not until dark," Martin shouted across the sand. "Eight minutes, by my calculations."

"Isn't he wonderful?" Ellen leaned over to whisper to me, a hot dog in one hand, a plastic wineglass in the other. Her second glass, but who was counting?

Yeah, if you wanted a Boy Scout leader. I smiled as best I could. She couldn't see in the near dark anyway.

My supposed date was checking his watch by the firelight, as impatient as the kid next door. I could have told him the real show never started on time, but people up and down the shoreline had campfires and sparklers and small rockets. Some of the big houses along the shore had impressive, expensive, noisy fireworks we could see, hear, and smell from the beach. So there was plenty to watch if Barry bothered to look around. Kids had those glow stick things around their necks so that their parents could find them, and an armada of boats cruised out past the breakers, their running lights brightening the distance, their flares streaking across the sky. Stars started to show up, and the moon left silver ribbons on the ocean. Scenes like that could steal your breath.

Barry had another glass of wine and complained he should have brought a six-pack. Martin and Ellen shared a burnt marshmallow, more wine, and a sticky kiss. Oh, boy. I made mental notes of the background for my story and how I'd draw it. I took some experimental pictures with my digital camera for future reference, but the private firecrackers didn't stay up long enough for me to get what I needed. The official ones would, I knew. I wasn't sure how I'd work the scene into my new book, but how could I have a fire wizard with no blazing stars in the dusky night? No dueling flamethrowers? No sky-rockets?

"Damn, we could have come an hour later," Barry bitched. I was expecting him to start kvetching about needing a bathroom like the overtired, sugared-up kid at the next blanket. Instead, he wanted more information about how Paumanok Harbor's fireworks never got rained out when Montauk's did, eight miles away.

"Luck of the draw," I improvised. "And they're on the ocean side. We're on the Sound side, Block Island Sound, which meets up with the Long Island one that everyone knows. Sometimes there's fog on one shore, bright sun on the other. Martin can explain it better."

And at great length. I tuned them all out and walked away to photograph the Coast Guard cruiser and its roving searchlight. They patrolled the water so no boat wandered into the marked-off area near the fireworks barge or where sparks could land, the same way the police drove three-wheeled beach buggies through the crowds. As it got darker, I wondered how they avoided all the children and dogs and entwined couples.

Boom!

I turned fast, but forgot to raise the camera. A brilliant red cluster rose high into the night.

Ooh!

White squiggles spun around the red with a high-pitched whistle.

Aah!

Finally, blue sparks shot through the falling screamers higher still.

Everyone cheered. It was like the Fourth of July after all.

After that, the show picked up speed, with one dazzling array of colors and shapes and heights after another. The smoke barely cleared from one cascading giant chrysanthemum than another erupted with a shimmering waterfall of multiple rockets. The burning colors swirled, circled, bled into each other time and again while the crowd clapped and cheered. I didn't know if we were watching Catherine wheels, Roman candles, girandoles, or pinwheels. I'd have to look up technical names later. My favorites were the offshoot sizzlers that whistled as they raced around. My father used to say they were scurrying mice, chasing their tails.

There was stuff I'd never seen before, and I'd seen some of the best. Give East Hampton credit; they did things up right when they did it.

Barry thought Macy's put on a better show. I wanted

to tell him to shut up. Instead, I moved away, taking pictures, getting lost in the entirety of the night: the ground-shaking detonations, the acrid smell, the wispy smoke that drifted back across the moon, the happy chorus of oohs and aahs every time another rocket went up. I marveled at the different colors, different patterns, different durations before the embers burned out or fell safely to the ocean.

I could almost see my hero stepping out of a ball of fire. He could make the stars spin, set the waves aflame, make day out of the darkest night.

He could ... make a bright yellow smiley face high overhead? With a glowing garden of iridescent flowers hung beneath it?

The crowds roared their approval. I had to laugh. I guess he could, if he wanted. If the Gruccis could work this magic, think what a fire wizard could do.

The next image was a multicolored peace sign. Not a great one because it listed to one side, but it was recognizable, as were the scores of white doves circling around it. The thousands of watchers along the shore were almost hoarse by now, their hands sore from clapping.

They found the strength to cheer East Hampton's emblem, a flaming windmill with its vanes spinning in different colors.

More clusters soared up and opened out, with more squealing mice-rockets, vast flower shapes blooming across the sky, turning the night bright enough to see Barry tipping the wine bottle up to his lips to drain the last of it.

"Isn't it wonderful?" I asked.

He shrugged.

Ellen was sitting in Martin's lap, making out. Couldn't they have waited ten minutes? There were kids nearby, maybe Martin's students. And they were missing the explosions of vibrant, moving colors. I snapped pictures, of them, of the watchers, of the amazing starbursts the technicians had created.

Then came the finale, a red, white, and blue flag surrounded by a crescendo of shooting stars in every direction, noise that drowned out the crowd's appreciation. Boomer after boomer roared as the flag winked out, filling the sky with every color of the rainbow from straight overhead to the horizon. New images appearing, a school of leaping, glowing fish, a flock of birds winging across the night, another meadow of living flowers that seemed so close you could reach out and pick one, as a gift, an offering.

And then silence. The crowd was as awed as I was, with no words to describe what we'd all seen. "Wow" didn't half express the feeling, but I heard wows from every side as the last glowing flowers drifted away, except one.

"Holy shit," Barry yelled. "Those are sparks, and they're headed here!"

Sparks? That was impossible. He put his hand out, though, to swat at a flicker with the empty wine bottle. He missed and cursed louder, grabbing at his hand. "Damn, I got burned."

More tiny embers were falling near us.

"Run," the people closest to us started yelling. "Fire!"

I stared up. "No, they're just lightning bugs."

"They're too big for fireflies," Martin declared. "Furthermore, fireflies do not bite."

It didn't matter. People were running toward the nearest beach paths to get away. Then they ran right over the dunes in a panic, picking up more ticks and chiggers that caused far more damage than fireflies ever did. The frightened hordes left their fires, their garbage, their blankets and chairs, and maybe their children for all I knew.

The burning flowers had all dissipated, leaving the beach in total darkness and disarray except for Martin's D-cell lantern, the occasional flashlight, and the beach patrol buggies' headlights as they tore around, urging caution, an orderly exit.

"No need to panic, folks. There was one gust of wind that carried a couple of sparks. Clean up, put out all fires."

No one in our immediate vicinity stayed to listen, even though the emergency had passed. So Martin and Ellen and I carried buckets of water to put out fires, using the shovel to spread the coals and kindling. We filled our garbage bag and took our own trash, but that was all we could do in the dark.

Barry was still nursing his fingers, so Ellen and I carried the garbage to the nearest cleared path where cleanup crews could find it in the morning. Then we went back to lug the slightly less heavy cooler to the paved parking lot that was almost empty by now. Martin and his lantern led the way with the chairs. Barry carried my blanket.

I left them there to go get the car, still half a mile away. I had my little dog-walking flashlight clipped to my belt, so I didn't mind. And I could swear I saw fireflies lighting my way.

When I got back with the car, Martin and Ellen were locked together on the cooler, heating it up like teenagers. Barry paced around, muttering about small-town bozos who shouldn't be allowed near explosives, and how there'd be lawsuits in the morning.

"But didn't you love the fireworks? I thought whoever they hired did an amazing job, and everyone else had a great time until you scared them."

"Me? I was the one who got burned."

"You got stung, or maybe you got an allergic reaction. No one else felt a spark."

He muttered something I couldn't hear, thankfully, or I might have stopped the car to throw him out. Instead I tried to lighten the mood for Ellen's sake.

"Didn't you adore those peace doves, and the flying fish?"

"What doves is she talking about?" Martin asked her.

Barry grumbled, "I never saw any fish, just those really annoying screaming meemies."

"What about the flowers? They were incredible."

No one said anything until Ellen laughed. "That's why we teach science and you write books. You always did have the best imagination of anyone I ever knew. You'd look at a cloud and see a rhinoceros with a butterfly on its ear."

No birds, no fish, no flowers? I kept my mouth shut for the rest of the ride home.

I dropped my passengers off at Martin's house. He invited us all in for drinks and dessert, but I said I needed to check on the dogs. And my sanity. I'd print out the camera pictures to prove I wasn't crazy or delusional. Martin could bring Ellen home later, unless she spent the night at his place. Her choice.

Ten minutes later I drove up Garland Drive, the dirt path that passed my mother's and Aunt Jasmine's houses on the way to Grandmother Eve's house, fields, and farm stand. The road had no lights, but it was well lit by the moon tonight, I thought. Until I got to my own front yard.

Flowers were blooming. That was nothing unusual for late August, but these were incandescent roses seven feet off the ground, on the lawn, where no rosebushes were planted. They waved and bobbed, as if welcoming me home. Then they separated into individual flames that danced close enough for me to see they were the same oversized fireflies that stung Barry. I kept my hands at my sides. My heart was in my throat.

"Hello. You don't really belong here, do you?"

They didn't answer. They didn't show up on my digital camera, either.

Uh-oh. I'd done it again.

CHAPTER 5

NO, NO, AND NO. I did not call up any kind of fire-fly. If—and I am only saying if—I could conjure up an enchanted being from another world, an airborne match wouldn't be my first choice.

Yes, I'd been thinking of a hero who used fire in the fight of good versus evil. I did not wish for, pray for, or cast incantations for some bugs that could burn up Paumanok Harbor. I had a story in my head, not a gate-crashing insect invasion of Earth in my front yard. When I was fantasizing about a new story, I never, ever thought about another world that was supposedly a parallel universe, filled with magical, telepathic creatures and separated from us by spells and glamour. Last spring, I'd never heard of a world called Unity. Half the time I didn't believe it existed, until one of its residents landed on my doorstep. But I never called them, I swear!

I went back outside, leaving the dogs indoors, to their displeasure. The sparks of light still twinkled here and there, just like on an ordinary summer night filled with the scent of honeysuckle and the sounds of peepers and crickets. Not so ordinarily, the brightest sparkles quickly flew into formation as a tree. No, a burning bush. Holy hell, had they read the Bible? Had they posed for the Bible?

I shook my head, and the bush dissolved into a ball of fire at the level of my head. I didn't feel threatened, not when the ball bounced and swayed playfully. The bugs seemed to be dancing to a merry tune only they could hear. I couldn't hear their voices, out loud or in my head, but I sensed the hundreds of flies packed close together were happy to see me.

I was not happy to see them. "Shoo," I said. "Go home." I was careful to keep my voice low and my hands at my sides, mindful of the blister—a tiny one, for all his complaining—on Barry's finger. It wouldn't do to antagonize small visitors with big powers.

Gentle verbal commands didn't work, so I visualized a different place, one with big red trolls and snow-white horses where the language was half vocal, half mental. "Go home," I said, and thought it as hard as I could.

Either my mind's pictures didn't look like their home or my telepathic powers were zilch or insects didn't understand English, but they bounced around into a cloud of softly glowing lights, a swath like a comet's tail. They weren't going away.

I slowly raised both hands, palms up, in a show of nonaggression. Two of the creatures separated from the swarm and flew close, then landed on my hands, nearly filling them. If the fireflies had been spiders, I'd have fainted. Bees, I'd be screaming and running. Mosquitoes, I might have slammed my hands together. Instead I felt no fear or repulsion, no scorching pain. There was only a slight tingle and a warmth in my hands, almost a lover's caress. "That's right, I'm a friend."

Maybe they were inspecting me the way I was studying them, because the two advance envoys took off and flew around my head, my hair, down to my feet, then back to their buddies as if they were reporting in. I still couldn't hear or sense what they were saying, so communication wasn't working. Hell, they were bugs; I was an accidental esper.

They looked like a lot of earthly insects to me, whose usual contact with the bugs was to panic at anything with a lot of legs. Long Island lightning bugs weren't a tenth the size of these green gossamer-winged wildlife, and didn't have coruscating blue eyes that appeared to reflect intelligence. If I recalled right, our fireflies glowed at mating season to find each other. They glowed from a chemical reaction, not from internal combustion in their abdomens.

"Please go away. People here will not understand. They'll be afraid. They might try to hurt you, like Barry did."

People—especially nonpsychics—wouldn't see the aliens the way they actually looked. They'd see lasting sparks, or they'd see larger than usual night fliers out courting, almost-familiar things their minds could accept. Only I, by some weird stroke of luck, could see whatever got across the gates between worlds. Luck? Why couldn't I win the lottery if I was so lucky? No, I was stuck with the kind of good fortune that let me be rare, misunderstood, and helplessly ill-equipped. I have no idea why I was chosen to be a link between the two worlds, a Visualizer, unless it was the ancient amulet I wore around my neck, made from my mother's wedding band. The linguists from the Department of Unexplained Events had translated it as: One life. One heart. I and thou. One forever. Maybe the bugs recognized it as something from their world. Maybe it spoke to them. It sure as hell didn't speak to me. I hadn't found my one true love, only beings that couldn't, shouldn't, exist on Earth. I saw the troll while others saw only the chaos he caused.

"Listen, guys, nothing from Unity is supposed to

come here," I explained to the fireflies in case they didn't know. I felt like an absolute fool for talking to them, but what else could I do? "No one here is supposed to see you, not ever. Not even as an image on a camera lens. Those are the rules."

Without knowing how, why, or when, I kept breaking those interdictions. For a minute I was filled with pride and wonder at the shimmering blessing I'd been given. Then I wondered what I was supposed to do with flying cockroaches with incendiary instincts.

Who could I ask for help, when no one else saw the fireflies for what they were, only the trouble they left behind?

I did not cause the trouble!

"Go. They'll blame me. Or make me find a way to get rid of you. That's not my job. I'm an author, not an exterminator."

I shouldn't have said the word, or thought it. The bugs' behinds burst into flame.

"No, I won't let anyone harm you." I hoped. They must have understood something, maybe the hope part, for they went back to glowing. "But you have to leave, really. You won't like the dirty air or the polluted water. Or the people. They're not like the ones you're used to." Who might speak Insect the way my city neighbor Mrs. Abbottini spoke Italian.

I tried not to think about flyswatters, electric bug zappers, insect repellents. My God, the health department might still be doing vector control to kill mosquitoes. "You could get soaked with poisons. You have to find your way back. I know there's a gate in Paumanok Harbor."

That's why everything weird showed up here. Well, not everything if you count yetis and the Loch Ness monster and UFOs. But enough bizarre stuff happened in the tiny Hampton's stepchild that we were getting our own branch of England's Royce Institute, with its Department of Unexplained Events.

Paumanok Harbor still had tourists. It did not need any more hassles. I didn't need them either, not if I wanted to get back to my uneventful life in Manhattan.

"Scram. I'm leaving here soon, so you'll be on your own. No one will appreciate how pretty you are, no one will be your friend." Maybe I was projecting enough of my own angst to get through to them. I didn't know if they had hive mentality—or no rationality whatsoever— but the swarm dissipated, tiny sparks separating to look like low stars scattered across the night.

I went in and did what any mostly nondrinking person would do under the circumstances. I ate the rest of the bag of Oreos.

Ellen never came home; I never went to sleep. As early as polite in the morning, I phoned my father.

"Hi, Dad. I'm calling to see how you're doing, and if you've sensed any bugs."

"You've got the flu, baby? Should I send your mother home?"

Sure, if he wanted to kill me. "Not that kind of bug, Dad."

"What, Bugs Bunny? A Volkswagen? You know I don't like foreign cars. That's why your mother went out and bought a Subaru, just to spite me."

"The Outback is a good car. I meant—"

He lowered his voice to a whisper: "You think someone is tapping your phone? That's what happens when you mess with those secret initialed organizations."

"No, Dad, I'm talking about real bugs. Insects. Big flying things."

"You should see the size of the bugs we've got here in Florida. And fire ants! The exterminators are as busy as the EMTs. But no, I've got no worries about real bugs,

Willy, so I'd guess whatever's around is no danger to you."

"Thanks, Dad."

"Just . . . maybe."

"Maybe what?"

"I'm not sure. You know how it is, I just get feelings. Words, images, bad dreams."

My father's presentiments seldom made sense at first; they often came true later. "So what are you sensing now?"

"Maybe. A scary *maybe*. I'm sorry, baby, I can't tell you any more. It's turning and hazy."

Or crazy. "Thanks for trying. Forewarned is fore-armed, right? That's what you always say."

"Right. Remember the old tables. I get shivers thinking about them."

The eel on the boat table was bad enough. I put that and *maybe* from my mind and took the dogs for a walk. I searched bushes and flowers, trees and high grasses, but saw no blue-eyed firebombers.

No one who'd gone to the fireworks show mentioned any trouble, according to Kelvin, nothing but the usual traffic jams and fender benders. This being Labor Day Monday, I called him at home to check on Barry's car.

"I think you should get him out of here as soon as possible. He might have seen something he shouldn't have."

"Shit, Willy. What did you do now?"

"I didn't do it! Why does everyone always blame me? Besides, maybe they're gone now."

"Who? What?"

"Nothing to worry about. But maybe you could have the mayor nearby when Barry comes to get the Mer-cedes. You know, to help him forget how a spark fell and burned his finger."

"I can try, but His Honor the Mayor never remembers his appointments. And so what if some jackass sues East Hampton? It's got nothing to do with us, does it?"

"Uh, not exactly. That is, no. Not at all."

I heard him curse again, away from the phone. "If that's the truth, Willow Tate, then why does my toe itch?"

Ellen came home before I had to answer, thank goodness. She told me she was going to pack up and take the late train—but she was coming back next weekend.

"I'd hoped to be back in the city by then. I'm not sure—"

"Martin invited me to stay at his house to work on the new honors program."

"Oh." That was all I could think of to say. "Oh."

"I know he's not your type, but we have a lot in common and get along great. You could try to be happy for me."

"I am. Sure. If that's what you want."

Good thing Kelvin wasn't around to hear the lies or he'd scratch his toe bloody. Martin Armbruster was dull as dust, pedantic and pompous, nitpicky and punctilious. And at least ten years older than Ellen and had more hair in his ears than he had on his head, except for the threadbare comb-over. To say nothing of the fact that she lived in Connecticut and he lived at the end of Long Island, and both worked five days a week at jobs they loved. Half their weekends would be spent traveling between the two places. "I hope it works out. Email me your plans and I'll let you know if I'll be around."

"Great. Maybe we can do something together again. Barry's staying, too."

Damn. "I thought he hated the country, especially after he burned his finger."

"Oh, Martin put some first aid cream on it and said it looked more like a bug bite to him. Isn't he great?"

Barry or Martin? I wished them both to the devil.

Ellen wasn't done. "He likes you, that's why he's staying. He thinks your town is fascinating the way everyone knows everyone. Give him a chance, Willy. You two have a lot in common, too. And you both work freelance, so there's no problem with the schedules or distance. Martin's renting him the room over his garage by the week. Isn't he yummy?"

Barry or Martin?

My cousin gave me a suspicious look when she finally got out of bed after a long night at the restaurant.

I spoke before she could. "I didn't do anything!" Somehow she always knew when I was in trouble. "All I did was tell a few polite lies to Ellen."

Susan lowered one eyebrow, the one with the hoop back through it.

"Don't bug me, all right?"

Bad choice of words.

The fires started that night.

CHAPTER 6

AT FIRST EVERYONE THOUGHT it was kids playing pranks before the first day of school, throwing matches into the metal trash cans on the street, setting newspapers on fire on people's doorsteps, tossing firecrackers into mailboxes.

The police didn't catch the kids. By the time they got to the scene, the adolescent arsonists were long gone. Big Eddie's big nose didn't sniff out any sulfur or gunpowder or telltale body odor. Neither did his K-9 partner's nose.

The kids went back to school, the tourists went home, and the fires continued at night.

Now everyone blamed careless campers in the woods or sparks from the train brakes catching the weeds along the railbed. We'd had a mostly hot, dry summer, so brush fires weren't unusual or unexpected. I heard some muttering at the deli about getting the weather mavens to bring on some rain clouds to help the exhausted volunteer firefighters. They'd had to call on neighboring departments to come help, there were so many fires over so many acres of undeveloped land.

Then people started to get hurt. And nervous. And

angry. Maybe—there was Dad's dream twitch—I shouldn't have mentioned Barry's burned finger to Kelvin, but the townsfolk were starting to put two and two together, and getting Willow Tate. They would have connected the bugs to the fires sooner or later, anyway, because swatting at the insects caused sparks; killing one meant you better have a fire extinguisher handy.

I couldn't face the neighbors. I couldn't leave, either. What I did was put up posters, telling people of a newly discovered species of beetle. Big letters said VALUABLE. DO NOT INJURE.

Then people started capturing the lightning bugs, carefully, and bringing them to me for a reward. I tried to explain they were valuable to science, not me personally, which only made the locals mad. So I started paying a five-dollar bounty on healthy, unharmed specimens. Which I released into my backyard as soon as the bug-nappers left.

The other thing I did was try to communicate with the flight squadron whenever I could. I sat on my back porch every night, getting eaten by mosquitoes because I couldn't use the bug spray if I wanted the alien insects to come talk to me. My cousin worked late nights, thank God, or everyone in town would hear that I was crazy, again. No one else saw a swarm of blue-eyed bugs, only falling sparks or larger-than-normal fireflies. No one else thought an insect could be sentient.

Maybe I was crazy, talking to them, trying to send mental images their way. But they came. They sat on my shoulders or on the wicker rocker next to me, or flew in a loose cloud while I urged them to leave. When the cloud appeared smaller or thinner, I begged them to stay in my yard where they couldn't get into trouble or draw attention to themselves or me.

Too late. Joanne at the deli slammed my sandwich down on the counter, without a pickle.

Walter at the drugstore put the Closed sign on his door when he saw me coming.

Bud at the gas station put expensive high-test in my car on purpose.

Mrs. Terwilliger at the library said my card had expired. She wouldn't let me take out any books because they might get burned.

Bill at the hardware store sneered at me while he displayed a new order of flyswatters in his window. He set the metal handles to playing the Bumblebee concerto.

Grandma Eve, my own grandmother, sniffed and told me to get to work if I wanted to see any of her beach plum jelly this year.

I couldn't get to work, not my work. I tore up my notes about the fire wizard, just in case. I'd work on something else, something safe. Bunnies and butterflies, good witches and princesses. Yeck.

Nothing came. No idea caught my interest, revved my engines, gave me that creative charge that was better than sex. (That's what I told myself anyway, since I'd sworn off men.) Now I had neither, a good man nor a good idea.

How come? I wondered. I'd always had plenty of fresh plots and new characters. Now I had none. This wasn't writer's block, when an author couldn't write. This was nothing *to* write.

Then a truly dreadful thought occurred to me. What if all my ideas weren't my ideas at all, but some slippage in the fabric of our world, letting in the unknown magic from Unity? What if everything I wrote as fantasy fiction was reality somewhere else? What if I was nothing but a channel for loose brain waves from another universe?

Then maybe I was nothing. I wish my father'd never put that dire word of uncertainty in my head. Maybe I had no talent. Maybe I didn't deserve my success. Maybe

I'd grow old and lonely and unfulfilled. I already had no friends. My cousin couldn't look at me without shaking her head. My mother hung up when I asked if she could talk to bugs, not just dogs. Even my dog distrusted me. In my self-doubt and despair, I squeezed Little Red too hard for comfort. He growled, got off my lap, and ran to hide in the closet, where he could chew up another pair of my shoes.

The only one in Paumanok Harbor who didn't blame me for the bugs, didn't demand I get rid of them, didn't worry about the fires, was Barry Jensen, the would-be writer. He thought the giant-sized fireflies were escaped from a private collection of exotic insects somewhere, which was what we told outsiders. He found them interesting, and me fascinating, he said, how I immediately leaped to help my neighbors. He wanted to write more about me, but also about how small towns pulled together and solved problems, how the volunteers selflessly gave up so many hours to keep the village safe.

He thought he could move back into my house now that Ellen was gone.

Yeah, right after the fireflies turned into frogs and hopped away.

Things got worse. An abandoned shed in someone's yard caught on fire. Then a vacant beach cottage burned to the ground before anyone noticed the flames. Martin Armbruster's comb-over got scorched when he netted one of the bugs, then tried to bring it into his class to study. And Janie, who cut my hair, called to say she had a package to deliver.

"Here, you caused this," she yelled as she pulled up at the house and started unloading paraphernalia and her "package." "Now you can take care of it."

"But I . . . I don't know how . . ."

"Your aunt will be home soon to help, or you can ask

Mrs. Garland. I wrote down everything you need. You can learn the rest, the way everyone else does."

My grandmother wasn't answering her cell. My aunt couldn't leave school early, not with the kids super-rambunctious on the first days after vacation, amped on the town's fears and furors. My cousin Susan decided to take the week off from the restaurant now that Labor Day had come and gone. She went to Manhattan, to stay in *my* apartment, since I wouldn't be there. I almost cried when she left. Not that I'd miss her. I missed my apartment.

Crying couldn't help. So I called Ty Farraday, the horse whisperer. He was kind and concerned, but he had no ideas. And no, he couldn't come to Long Island right now. He had performances booked and horses to train. He needed the money to build the horse-rescue ranch here in Paumanok Harbor.

"There mightn't be any Paumanok Harbor unless we solve this problem."

"Then you better ask his lordship in London."

Which was precisely what I didn't want to do. His lordship was the son of a British earl. He was also my former lover, my almost fiancé, and my mother's dream of grandchildren gone down the tubes. Oh, and he could translate some of the language the insects might use or understand, if he deigned to come to my aid.

He didn't. "I don't know anything about insects. We got a reading of some paranormal activity on the Eastern seaboard. I suppose I'm not surprised you're in the middle of it."

That didn't sound lover-like to me. It sounded downright nasty and unsympathetic. "It's not my fault."

"It never is, is it?"

So he hadn't forgiven me for getting involved with Ty so soon after breaking our engagement, even if he'd started seeing Martha from the real estate office. We'd never really talked about it, so I tried now. "Listen, I am sorry things did not work out between us. I am sorry I thought we could get married and live happily ever after. I am mostly sorry I realized we couldn't."

"We could have if you'd given us half a chance."

"No, it was never going to work. As my father says, we have to build a bridge and get over it. Besides, this is not about you and me. You are the highest member of the Department of Unexplained Events I know, so this is business, not personal. The bugs start fires when they are threatened, and now the locals feel threatened, so they are out for blood. Or ichor, or whatever you call an insect's blood. This is not a good combination. The people on a witch hunt and the insects defending themselves could destroy the Harbor or bring it to national attention your people would not want."

He exhaled loudly. "I understand, Willy, but there is nothing I can do. We can send people, but no one knows anything about your bugs. I've never come across any references to them in the old books. We don't have so much as a word for them."

"You could come brainstorm." Or hold my hand, but I didn't say that.

"I'm sorry. You're on your own."

I always was. "You didn't come help with the horses, either, not until we had it almost under control."

"You didn't come meet my parents the way you promised."

"I never wanted to go there. I agreed to go to make you happy. Now you can be happy we aren't married."

"I am. You can bank on that. I never wanted a clinging, managing kind of wife. I thought you were independent and honest."

That hurt. "Well, I thought you meant that crap about 'One life. One heart,' on the back of my pendant."

"I did, but the only time you remember it is when you need something. All you ever wanted was a white knight to ride to your rescue, then get out of your way so you could keep your comfortable little corner of the world neat and uncomplicated. Someone to take out the trash and check the air in your tires."

"Well, all you wanted was a mother for your children. A mother with talent, who'd be happy living in your shadow halfway across the world from everything she knew and loved."

He sighed again. "Listen, you are right. This is a waste of both our time. We've both moved on, we're over. I'll ask around to see if DUE has anyone in the field who can help in any capacity. Okay? I'll get someone there in a couple of days."

"Days?" I panicked. "But what about the baby?"

He panicked. I waited while he picked the phone up from the floor.

"Grant? Are you still there?"

His voice came back on the line, raspy from choking. "Baby? Are you pregnant? If you are, I didn't do it!"

That was my line. "She's not my baby. Not our baby." And not my father's turning Maybe either.

"She's a burning baby. Janie from the beauty parlor's niece's daughter." The one who was asleep in my bathtub right now after catching her house on fire and injuring her mother.

Grant was so relieved I wasn't suing him for child support that he listened while I explained why I was temporary caregiver to a ten month old. I told him how the toddler had caught a bug, put it in her mouth and bit down. Now when she cried, she spewed flames. Janie had to go to the hospital with her niece, Mary Brown. Mary had divorced the baby's father, Roy Ruskin, because he was a drunk, a doper, and a spouse abuser, according to Jane. Then he'd been arrested for refusing to pay the court-ordered child support and now Mary had an order of protection against him. He couldn't be allowed near the baby.

"But you can? Is everyone in that town crazy?"

"Excuse me, but you did think I could raise your children."

"We'd have a nanny." He went on before I could tell him what he could do with his nanny and his blue-blooded brats. "Tell me why you have the fire-breathing baby."

"Well, they can't send her to day care with the other kids, can they? And there are no other relatives in the state. Besides, Janie doesn't want any of the neighbors to know about the danger. Can you imagine what they'll do to poor little Elladaire if they think she's starting all the fires?"

"Worse than handing her to someone who's never held an infant?"

"I've done fine with her, I'll have you know. I took her to the beach—with sun screen and a hat—where nothing could get burned. She had a wonderful time, and now she's all tired out. I have a bottle ready the second she wakes up, and Jane promised she'll be back tonight. I don't know how safe she'll be with Elladaire. Babies cry!"

"Shite." He pronounced it the British way, but I understood.

"They do that, too. I need help!"

"You need a keeper, Willow Tate."

CHAPTER 7

I NEVER SAID I WAS BRAVE.
Planes, snakes, subways; they didn't make the top
of the list of things I was afraid of. Add boats, bats, and
taxi drivers with eye patches. My grandmother, coyotes,
hair dye, tornadoes, the gynecologist. Going crazy like
my paternal grandmother, turning into a witch/bitch like
my maternal grandmother, turning into my mother!
Getting cancer like my cousin, living the rest of my life
with my cousin. Sharks. Choking when I am alone so no
one can perform a Heimlich. Being alone when I am
eighty. Talking in public. Forgetting to send in estimated
taxes. Catalytic converters, global warming, and reli-
gious fanatics of every denomination. You know what
scares me most? The idea of being responsible for another helpless human being.

I had a baby. I had Mary Brown's daughter for a few
hours only, but Elladaire had to be protected from herself, from a zillion dangers everywhere, and from my
own inexperience and incompetence. What if I dropped
her? Or fed her wrong? My house wasn't baby-proofed.
Neither was Little Red. None of us was fireproof.

The trick was to keep her from crying, which meant
keeping her happy. Half the time I didn't know what

made me happy. Oreos and ice cream? A walk on the beach? A nice royalty check? Not applicable. Elladaire could barely walk or talk. And she might miss her mother, or cut a tooth, or bump her head. Hell, she might be afraid of strangers. I reread the lists Janie'd left me.

Do they make tranquilizers for babies? I'd read how centuries ago they gave infants gin to keep them quiet, rubbed liquor on their sore gums, fed them beer to help them sleep. I was tempted.

Elladaire was a sweet little munchkin, though, who gave cute drooly smiles and played patty cake and peek-aboo and this little piggy and held up both hands to be carried, and I thought I was going to die before Jane came back. I knew damn well they made tranquilizers for adults, but I was afraid of falling asleep. I couldn't take my eyes off the kid for a second.

Her mother was going to be all right, Janie reported, but they sent her by ambulance to a specialized burn unit elsewhere on Long Island. Who knew how long she'd be there?

Janie stopped off on her way home from the hospital to buy a crib with metal bars and six fire extinguishers, three for her, three for me. Cripes.

Infant apparel had to be flame-retardant by law, she told me now, after I'd kept the poor child naked all day except for her diaper, which was usually so wet it couldn't have caught fire.

"I don't think Elladaire can burn herself," I told Janie. The fireflies never did, or there'd be no fireflies.

"But she can burn down everything else. You've got to do something, Willy. I can't tell my customers I'm canceling their hair appointments because my grandniece is a time bomb. I sure as the devil can't take her with me to the salon with all those chemicals."

"You could tell them you have to take Elladaire to visit her sick mother. People will understand."

"I need the money to help pay Mary's bills. Her insurance won't cover half the expenses and that bastard she married won't cough up a dime."

I gave Elladaire a good-bye kiss. "I've asked for help. I don't know what else to do."

"Well, you better start praying. I'll drop her off in the morning."

Great, Janie had Elladaire when she slept from seven to seven. I had the infant arsonist when she was awake. What if it rained and we couldn't go to the beach? I read the directions on the fire extinguishers.

"Grandma, you know those drops you gave me for the dogs, to keep them calm? Are they safe for people?"

"Of course."

"What about babies?"

"This better be for one of your stories, Willow Tate, or I am disowning you tomorrow."

Next, I asked the only real experts I had. I was used to them by now, and not afraid to stand outside in the dark and talk to fire-flinging beetles. They whirred and whizzed around leaving trails of tiny shooting stars, but they offered no answers. I gave up and started inside. I had to let the dogs in from their fenced-in area at the side yard first, so I walked around the house. One of the lightning bugs must have followed me, then tried to investigate the old shepherd.

Who knows what a dog sees? A bug? A spark? The dog snapped at the insect, and the insect torched back.

There was a lot of frantic crying, yelping, and running in circles. The dog was pretty upset, too.

I called the nearest vet in Mom's address book. Most likely his answering machine would direct me to the all-night veterinarian clinic in Riverhead, but that was almost forty minutes away! I begged him to pick up.

For once my wish was granted. Dr. Matt Spenser had several emergencies that day, so he was checking on patients at the animal hospital, next door to his house. He knew my mother, the work she did, and her dogs. He told me to come right over.

We had a handful of vets on the East End, in East Hampton, Montauk, and Sag Harbor, which left Amagansett, Paumanok Harbor, and Springs with none close by. Matt Spenser filled a big gap.

He filled the examining room, too. He stood at least six-two, with the body of a football player. His light brown hair was long and tousled, as if he didn't have time for a barber. He had on an old shirt with bleach holes in it. Even if I didn't know he was divorced, I would have guessed. I guessed his age at about forty, his love for his job about a hundred percent.

He gave Buddy a shot for pain, some salve for the burn on his jaw, and a soft treat from the jar on the counter. He offered me a glass of water.

"I'm sorry, there's nothing stronger here. You look like you could use a scotch."

"That's okay. I don't drink."

"Me neither."

He went back to talking to the dog, although he had to know Buddy was half deaf. "Good boy. You'll be fine. I know it's scary, but it's over and you can go home to your pals and your soft bed."

I didn't know about Buddy, but I felt better listening to his calm, soothing voice. What a nice man. I sighed in relief that he'd answered the phone and fixed my dog.

He looked over at me. "Don't worry. Mostly likely he won't remember anything about tonight."

"I hope he remembers enough not to chomp on any more lightning bugs."

Dr. Spenser kept stroking the dog. "You know, I see a lot of insect stings in dogs and cats. They're always putting their noses where they don't belong. The bites I'm seeing now are different, though, more like burns. I worried about the first cases I got last week from Paumanok Harbor, because it looked as if someone was holding a cigarette to a dog. I was ready to call the police, the Animal Control officer, and the ASPCA, but then someone brought in another dog. And another, from a different neighborhood, on different days. The owners were people I knew, people like you who really love their animals."

Buddy was my mother's dog, but I didn't need to tell him that. I needed to give him the current theory I was trying to promote. "It's a new strain of beetle, I hear, that carries some kind of acid. People are talking about Plum Island where they do those animal experiments."

"This isn't hoof-and-mouth disease."

"No, but it's never been seen before."

"A lot of things in Paumanok Harbor have never been seen before. Like your mother's uncanny communion with canines. And how the guy at the drugstore always knows when I've got a hot— That is, he knows more about my personal life than I do."

"Walter believes in safe sex."

"So do I. That's why I run spay and neuter clinics every month. It's not the same. And one of your neighbors brings her imaginary dog every year for his physical."

"That's very kind of you to play along."

"Who's playing? I swear I can hear the dog's heart beating. That's just the tip of the Paumanok Harbor iceberg."

"But you like it here?"

"I love it. You never know who or what'll walk in the door next." He gave me a smile, to emphasize his point.

"Um, well, the air is purer here and the people are, uh, creative thinkers."

He laughed. He wasn't buying my explanations, but he wasn't calling me a liar, like a bunch of the lie-detector Harborites would have. And he had a nice laugh. "I don't think Paumanok Harbor's weirdness comes from the air or the locals' imaginations."

"Maybe it's in the genes," I said, laughing too so he wouldn't realize I was finally telling the truth.

"You know, I was one of the vets at the big horse show you guys put on."

"You did a great job, between the horses and dogs and sheep. Did you get to see any of the show?"

He nodded. "Some really amazing stuff. But the end got kind of hazy somehow."

Which told me what kind of man he was, besides nice. He was normal, ordinary, one of Them. One of Us would have seen and remembered a herd of iridescent white mares dancing and disappearing as the show concluded, despite the mayor's hocus-pocus.

"As long as you got to see Ty Farraday and Paloma Blanca, his Lipizzaner mare."

He looked at Buddy, but he spoke to me: "I saw them single you out of the whole audience."

"We, ah, became good friends during the preparations."

"Lucky man."

Hmm. "He's gone now."

"Stupid man."

Hmm, hmm. There was absolutely nothing wrong with a nice, normal man. Except I'd sworn off all men. I changed the subject quickly. "Thanks. I believe some experts are coming soon to get rid of the infestation."

He politely accepted the change. "That's good. So far I've seen nothing serious, but a plague of venomous insects could be dangerous."

He lifted Buddy down from the examining table with ease. The shepherd had to weigh a good sixty or seventy pounds, so the man kept fit. While he washed his hands at the nearby sink he asked, "Do you still have that feisty Pomeranian whose leg I had to amputate?"

"Who else would take him?"

He laughed again. "Well, keep him in at night when the fireflies are out. All that hair could turn into a catastrophe. Let's hope we get a storm soon. Insects don't like to fly in rain or wind. Either way, their courting season will be over soon, and they'll stop lighting up to find a mate. Or they might reach their age limits. I'd like to do some research on the species, so I know what I am dealing with for the next bite. Do you think you could bring me one?"

"NO!" I shouted. "That is, no. It's too dangerous to capture a live one, and I've never seen a dead one."

"Maybe I'll come out and take a look for myself. Where's the best place to find them?"

A parallel universe, but I couldn't reveal that. My backyard, but I couldn't encourage him. Matt Spenser was an outsider, a danger in itself to Paumanok Harbor and its residents. I had to keep him at a distance, even if I'd feel better having a calm, competent man for a friend, at the least. I tugged on Buddy's leash to get him headed for the door.

"You should bring him back in a couple of days for me to check the wound."

"I thought you said he'd be okay."

"What if he ate the bug?"

Good grief, Buddy'd be a blowtorch every time he barked. "No, he didn't. I saw the thing fly away."

"That's good. But bring him in anyway." He sent me another smile. "I'd like to see you again."

Oh. "Maybe my mother will be back by then. I'll tell her."

"An amazing woman, your mother. Do you know she's the reason I settled on this neighborhood? She convinced me this was the perfect spot for a new practice. She was right. And know what? She said I'd be happy to meet you. She was right there, too."

My mother ought to be sent into space to rescue Canis Minor. On the other hand, there really was nothing wrong with having a cup of tea with a nice, normal man. Nothing except blazing bugs and babies.

CHAPTER 8

PEOPLE ACTUALLY VOLUNTEERED for this?
I'm sorry, Mom, but your hopes for grandkids just went down the toilet, along with a lot of disgusting unmentionables. I admire women who can do this, who get real pleasure out of changing diapers, spooning slop into uncooperative mouths, singing the itsy bitsy spider ten times. I am not one of them. I doubt I'd feel any different if the infant were mine.

Elladaire is cute and lovable. I'd love to buy her books and stuffed bears and pretty dresses with flowers on them. Spend another day keeping her happy, keeping her from the electric cords, the dogs' tails, the house plants, the bric-a-brac, everything else dangerous, inedible, or irreplaceable? No thanks.

It was raining. No nonflammable beach. No playground. No stroller rides. I couldn't pop her in the car and head for stores that carried toys and baby videos and board books. Not when a single wail could set the car on fire.

"It's just you and me, kid, but today's the last day. Your auntie Jane can take over from here. I wasn't the one who let you teethe on a bug bigger than a praying mantis. I know it's not your fault, but I'm not cut out for this job."

It started too early, for one thing. Janie arrived with Elladaire before I could shower or change or make breakfast.

"Here's her oatmeal, her bottle, more clothes, more diapers. I have to meet with Mary's insurance agent about her house and how much fire damage they'll cover. Lord knows what they'll put down as cause."

Elladaire was fussy, which was a polite way of saying she was difficult. She spit the oatmeal all over my sleep shirt, threw the bottle across the kitchen, mashed her bananas and Cheerios into my hair when I picked her up, and peed on the couch while I was changing her. Her eyes filled with tears, her lower lip started to quiver.

I stood ready with wet towels and a fire extinguisher. I was exhausted, hungry, and filthy, and couldn't do anything about any of it because I couldn't take my eyes off her for a second, not until she took a nap. Here I was, wiped out and at my wit's end, and it wasn't nine o'clock in the morning yet.

Bad mother that I am, I found some idiot kids' show on the TV. A goofy clown sang and danced and flashed bright colors. Elladaire was fascinated. I put the wet towel on my forehead.

Then I heard the thunder. The rain was bad enough, but now we had an electric storm, too? Elladaire and I could hide in the bathroom. No, then she'd grow up afraid of lightning like me. For now she just seemed startled.

I wondered about the fireflies. Where did they go in the rain? For that matter, where did butterflies and ladybugs go so their wings didn't get wet? Under trees, I guess, though I've never seen any during storms.

I waited for the next flash or boom, but the thunder rolled on, louder, closer. Elladaire's eyes got wider.

That was not thunder, I realized, but a truck barreling too fast down the private access. It was most likely a wholesaler desperate for Grandma Eve's fresh produce. Or a manure deliveryman in a hurry to get back on the main street before our dirt road turned to muck in the rain. What if Elladaire and I had been walking down to the farm? Worse, what if the loud noise frightened the baby into crying? I felt like shouting to the dumbass driver what I thought, except this wasn't mid-Manhattan, and I couldn't use those words in front of a child.

The truck screeched to a halt in front of my property. Maybe I'd have the chance to vent my anger after all. I went to the door and saw a battered, mud-spattered camper stopped there.

"You're lost," I yelled, then pointed. "The farm is that way, and you are driving too fast."

The driver of the rusty RV rolled down his window. "You Willow Tate?"

A mad stalker? Elladaire's drugged-out father? An avid entomologist? An irate tourist whose campground was shut because of the brush fire danger?

"Yes, I am Willow Tate." I hoped my voice didn't sound as shaky as I felt. A stranger was getting out of the camper. He wasn't real big or broad, but he seemed threatening anyway. I couldn't tell his age from here, not through the rain, but he didn't move stiffly like an old man, or fluidly like a young one. He just seemed tightly coiled, controlled, determined. His light hair was buzzed short, but he had a scruffy start-up beard, maybe to cover some of the angry red marks on his left cheek. Damn, he'd been in a firefight with the lightning bugs, and lost. Now he was blaming me.

He took a couple of steps up the path to the porch where I waited. I clutched Elladaire a little closer to my chest. If he got too close, made a hostile move, I was ready. I wasn't any meek little pen pusher waiting to be shoved around. I had a weapon and I wasn't afraid to use it. "I'm sorry, baby," I whispered to Elladaire as I got ready to pinch her into crying. If this angry man thought the fireflies were bad, he hadn't seen a flame-throwing toddler.

He came closer still. Little Red barked furiously and ran past me to attack his ankle. The man looked down. He had more scars or burns on the top of his head. I couldn't help my imagination taking over. Here was the villain of my fire wizard book. This was one evil dude, the perfect foil to my do-good hero. I could see them fighting, casting thunderbolts at each other while a hapless village smoldered beneath the mountaintop confrontation.

Then he asked, "So where's the fire?"

On the mountaintop? I did a mental blink. "If you are a volunteer firefighter, you've wasted your time. There's no fire. Not now. "

"Of course not. I'm here."

Oh, boy. Angry and crazy, not a good combination. He ignored Little Red snapping at his pant leg and took another step closer.

He wanted a fire? I pinched Elladaire. She wailed, but nothing happened.

"Lady, it's raining. Are you going to invite me in or not?"

Definitely not. "I'm a little busy right now . . ."

"Yeah, I can see that. Listen, I spent the last week in the hospital, and was supposed to have a week's vacation. I drove all night to get here, without the pain meds that make me sleepy. So do you want my help or not?"

"Help?"

"You called for help with a fire problem, didn't you?"

"I called . . . DUE sent you?"

"Shit. Didn't you get the email? They said they'd contact you."

I stood aside so he could come into the house. "I haven't been able to get to the computer. The baby . . ."

"I heard all about the baby. She'll be fine." Without a by-your-leave, he scooped Elladaire out of my arms. Just in time, too, so I could grab Little Red before he sank his teeth into the guy's ankle.

The baby didn't like being plucked away, or strangers. Maybe she didn't like men, considering the father she had. She started to cry in earnest, but with tears, not sparks. The visitor jiggled her and made funny sounds. She stopped crying.

"How did you . . . ? That is, what did you do to make her stop?"

"Babies like me, that's all."

"Not the crying. The . . . the other?"

"I told you, I put out fires."

I turned off the TV, shoved a bunch of stuffed animals and plastic blocks off the sofa so he could sit, the baby on his lap. I nodded in her direction. "That's Elladaire Brown. The dog is Little Red. You already know I am Willow Tate. Who in the world are you?"

"Piet Doorn, at your service. Not exactly willingly, but I'm the best chance you've got."

"Pe-et?" He'd pronounced it in two syllables.

He spelled it out. "Like Mondrian. Only the artist's name is pronounced Pete. My mother thought that was too common, so she insisted on her own version. It stuck."

"What kind of name is that?"

"My grandfather's. His family came from the Netherlands generations ago. They like to keep some traditions. My sister is Katrinka. What kind of name is Willow?"

"A family tradition, too," I told him while I started the coffeemaker and put on a pot of water for tea. I put out two scones and the last of the farm stand's raspberry jam. "My grandmother named her daughters Rose and Jasmine. We also have a Lily in the family."

"What about Elladaire? That's a strange one, isn't it?"

The baby was playing with his keys. She looked up at him when she heard her name and batted her eyelashes. Flirting, at her age! And with such a peculiar man.

"Her mother was living with an abusive husband in a rundown trailer parked in a weedy lot. She wanted better for her baby girl, something prettier than the world she was looking at. Besides, her name is Mary Brown. She wanted a unique, elegant name for her daughter. I guess she made it up."

"Edie'll do for now."

He was making changes already? Just who did he think he was? "Her name is Elladaire. Tell me again why the people at Royce sent you?"

"That's easy. I put out fires. I don't know anything about bugs, but I do know about forest fires, oil field burns, electrical malfunctions, that kind of thing. They tried to send me to the war zone, but it didn't work. I could put out the fires, but I couldn't stop the explosions when the bombs hit the trucks. I saved a couple of soldiers, lost a couple before they pulled me out. That was hard. Brush fires are easier."

"But how . . . ?"

He bounced Elladaire on his knee and had her giggling. "How do the Royce descendants know truth from lies? How do you befriend beings no one else can see?"

"I don't—"

"You do something or I wouldn't be here. There's no explanation for any of it. Just magic. From what I hear, you should be used to it, living in Paumanok Harbor. Some people talk to dogs, some change the weather. I put out fires."

"You don't start them?"

"Nope. Never have, never could. My father couldn't figure out why his leaf pile wouldn't burn; my mother had to get a new electric stove. I was the only kid thrown out of Cub Scouts because he couldn't get a fire started. Neither could any of my den mates when I was nearby. I never tasted a s'more or had a charcoal fire barbeque. No beach parties around a bonfire, no romantic candle-lit dinners either." He looked toward the stone fireplace, a bit wistfully, I thought. "Never sat by one of those on a cold winter night."

I'd seen some strange stuff recently. This was bizarre, even by Paumanok Harbor's standards. "Show me."

He tipped Elladaire back and tickled her belly until she laughed out loud, which she'd never done for me. "See any flames?"

"She's too happy."

"Do you want me to make her cry?"

I'd tried that. "It's possible Elladaire finally got the bug out of her system, without your, ah, abilities."

"Sure it's possible. Light a match."

I got the emergency stash from the kitchen, a box of matches and candles and flashlights for when the power went out. "The matches must be damp."

His lips twitched.

I came back to the living room and tried the long fireplace matches on the mantle. One caught, sizzled, and died. The second didn't get that far. The battery-run grill starter couldn't cough up a spark. I looked around, then ran toward the kitchen. The electric coffeemaker was burbling, but my teakettle was still cold. I checked, but I couldn't start the gas range either. "Wow. Good thing there's electricity." I put a cup of water in the micro-wave.

"Yeah, I don't cook much when the power is down."

Elladaire started playing with the short stubble on his chin. He didn't seem to mind, so I asked something that was bothering me. "I don't understand how you got burned, then. Those are burn marks on your face, aren't they?"

He touched his jaw. "They'll do more skin grafts soon. And Royce has someone in Virginia who can make the scars fade. They've done it before."

"My grandmother has an ointment that works, too. I'll get some from her. But what I meant was how can you get burned when fire won't work around you?"

He looked at Elladaire, not me. "Sometimes you just have to run faster than the magic. I happened to come across a bad crash before the cops did. There was a kid trapped in a burning car. Someone had to get him out in a hurry."

So they'd sent me a real hero. Piet was the genuine article, not a construct of my imagination, not tall, dark, and handsome, and not a perfect cover model. I went to get his coffee and the scones. When I got back to the living room, Elladaire was asleep against Piet's chest. Little Red sat on the sofa next to him, shredding one of the baby's stuffed animals.

A real hero.

He looked over Elladaire's head and scowled at me. "Don't you go getting any ideas, lady."

CHAPTER 9

"IDEAS? WHAT KIND OF IDEAS? Thinking up new stories is my business."

"This isn't anything new. It's love and marriage and forever after. So don't look at me like your next meal."

I gasped. "I wasn't—love and marriage? Why, you arrogant jerk. I just met—"

"Shh. You'll wake the baby. I meant I'm not the marrying kind, no matter what the bastards at Royce tell me is my duty."

I had a hard time getting enough air in my lungs for another gasp. "They sent you to marry me?"

"They mentioned you were single and attractive. Twice. They've been pushing every unattached, talented female at me since I was seventeen."

"How old are you now?"

"Thirty-eight. Feeling a hundred and eight some mornings. That's why they yanked me out of Iraq so fast. They're afraid of losing my genes before I get killed. I donated sperm to the cause, but they aren't satisfied. They suggested I wouldn't take so many chances if I had a family. It's all about crossbreeding with them."

"They must have taken lessons from my mother."

He thought about that, idly stroking Elladaire's

back, ignoring the trail of drool she left on his shoulder. "I guess they push females harder. That ticking clock and all."

"After spending a day with Elladaire, my clock is set at zero. I'm not doing it. No matter what anyone says, I am not having kids to please a committee. If I were thinking about having a family, I wouldn't let a bunch of mad scientists pick me a mate. I'd feel like a zoo animal in a captive breeding program."

"You could change your mind for the right man."

Now I sneered at him. "Like someone who runs into burning buildings for a living? Not likely."

He laughed. "Sometimes I just sit on mountaintops, keeping brush fires away from power plants and observatories."

"That's just as dangerous. With just as much travel, hopping from calamity to catastrophe."

"So you're looking for a safe man who's around twenty-four/seven?"

"I am not looking, I told you. And no, I'd hate having someone underfoot all the time, safe or not." Having Ellen around for a week proved steady company was too much. "I need time to myself, for my work, for my thinking about work. A weekend companion might suit me better." And keep me from that black hole of loneliness. "What about you? Do you ever think about spending your life with one woman?" I wanted to ask if he ever got lonely, but that was too personal, no matter how we were talking about love and marriage.

He drank some of his coffee and eyed the scone, but his hands were full of Elladaire. I got up and spread jam on it for him. See how domestic I could be? He took a bite and "hmm-ed" in satisfaction at the taste before answering. "I thought I'd like to come home—I have a place in California, close to the worst fire zones—to home-cooked meals, a clean house, and someone who accepts me, scars and all. So I hired a live-in house-keeper."

Before I wondered what other comforts the house-keeper provided, he said she was sixty-eight, and her husband lived in, too, to caretake the house and yard. Their nine grandchildren were always around, which is why he was so comfortable around babies.

"If I did go looking for a wife," he went on between bites, "I definitely wouldn't pick one who attracted trouble like a magnet. I have enough drama in my life."

Was he talking about me? "I don't need any more stress, either. I couldn't handle worrying all the time if my husband was going to come home in one piece, or in an urn."

"Good. Then we're both safe from any pressure from the Institute."

"Good."

He'd finished his scone but still looked hungry, so I fixed him the second one, mine. I ate some of Elladaire's Cheerios with my tea. While he ate, I thought of a hundred questions I wanted to ask.

"Who pays you? I mean, who do you work for? Who decides where you should go? Royce Institute in England? DUE in this country? The government?"

He blew out a breath, then brushed crumbs off the baby. "The government? They barely know I exist, thank God. Except as a fireman, of course. That's what's on my tax return. It's the oil companies who'll pay anything to keep their profits from going up in smoke. That way I can volunteer to the Park Service or local fire departments, wherever I think I'm needed. The Department of Unexplained Events doesn't find a lot of work for me, but I go when they are in my kind of trouble. It's fun. You never know what you'll face with their situations, like now."

A carnival was fun. *Saturday Night Live* was fun.

Fighting fires or fireflies? Not my idea of a good time. "What about the Army? Someone had to know what you can do to put you there."

"Kids were getting killed. I wanted to go, to see if I could help. The people at Royce got me embedded as a firematic scientist testing a new airborne fire-retardant. Half the time I forgot to open the damn canister to make it look good."

"No one noticed?"

"Not when shrapnel started flying and trucks flipped over and men had to run for their lives. It's the same on a city fire call. Everyone has so much equipment it's hard to tell what I'm doing. Usually everyone's so grateful to have the fire contained, they don't ask how. I tell them the formula is still being tested, if anyone tries to get hold of some of my 'invention.' I explain it doesn't work reliably enough to hand over yet, and there may be side effects. Guys keep their distance."

"How far does it work?"

"The range of effectiveness depends on whether I'm inside or out, in an open field or a forest, with high or low visibility. Sometimes I can throw a circle of protection about as far as I can throw a ball. Other times it's a narrow cone as far as I can see. Mostly it's a ten-to-twenty-car-length range."

My fingers itched to sketch what my mind was picturing. "That's one amazing gift you have."

He touched the scars on his cheek. "Not always a blessing, as you can see. Saving lives, houses, forests—there's the reward that makes it worthwhile."

"I'm sorry to be so curious. It's fascinating, though."

He waved that aside. "No problem. It's a relief to be able to talk to someone about my talent without lies and evasions."

"Untruths won't work around Paumanok Harbor. Too many locals have Royce blood in them."

"Yeah, they briefed me about being careful what I say. You've got a circus worth of curiosities in this place yourselves. A regular wizards' convention."

At least he hadn't called us a witches' coven. "It's not all that obvious. I never realized anything was strange about the Harbor until a few months ago. I thought the year-rounders were simply teasing the tourists, or were plain nuts. And half the population is normal."

"Dull, you mean."

I thought of the vet, Matt Spenser. "No, not dull. They have full, ordinary lives. My friend Louisa is one of the most contented, fulfilled people I know. She married the man of her own choice, has a great career, a terrific family, and she doesn't have to hide her talents or tell lies to her neighbors. There is nothing wrong with normal."

"You're not."

"I'm a writer and an artist, the creative type. I get away with being eccentric. The other paras in town accept each other's powers the same way other people accept a smart kid or a good cook or a tennis ace."

"You're a little different from your run-of-the-magic clairvoyant or telekinetic, according to my contact at DUE. Your file is so classified I'm not sure it exists, but you are definitely a person of interest to them."

"You mean how not even the psychics in town know the history of where their talents come from."

"Unity."

So he knew about the world of magic that touched ours. That was a relief, too. "I never heard of it until last spring. Few people here are aware of its existence, still. It's a bigger secret from the world than Paumanok Harbor is."

"But you can touch it or influence it or talk to its envoys."

"I haven't been able to communicate with the lightning bugs. I sense that they like me. They'll come visit without starting fires, but I have no idea what they're thinking."

"You'll figure it out. But tell me about yourself, meanwhile. How did such a good-looking, intelligent female avoid the matchmakers for so long?"

I had to smile at the compliments. "I stayed away from Paumanok Harbor as much as I could. I refused to go to Royce University or take any of its classes. And I grew deaf to my mother's lectures. I was home free for awhile. Now, though, if I need help, no one shows up except appealing, attractive, unattached men. Never an old guy or a woman or a teenager."

"They're not stupid at the Institute. Danger and adventure make for a fast introduction and adrenaline is an aphrodisiac. You're branded into each other's souls before you can shake hands."

"Exactly. I was half in love with both men they sent despite my intentions." I quickly raised my hand. "Not that I intended to keep either of them. Not for long, anyway."

Piet was right; it felt good to talk about my life, about issues I couldn't discuss with anyone else. "You can't build a foundation for marriage on instant attraction, on shared jeopardy. I cannot give my heart and soul to a nomadic troubleshooter, a soldier of fortune, even if he tells fortunes. I refuse to commit myself to a man who walks a tightrope between life and death."

"Thanks. That lets me sleep better." He meant it, that he was happy I wasn't interested in him. I guess I could take that as an insult, but I chose to consider it an honest response. Piet Doorn didn't play games. I appreciated his openness.

"So who'd they send?" he wanted to know. "It wasn't in the notes they faxed."

I took a deep breath. "Grant, Viscount Grantham, and Ty Farraday."

Piet whistled softly between his teeth. "Major league heavy hitters. They must really want your genes passed on."

I checked to see if Elladaire was dry, before she leaked all over Piet. "No babies for me. I'll leave my books for posterity."

"You could change your mind," he said as I laid out a fresh diaper for when she woke up.

"I reserve the right to change my hair color, my address, and my mind, always. But I'll be the one to change it. No one is going to tell me what to do."

He raised his coffee cup. "I'll drink to that. And to our clearing the decks, so to speak. We should work well together, now that we understand our positions."

"Sure." I felt comfortable with Piet, with none of that edgy, anxious energy of trying to impress a new man. Now I wouldn't have to worry about fighting off any sparks between us. Hey, the dude extinguished fires! Except he looked better than good, drowsy on the couch. Maybe I felt a tiny glow.

I asked if he wanted another coffee, but he said he'd had enough caffeine, trying to stay up for the all-night drive. But Elladaire was still sleeping, so he couldn't leave. I went back to our previous conversation. "What about you? Do you think you will ever change your mind about settling down? Having a wife and kids?"

"Who can be a widow and orphans at the drop of a match? A collapsed ceiling, falling oil rig, blowing propane tanks? I can't control any of that. Maybe I'll reconsider my options when I'm too old to hop in the camper or race for a plane. If anyone will have me then."

"They'll have you."

He smiled, showing a tiny gap between his front teeth. "So are we partners?"

"Equal partners. I am no one's assistant, and I don't take kindly to orders."

"Sure. It's your town, your bugs."

I sat back in my chair, more relaxed than I'd been since the fireflies appeared. Certainly since Elladaire appeared. Little Red left off hunting for Cheerios and jumped into my lap. "We're good."

Piet stared at my bare legs and smiled again. "Of course I'm not opposed to having a partner with benefits. You know—a little work, a little play."

CHAPTER 10

SO MR. NON-COMMIT played games after all. Before I could tell him what I thought of his suggestive remark—what *did* I think?—someone knocked on the door.

Little Red started barking, which woke up Elladaire, which had me panicking. If she started squalling, how could I explain to the UPS guy or a Jehovah's Witness that a baby caught his shirt on fire? Or maybe an ordinary person would only see projectile vomiting that left scorch marks. Not good.

Piet smiled reassuringly. I opened the door. There was Barry, looking like an Adonis in the rain with a yellow slicker. There was Little Red, attacking his pant leg. The big dogs on the porch looked up and went back to sleep.

"Barry? What are you doing here?" I knew we didn't have plans for today. Or any other day.

"I guess I should have called first."

"Yes. It's early." And he should have seen the camper in front of my house.

"I thought you'd be up working. I wanted to get a picture of your work space for the web article." He held up his cell phone camera.

He knew damn well I set up my studio in the dining room when no one was coming for dinner, but my laptop was upstairs in my bedroom. "This isn't a good time."

"I can tell." His gaze went from my bed-head hair to my oatmeal-stained nightshirt, the one with frogs on it, to the dog-chewed slippers on my feet. Then his gaze travel past me to Piet, a crying baby in his arms. "What the f—"

It was none of his business, but I didn't want to be rude to someone who might help my career. "I'm babysitting and a friend came to help."

Piet got up and shifted Elladaire to one arm so he could shake Barry's hand when I made the introductions. Barry didn't offer his. He sneered at Piet, at his scruffy beard and his scars. Mostly he sneered at Piet's sleepy eyes. I know he thought Piet had spent the night, but there was nothing I could do about that.

"He's great with babies," was all I said.

Elladaire started screaming, contradicting my words. Yikes! She could make one hell of an article if she spit out sparks. I asked—or begged—Piet: "Are you sure she won't . . . ?"

"Edie's fine," he answered. "What web article are you talking about?"

I told him about the free publicity Barry was going to get me and my books, how important it was for an author to be "branded" on the web, how Barry hoped to be an author someday.

"Listen," Barry interrupted, "I need to get going on the interview. My boss thinks it'll be a big deal, bring us lots of viewers, sell more ads. He wants it soon."

"Maybe we can get together in a couple of days." After Piet and I disarmed the fireflies and saved the world.

Handsome Barry didn't look so hot with his eyes narrowed and his cheeks flushed with angry red blotches.

"So playing house comes before your career." His lip curled. "I thought you were different."

He was jealous, with no right to be. And ugly about it, too. And rude to stare at Piet's burn marks or belittle my career choices. "I think—"

"I'll let you two have a little privacy," Piet said before I could speak and destroy any chance of having a favorable article about my work. "I need some stuff from the camper anyway. Here," he said to Barry, "why don't you hold the baby so Willow can grab her hell hound before he goes ballistic?"

"I don't want to—" Barry got an armful of enraged toddler anyway. "Damn it, she's sopping wet."

And Little Red peed on his shoe.

"I'm sorry about that." Piet went to the kitchen sink to fill his cup with water to take a pill. "If you had a thing going . . . ?"

"We didn't, and don't be sorry. It's his own fault for coming without calling, and when I had company. Besides, he had no right to be rude."

"He was jealous. That makes a man act like a Neanderthal. You sure he didn't have anything to be jealous about?"

I put as much vehemence as I could into my "Yes, I am sure."

Piet smiled. "Still, watch out for a guy who doesn't back off when he's challenged. Do you think he'll write his article now?"

"I don't care. It's more important for us to make a plan for dealing with the lightning bugs. Then I can get back to my books and let my work speak for itself. I was never sure about going so public anyway. I like people not knowing whether Willy is a man or a woman."

He checked out my nightshirt that was now plastered

to my chest with Elladaire's spilled bottle. "She's a woman, all right."

"Ahem. We need a plan."

"I'm working on one right now." He was changing Elladaire's diaper. What a man!

"Seriously, what should we do about the fires? You can put them out if we find them, but you can't stop them from happening, and you can't be everywhere. Or stay forever."

"First, we reconnoiter. No, first, I take a nap. I'll be no good to anyone if I fall asleep on the job. Then we'll look around town, see if we can discover what people know, where the fires are, and why. The why's your job."

"Mine?"

"You have to find out why the bugs are here, what they want. The troll came to claim his half brother. The night mares might have arrived by accident, but they stayed to rescue a lost colt. It's my understanding that the aberrant travelers can find their way back whenever they want. So the bugs must have a reason for not going home."

That made sense. Impossible to comprehend, but reasonable. I couldn't imagine what motivated a bug to do anything, other than food and sex. Like a man, and I managed that species equally as badly.

"So is there a cheap motel anywhere close?" Piet asked. "I don't relish sleeping in the camper with no hot water."

I didn't have to think about my answer. "We're partners, right? I have a spare bedroom. It's my mother's, but she's not due back until she finds homes for a hundred greyhounds. It has its own bath, with plenty of hot water."

"Sounds like heaven."

"But only if you watch Elladaire for another couple

of minutes while I shower and change. Then I'll take over. We're good at stacking the pots and pans."

Twenty minutes later I was back on baby duty, back to worrying. I should have asked if the fire-suppression thing worked when Piet slept. I didn't want to find out the hard way.

"How about some goldfish, Edie?"

That lasted about five minutes. Babies had the attention span of a flea, and this one wanted Piet.

"He's resting, sweetie. He'll be back soon. Please don't cry."

Except his last words before shutting my mother's door were "Trust me."

"Okay, Elladaire, you can cry."

I put the TV on for her and called my grandmother. "You know that stuff you have to make burns heal and scars go away?" I asked.

"So you *are* responsible for those fires! I tried to deny the rumors."

Thanks for the vote of confidence, Gran. "No, I am not responsible. And Mr. Doorn had the burns and the scars before he got here. He's a fire specialist who's just arrived to help."

"Very well, I'll make up a new batch of salve. Bring him to dinner."

Oh, hell. I hated eating at Grandmother Eve's. She wasn't above experimenting on the family and you never knew what you were eating. Or what she'd say. An order was an order, though. "Okay. We might have a baby."

"You just met him!"

"I mean a baby with us. I'm minding a friend's child."

"Is your friend insane?"

Thanks again, Gran. "Mary Brown is in the hospital. Janie had to go help her."

"*That* baby? I heard whispers about her. The rain is stopping. We'll eat outside."

"You don't have to do that. Elladaire is fine. Piet took care of the little problem she had. I don't know if it's permanent yet, but she's not a threat as long as he's here."

"Thank the goddess. What does he like for dessert?"

Janie had left me a baby car seat, in case I had to take Elladaire with me somewhere, like the hospital. As if I knew how to install one of the contraptions.

Piet did. We were off.

Our first stop was the Fire Department, for Piet to offer his assistance. Micky, the kid who maintained the trucks and the building, called over to Town Hall for the captain, who was also the village building inspector. While we waited, Micky proudly showed Piet the shiny equipment. I bet Piet's would make him cry. His fire-fighting equipment, that is. Micky was gay; Piet wasn't. Micky's ESP told him every time; that flutter in my innards told me.

The fire captain came and gave a hard sniff after Piet volunteered his expertise. Mac didn't ask how Piet could help, or why he'd come. The stranger was with me, which meant everyone was better off not knowing. "You'll do," he said and tapped his nose. "I can always tell a good firefighter. There's a smoky smell to them years before they join the department and years after they retire. You'll be welcome." Except Mac's pipe tobacco wouldn't light for some reason. He gave Piet a beeper for direct communication and a police scanner to monitor the fire calls.

We paid a courtesy call at Town Hall next. The mayor remembered to come to work that afternoon, but he forgot about the fires.

Chief of Police Haversmith, whom everyone called Uncle Henry, was glad to have outside help, but he wanted to know a little more of what I was bringing to the town this time. "He's been with the Army and the Forest Service, and knows a lot about scientific firefighting. He's got this new technique, a canister filled with—"

"Bullshit." Uncle Henry belched, excused himself, and reached for a bottle of antacid tablets. "Damn it, Willy, you know what lies do to my stomach."

Piet grinned. "You warned me."

"I wanted to prove it."

Uncle Henry put his pills away. "Just don't let him stir up more awkward questions no one can answer. In fact, might be better all around if you let folks think you've landed another prospect."

"Uncle Henry!"

"They're going to suspect that anyway. He's staying at your house, isn't he?"

Grandma Eve had already been on the phone.

Piet said that wasn't such a bad idea. DUE warned him against being too obvious, as always. So I let him hold my hand when we left the police department.

While he fastened Elladaire in her car seat, Big Eddie, the young cop who ran the K9 section, the arson squad, and the missing persons department when he wasn't giving parking tickets, whispered to me: "I think this one is a keeper. He smells of antiseptic and milk and your mother's shampoo. Nice."

Okay, he was a nice guy. He opened my door for me. So what? We were partners, nothing else. We split the lunch bill at the deli, and let the village gossips make what they wanted out of that. I paid for Elladaire's grilled cheese sandwich. He left the tip. And bought me a chocolate bar on the way out.

Very nice.

CHAPTER II

PIET WANTED TO GET FAMILIAR with the village, so we went on a tour through Main Street on the cloudy, cool late morning. Elladaire's stroller, diaper bag, bottle, toys, blanket, sunscreen and hat took more time packing than I needed for a weekend.

Downtown was déjà vu, with differences. I'd done the same route with Barry only a few days ago. This visit wasn't as fraught, because Piet knew about the Harbor's quirks. I didn't have to explain how we had a blind postmaster, or how the barber gave a thumbs-up for Piet's strong power aura or how Joanne at the deli knew the way he liked his coffee. By now everyone who mattered knew what baby we pushed, and that Piet made her safe to take out in public. What they thought about us together was easy to tell, without any added perceptions. Smiles, nods, and a "Come see me," from the jeweler whose engagement rings told him if a match was right said it all.

"Nice friendly town," Piet noted, the same as Barry had. Sure it was, now that I had a man of talent, a possible problem solver, with me. Suddenly I wasn't espersona non grata.

I told Piet not to go into the drugstore when he

wanted to get a newspaper and a new toothbrush. And end up with a sack full of mortifying condoms? I volunteered to go while he stayed outside with the baby. I wanted to pick up some videos and books for her, I explained, which was true.

I wanted to get some books about the fireflies, too, so I could compare beetle pictures without having to flip through a hundred computer screens and links. The problem was, I didn't know if Mrs. Terwilliger would let me into the library, even if I left the pint-sized threat of fire outside with Piet. While I stood on the sidewalk, debating whether to confront the dictator of the Dewey Decimal System, the eighty-year-old librarian came outside. To see if the grass was dry enough to hold the reading group on the lawn, she claimed. I didn't believe her, not when she handed me a tote bag filled with books.

"Bring them back on time. They are all checked out properly," she declared.

I didn't doubt that for an instant. Or that the books would be about beetles, babies, and burns. She'd put in a couple of books for Elladaire too, and a history of Paumanok Harbor for Piet.

"How did she know . . . ? Did you call ahead?"

I smiled. "How do you put out fires?"

"Got it."

I took him to our new arts and recreation center so he could meet my friend Louisa, who had absolutely no para-skills. Louisa, who was immensely pregnant, was directing a man on a ladder hanging pictures for a new gallery show while she tried to design a brochure for the opening, feed her son a yogurt, admire her daughter's crayon drawings on the floor, and talk to her husband on one phone, a newspaper editor on the other. A harried assistant, a frantic artist, Joe the Plumber, and fifteen kids wandering in for the after-school programs waited for directions. She waved to me and yelled across the room: "You look good with a baby, Willy. Want two more? My babysitter is sick."

I waved back and left quickly.

"Normal, huh?"

"But not dull."

Outside again, a cold drizzle turned the town gray and dreary, so we halted the tour and got back in the car. Piet wanted to see the sites of the recent fires, following the list Mac at the firehouse gave him.

We saw scorched trash cans in the center of town, but everything in or around them had been swept up and sanitized days ago. A few of the torched mailboxes on the side streets still waited for repairs. Ignoring the rain, Piet got out and touched and smelled and walked around six of them.

He did the same at the charred old shed behind the bowling alley while Elladaire and I read the new books. The Wheels on the Bus book had wheels that turned! What would they think of next?

Piet came back with a handful of dirt or leaves that he wanted to examine later. I found my mother's stash of pooper-scooper bags under the backseat for him. He stuffed some in his pockets while I drove out to the demolished beach cottage.

You could smell soot, even with the rain and the distance from the house where I had to park the car. A narrow crushed-shell path led down to the ruins on the shore, but you couldn't see much from here.

"Do you have to go? It's awfully far away. And I think it's raining harder."

"I have my rain poncho."

"The county arson squad's been here, and the insurance inspectors. None of them found anything. Big Eddie sniffed for accelerants, anything suspicious. I thought the cause of a fire was not your field of expertise."

He was pulling the plastic raincoat on over his head. "I've seen a lot of fires," was all he said.

"But you won't see Elladaire from there." That was my main concern, of course, not that he'd get wet or waste his time. "The building could be out of your range." He'd said his extinguishing distance varied with weather and terrain.

"You want me to take her out in the storm?"

The baby's lip was quivering already, and her eyes started to fill with tears. Her Pipi was leaving. "Do you want her to cry in a closed car when you're gone?"

"Damn. How far is it to the house?"

"How should I know? I've never been down that path."

"It can't be too far. People have to carry groceries and get fuel deliveries."

"It's a beach cottage. Sorry, it *was* a beach cottage. I think they said there was no furnace to malfunction, only a fireplace and an electric heater. Neither used recently. The place didn't rent this summer, with the poor economy." I gave Elladaire a dog squeaky toy I found under the seat when I looked for the poop bags. She put it into her mouth. Oh, hell. But she stopped crying. "What if you're not looking at her?"

"I'll walk backward, okay?"

Down the steep path? "Don't be absurd. Go. Listen if I call."

"You really are a worrier, aren't you?"

"World-class. It runs in my family, on my father's side. I'm sorry; I don't mean to be a nag. That's from my mother's side."

"Don't apologize. It's kind of cute."

Cute? I'm waiting to be turned into a charcoal briquette and he thinks it's cute? "Are you sure your thing will still work if you're out of sight?"

"My thing is working fine." He gave a devil's grin.

"My fireproofing works unless I'm unconscious. That's the only way to turn it off. A doctor from DUE tested when I was a kid having my tonsils out. They checked again during the last surgery. Not in the OR, of course. But one of their agents tried to use a cigarette lighter before I recovered from the anesthesia. The lighter worked." He got out of the car. "I'm wide awake now. You and Edie will be fine. Trust me."

I did, except. Except Elladaire was cranky and tired of being in the car and he was gone for hours, it seemed. So what if my watch said ten minutes? What if he'd fallen and was unconscious after all? I wrapped the baby in a hairy dog blanket from the trunk. I drew the line at giving her a dog biscuit to teethe on, but I thought about it—and picked my way down the path with her in my arms. The cottage was a sad heap of charred timbers at odd angles, facing what must have been a beautiful view of the bay on a clear day. People loved coming here once, I thought, with the beach in their backyard and no neighbors in sight. Of course if there'd been neighbors, someone might have noticed the fire before it got out of control.

Piet circled the house. He'd stoop, put something in a plastic bag, then circle again, farther and farther away from the ruins. At last he pointed back up the path. I handed him Elladaire, who'd gotten heavier by the minute, then hurried to the car ahead of him to start the engine and warm us up. When he got in, he told me he'd found some dead beetles. Once we got back to my house, we'd look through the books to see if they were a recorded species or not. The arson squad would never think anything suspicious about bugs in the undergrowth, I conceded, and Big Eddie would ignore their smell as a natural part of the countryside.

Sight unseen, I was sure they were my fireflies. And guilty, like everyone assumed. Damn. I didn't want to think of the lovely creatures as malicious criminals.

Piet picked up on my upset. "A couple are squashed."

"Sure, with all the firemen dragging in their equipment, then the investigators going over the area."

"I don't think that's it. If your bugs set the fire on purpose, they wouldn't have killed their buddies. Two were missing wings. I think they were tortured to make a blaze."

"Who could do such a thing? They're gorgeous and shine with all the colors of the rainbow, and they're smart enough to fly in patterns. You'll see tonight, if they come."

"How can I see? I'll shut the fires off."

"They're magic. Maybe yours won't work."

"You better hope my magic is stronger than theirs or I can't help."

Janie looked exhausted when she came to fetch Elladaire that afternoon. This was the first time I'd ever seen the hair stylist with her own hair in a rats' nest. She was haggard, but relieved.

"I was worried I'd get here to find the place surrounded by fire trucks and police, I'm glad you had no trouble, but now I'm afraid to face another night with her, I'm so tired. I stay awake the whole time in case she wakes up and starts crying."

"Why don't you leave her here tonight?" I heard a stranger saying. Cripes, the stranger was me. "She isn't crying fire anymore, but I don't know what will happen if she's away from Piet."

She never heard my two-syllable pronunciation. "Pete, you are a godsend."

"No, only a one-trick pony. I don't know if I can cure her. Maybe with another day or so the bug juice or whatever will pass through her system. She's a sweetheart. I'll be happy to look after her tonight so you can get a good sleep. Your niece is going to need you well rested when she gets home."

"You can't imagine how grateful I am." Janie threw her arms around him. "I'll fix up that beard for you whenever you're ready. You'll be as handsome as a fairy-tale prince or an English lord when I get done."

I caught the reference to my former fiancé, Lord Grantham. And the slight to my new partner. "Piet is handsome right now."

Piet smiled. Janie said, "Oh, by the way, Willy, you need to fix those roots."

I had a lot to think about, besides what to wear to my grandmother's for dinner. While Piet played with Ella-daire, I considered that the fireflies might not be guilty of the recent mischief. Elladaire only spit flames when she was upset, frightened, or hurting. Perhaps the light-ning bugs did the same, like when Barry swatted at one of them and Buddy snapped at another. Both got burned. So maybe some kid thought it'd be fun to stuff one in a mailbox with no escape, the way adolescents tossed cherry bombs. Or crush one and throw it in a trash can to see what happened. Then the pranks esca-lated into something dangerous and nasty. Who hated Paumanok Harbor that much?

I didn't know. I tried to think about my writing in-stead while I took a shower. I still had no new ideas, re-jected my old ones. That left something borrowed, something blue. What could I do with the Creature from the Blue Lagoon?

Or with the hero who offered to give Elladaire a bath because I was afraid of drowning the slippery kid?

Dinner at my grandmother's started fine. She made in-credible vegetable lasagna, and wrapped Elladaire in a

towel to keep her clean. She didn't pick on me or inter-
rogate Piet, not at first anyway.

When I mentioned how we thought the fireflies had
been forced to defend themselves, she told us that talk
around town had them spotted out in the wetlands east
of Paumanok Harbor. It was a flat stretch of land on the
bay, intersected with drainage ditches to keep the area
from flooding. Clams, mussels, and all kinds of shore
birds made their homes in the muddy, brackish manmade creeks. Men made osprey nests on poles, too, to
bring the fish hawks back from extinction. It was a wild,
empty area, full of reeds and weeds and phragmites, the
perfect setting for my swamp monster.

"They also say a beaver is out there, because of all the
destruction some clammers saw."

"Come on, we haven't had beavers on Long Island
since Indian times."

My grandmother insisted one had been seen last
spring in East Hampton, with a lot of gnawed and felled
trees to prove it. The naturalists reasoned that one had
swum or rode a log over from Connecticut. "There's no
reason that poor lonely creature couldn't come east,
looking for more of its kind."

"There are no trees in the flood plains, nothing for it
to eat or build a lodge out of. No beaver in his right mind
would come there."

"I suppose you're right," Grandmother Eve said,
passing around the salad bowl. "Besides, people are always swearing they see monsters out in the swamp. We
used to tell children that the bogeyman lived there, so
they wouldn't think of exploring the sinkholes and stagnant water."

"So what's there now?" Piet asked.

My new, old, borrowed idea. I lost my appetite.

CHAPTER 12

SOME COOKS GET ORNERY when their efforts and artistry are ignored. Grandma Eve got even.

"I suppose that father of yours told you about the hulking monster living in the marshes. And you believed him, didn't you? If so you were the only child in Paumanok Harbor to take the fairy tale seriously after they turned ten. For that matter, you're the only one who ever held stock in any of the doom and gloom that man spouts. We all swear that's why you're afraid of the dark and everything else."

"I did not believe a swamp monster lived in the lagoons—that is, the wetlands." Then. Now I had my doubts. "Any more than I believe some poor beaver is hanging out there. And I am not afraid of the dark." Lots of people slept with a night-light on. "And my father's premonitions always come true, simply not in expected ways."

"Hah!" My grandmother wiped Elladaire's face so hard the kid had towel burn.

"Your father is a precog, isn't he?" Piet asked in an effort to fend off an obviously ongoing family argument, at least until he finished the best meal he'd had in weeks.

"Pea-brained worrywart, more like," Grandma told him.

I glared across the table, but told Piet, "Yes, he senses the future. Future danger, specifically, for people he is close to. Like many other oracles throughout history, his warnings are subject to interpretation. He's very protective but not very precise. At least he tries to be helpful," I said with another glare.

"Hah!" came again from the family matriarch, which Elladaire took for a laugh so she imitated it.

I wasn't laughing, not when the old biddy belittled my father. "Dad never pretended to be a rustic countryman. He prefers the city and the dangers there to whatever lurks in swamps. My grandmother thinks it's heresy to find fault with Paumanok Harbor."

Since Grandma Eve knew she wasn't going to shake my faith in my father, she turned to Piet. "So what do you call yourself?" she demanded of him.

He put down his fork, reluctantly. "Uh, Piet, with two syllables."

"No, what *are* you?"

"Dutch, mostly." He eyed the plate of toasted garlic bread, hoping she'd pass it.

Not until she was finished grilling him, it seemed.

"Do not be impertinent, young man. What do they call what you do?"

"Oh. Lucky, mostly. But the record keepers at Royce list me as a fire-damp."

I waited to see if he had nerve enough to ask my grandmother what people called her. Most terms were unspeakable in front of Elladaire. I suppose an herbalist would describe her strength. She could make anything grow, and she could make any plant into something tasteful, healthful, or effective, for whatever effect she wanted. She was always cooking up something to cure heartburn or heart attacks or heartache. And she could read tea leaves.

If it walked like a duck, quacked like a duck, Eve Garland was a ducking witch.

Which meant I kept my mouth shut for the rest of the meal.

"Tea?" she asked.

Not on your life. Or mine. I said we didn't have time to stay that long, even if she had mixed berry pie. "It's past Elladaire's bedtime, and Piet traveled all last night and—"

"And you don't want me to look into your future. I understand that, Willow. What I don't understand is how your mother raised such a thick-headed child."

Eve had been demanding to read my fortune since I was seventeen. And she wondered where I got my stubbornness?

She didn't speak to me, but to Piet: "Her lummock of a sire wanted her raised like an ordinary, unexceptional child. He refused to let anyone test her. Now look where we are; she doesn't understand what she does or know how to control it. We all suffer for her ignorance."

Before I could try to defend what was, in truth, the truth, Piet spoke up. "From what I hear, Willow has done incredibly well in difficult situations no one could anticipate. According to the department, her talent is so rare no one could tutor her. They also told me that your little enclave here might have been wiped out without her."

"Hmph. If there is a monster in that bog, it's her fault, I swear," she muttered, but brought out the pie. "Well, everyone wants to know if you two are going to get rid of those plaguesome bugs. May I read your leaves, Mr. Doorn?"

"No, ma'am, I hate tea. Never drink the stuff. Besides,

I know I can shut the bugs down when I find them. You've seen what happens when I don't."

"Then you don't believe the outcome is already decided, waiting to be actuated?"

"I believe anything is possible, ma'am, because I've seen a lot that is impossible. Willow and I will do our best no matter what the leaves say, and that's all anyone can ask."

"Very well." She gave him a jar of her special salve for his burns. "Do you believe this will work?"

"If you say it will, then I have confidence the scars will heal."

"What I say is not the point. If you don't believe for yourself, the recipe won't be effective."

"It's a placebo, then?"

"Why would I spend all afternoon in the stillroom if I doubted its success? You have to help it along, is all." She turned to me. "You should take that to heart, Willow. Believe, and toughen up your backbone . . . and get your roots dyed."

"Thank you for a lovely meal," I said, relieved to get off so easily. And to have the rest of the pie to take home.

Then she said, "Oh, that man your mother married called when he couldn't find you at home."

"That man is my father."

"Which explains a great deal. It does not excuse it."

I wrapped Elladaire in her blanket, not the dogs' this time. "Thanks for having us. I'll let you know what we learn so you can tell the rest of town." She would, anyway.

"He said he had a warning for you."

"You waited till now to tell me?"

Grandma scowled. "What difference does it make? His premonitions are for the future, when they make sense at all."

They did, but usually when it was too late to do anything about them. Others I never figured out, like his old tables. "What was it this time?" I pasted a smile on my face so Piet would understand not to take my father's pronouncements too seriously.

"He said to watch out for a boil on your ass. I'll make more salve."

Could a person die of mortification? If so, I would have been buried almost twenty years ago, after running naked though an outdoor cocktail party when a snake slid over my foot. Better not to dwell on why I was naked, but it involved a blond lifeguard and an old swimming hole. No one in the entire village ever forgot, despite my begging the mayor for help.

This was almost worse.

"I don't have— That is, my father's alarms are sometimes garbled. I bet he means I should stay away from broiled bass. Sometimes the stripers have too much mercury. Or he could be telling me not to boil water in a glass. That's it! I did once and broke my mother's favorite Pyrex pot. It made a mess and she—"

"Don't worry. I'll help you put on the ointment."

"I don't—"

He was choking, trying so hard not to laugh that he woke up Elladaire, who was half asleep on his shoulder while we walked home down the road. I laughed also and felt a lot better for it, until I spotted a hulking bulk on the porch. Lord, don't let it be another monster. I already had all I could handle.

In a way, a port-a-crib is worse than an alien ogre. I couldn't figure out how to open it, for one thing, and it meant Jane thought Elladaire was mine for the duration, for another.

I did not want a baby. I wanted my life back. My work, my apartment, my mean little dog. I didn't want to be wiping noses and butts and sticky fingers all day. And, yeah, I didn't want an interesting man paying more attention to a babbling baby than to me. We should be making a plan for dealing with the fireflies if they appeared tonight, not making a bed and a bottle and how the hell did women do this?

Piet set the crib up in the living room. We'd move it upstairs later, but this way we could hear Edie if she woke, while we went outside to wait for the bugs. I brought the big lantern flashlight, two bottles of water, the insect book, a hooded sweatshirt, and my drawing supplies.

"I wish we had a plan."

"I wish I had more of your grandmother's pie."

I'd left it on her table when I hustled the baby and Piet away. "Sorry. She sells them at the farm stand. I'll buy one for you tomorrow. Meantime, do you know any telepaths or empaths we could beg to come help? We need someone who can communicate with the swarm."

"I know a busload of espers, but I never heard of one who'd ever seen an alien animal, much less spoken to one. Nor am I acquainted with any bug-hunting linguists. Sorry."

"It was a long shot. I called one of our weirdest characters, old Mrs. Grissom who talks to her decades-dead husband. She gives reports back on his opinions and advice on any number of subjects. Neither one of them had any suggestions for dealing with the pyro-beetles. Mrs. G did hint that I was crazier than she was. She only spoke English, not insect."

"You said your mother turned you down, too. She only talks to dogs. And your cowboy speaks horse. What else have you got?"

"A crayon."

"That works for me." He pulled me down to the wicker love seat he'd dragged out to the lawn. "Like I told your grandmother, we'll do the best we can."

"But what if you frighten them away?"

"Then I'll cruise downtown, maybe find those wetlands, see if the fire department has any calls."

"And leave me to handle Elladaire and the flamers by myself?"

"She's asleep and they like you. Everyone likes you, even your grandmother. She doesn't understand you, but anyone can sense the love between you."

"I'll take the bugs." I started sketching. The only plan I'd come up with was to use scratchboard and a stylus. That's the hard paper with a black coating that you scrape off with a sharp pointed tool to make multicolored designs. Maybe the night flyers could associate with the inky dark background and the bright colors. I etched a sheet full of bugs, spending extra time on those lacy wings and big eyes, sending my thoughts and mental images as well as words. "Come on, buddies, come talk to me. I'm all you've got."

Piet whispered, "I see them."

I didn't take my eyes off the board on my lap. "What are they doing?"

"Pretending to be firecrackers, it looks like, or shooting stars, diving around way overhead."

I scratched out a bursting chrysanthemum with cascading fountains of light. I looked up, and there it was.

Piet whistled. "You really can talk to them."

I flipped to a fresh sheet. I scratched out Piet and me on a chair, and a ball of tiny dots over our head. "Come on, guys. Let me know how to help."

The ball formed, and then disappeared.

"No!" I wailed. "You've killed them!"

"Sh. They're there. The fires are gone, is all."

"They're scattering!"

"Maybe your father meant a roiling mass, not a boil on your ass."

"No, they're upset. They need the flashes of light to

see each other. You put out the fire, so they can't fly together. Do something."

He raised the flashlight into the sky, showing widespread individual insects, not a knot of wings. In the light, some re-formed their circular gathering shape, but others flew off out of the lantern's beam. They all seemed confused, unfocused, and in distress, like a beehive when the queen's gone missing.

"Higher, go higher," I shouted, "out of his range. He's a friend, but he doesn't like fire. And you"—I kicked his leg—"dial it down if you can. They are not incendiaries!"

How do you visualize higher? I dropped the heavy flashlight and held my second picture up overhead, as high as I could reach. Then I stood on the wicker sofa, with Piet holding my legs to keep me steady. "Higher, go higher."

And they rose, without the sparks, but casting a soft glow. Fire wizard One, fireflies One. A draw. I drew as quickly as I could by that dim light. Piet with his hands out, welcoming, points of light landing on his head and shoulders.

"I'd never have believed it," he whispered in awe. Hundreds of hard-shelled beetles landed on us, with no fire, just warmth and a feeling of comfort.

I let out a breath. "There. See? No harm. You have each other, and us. You are still beautiful. Piet is beautiful, too."

I could hear the hum of thousands of wings. I didn't know if they understood my words or what they were saying back, which was so frustrating I could weep, but I kept talking, trying to create images in my mind that they might relate to. I was a Visualizer, after all. People hugging, people holding their hands out in peace, that big peace sign from the East Hampton fireworks.

"I don't know what you want or how to help you. I

need you to tell me, or show me if we cannot talk. Why
have you come?" I grabbed up my board and the
wooden stylus and drew a fire with an angry face. "I
know one of my kind hurt your kin, and I know we have
to stop that person, but why don't you leave if you are in
danger? Not everyone cares for you or admires you the
way Piet and I do."

They rose up again, not high enough up to overcome
Piet's power but with a stronger glow, made more intense by their close formation. They did not have the
brilliance of fireworks, but they were visible against the
night sky. The warmth remained, and the whirring. Was
it the sound of their minds, trying to speak to me, or just
their wings?

"Show me." I held up a blank page.

First they separated and formed tiny knots of indi-
viduals, which shifted to the flowers I'd first seen at East
Hampton's display. "Is that your home, or do you like
our summer gardens better?"

The flowers drooped and disappeared.

"What did you do to them?" I demanded of Piet.

"Nothing. I think they are trying to show you something is wrong. Wait, they are lining up to make something else."

"What is it? I can't tell."

"A big bug?" he guessed. "Something with wings, it
looks like."

"Those aren't wings, they're fins. It's a fish, I think." A
huge fish, spreading across the sky. I fixed it in my mind,
its big eyes, its peculiar array of fins or flippers, six of
them, like a beetle. Then it—they—turned so the outlined fish was standing on its end as if the forks of the
tail were legs. "A merman? A hybrid?"

The fish shape righted itself and dove. I did not sense
the playfulness of earlier displays, but a great leaping,
like a dolphin breaking through the waves. I tried to cast

my mental picture and my questions back at them. "A big fish, chasing you? Are you afraid, so that's why you left home?"

They shifted to lots of little fish, again like I'd seen the first night they appeared.

"But you don't eat fish. That's what the book said. Don't go near the water if you're afraid. I try not to go on boats."

The whirring, buzzing got louder, as if they were as frustrated as I was. "Okay, I'm trying. So there's this big fishy thing. A friend?"

The lights got brighter, almost sparks. "NO fire!" I shouted out loud and in my own head. "I'll lose you. Piet really really has a thing about fire. He can't help himself."

I lost them anyway when a loud car engine roared up the private road. Piet stood, as angry as I was to be interrupted when we were finally making progress. Maybe his anger at the car extended his range, tamping down even the lesser glow. I'd have to ask how his emotions affected his talent, if it did at all.

I turned the flashlight to the sky. "Where are they?"

A man lurched out of a souped-up pickup truck. "Where's my kid?"

I lost the lightning bugs, but found Elladaire's father.

CHAPTER 13

NO WAY HAD I BEEN LOOKING for Roy Ruskin. He found me, though. I flashed the lantern on him while he stood by his big-wheeled truck. He put an arm over his eyes to cut down the glare. His arm was full of tattoos. His head was shaved. On some, either was a fashion statement. On Roy, they were the signs of a skinhead, a convict, or a gang member. Or all three.

"Edie's father?" Piet asked quietly.

"Yes, poor kid. Do you have your cell phone with you?"

Piet patted his breast pocket.

"Good. There's an order of protection against him, so call nine-one-one if he looks like trouble."

"He looks like he was born that way."

Roy lowered his arm and tried to light a cigarette. His lighter wouldn't work, of course, so he cursed, then threw it and the cigarette down on my lawn. That's the kind of jerk he was. "Hey, Willy, I've come for my kid."

"You're wasting your time, Roy. And you're interrupting our stargazing."

"That what you call it now? I don't see any telescope."

"I don't see a party going on either. You weren't invited, so get going. This is a private road."

"Come on, Tate, don't be so hoity-toity. A hundred people use this road every day going to the farm stand. 'Sides, we're old friends."

"I've never said more than ten words to you, and you know it."

"Yeah, but you're friends with Jane, my wife's aunt. That counts."

"Mary's not your wife anymore. You're divorced. And Janie is my hairdresser, nothing else."

"Then why'd she leave the brat here?"

"She didn't."

He started toward the porch. The line he walked couldn't pass a blind cop's sobriety test, but Roy kept coming, even after I said, "Your daughter is not here. Everyone knows I don't want anything to do with children. Janie would be crazy to leave a baby with me. Ask anyone in town." The word was Roy Ruskin had no aura or special talent, so I didn't worry about lying to him. I needn't have bothered.

"Jane said she left the brat with someone I'd never mess with. I figured your grandmother. Shit, no one messes with Eve Garland 'less they want their dick falling off. Then I heard you were shacked up with some hotshot imported fireman. What happened? Us local volunteers aren't good enough for you? Maybe they're not, the way things are going. Too bad I can't join the fire department, what with all the time they take for training."

I knew Roy couldn't join the fire squad because no one wanted a drunk and a stoner watching his back in an emergency. I defended the volunteers. "They do a great job. Piet has new technical training; that's why he came to help."

"And that's why Jane parked my kid here, I bet. Well, I can look after my own kin, and I aim to do just that."

"We can't let you."

"Is that supposed to scare me?"

Roy scared me. He must have threatened Janie if she told him anything at all. I only hoped she called the police after he left.

"Your lover boy don't look like much to me. Maybe you ought to try a local stud for a good time." The pig adjusted his privates in case I missed his point. "Or aren't we good enough for that either?"

He wasn't good enough to pick up after my dog. "Listen, Piet's a friend, that's all. And your daughter is not here." I waved my hand around at the porch, the wicker loveseat out on the lawn. "Do we look like we're babysitting, Roy? Go on home."

"Not till I see for myself. What if the kid got hurt in the fire? She needs her dad."

She needed Roy Ruskin like I needed a swamp monster. Meantime, his shouting was going to wake Elladaire, if Little Red's barking didn't. I'd locked the Pomeranian in the house to keep him safe from the lightning bugs. Now I wished I'd taken him out, to take his chances.

Roy came farther up the path, after he stopped to spit into the bushes. I didn't want him in the house or anywhere near the baby, so I started to walk toward him. "You go up on the porch to put the lights on," I whispered to Piet, "and start dialing while your back is to him. I can handle this."

Piet muttered, "You really are crazy," but he stepped up onto the porch, the cell phone hidden in his hand. I saw him looking around for a weapon, and he squinted at the big ceramic mosaic pot filled with trailing petunias. "Don't you dare. My mother brought that back from the Keys. She loves it."

I met Roy halfway to the house. "Your little girl is not here, and you know you are not supposed to go near her anyway."

"She's mine, ain't she? They take half my paycheck to pay child support, don't they? My wife's in the hospital, so now I get to take care of her."

"Mary's taken back her maiden name, Roy, to have nothing to do with you. And you're in no condition to care for a baby."

"You saying I'm an unfit father?" His hands clenched into fists.

He was an unfit human, but I wasn't stupid enough to say that. "Think about it. You don't have a crib or a carriage or a car seat. And you'll be going out fishing. Who will look after her then?"

Janie told me Roy worked in Montauk now, on one of the long-liners that went out on the ocean for weeks at a time. He'd been fired from Rick's boatyard when he broke Mary's wrist. Rick wasn't having any wife beater on his payroll. Roy lost his next job at the bowling alley when he was arrested for ignoring the court order to pay his back child support. An automatic pat down turned up several illegal substances. The judge sentenced him to time served, so he could keep working, to keep Elladaire in Pampers. The fish-packing plant in Montauk sent him packing when he got arrested again after pushing Mary down the stairs. One more infraction and he'd go to jail for serious time. "You don't want to break any more rules, do you? Go home."

"She's my kid! That bitch Mary took everything I had, the trailer, my car, my big screen TV. Now her and her shyster lawyer don't leave me enough to live on."

"You've got a nice truck out there."

"It's Frankie's, on the second crew. I use it while he's out on a fishing trip."

I wondered if Frankie knew that. "I'm sorry for your troubles, but I can't help you."

"Won't, you mean, like everyone else in this friggin' town." He took another step closer, too close for my comfort. Sweat trickled down my back. I wiggled my fingers, hoping Piet got the signal to dial, fast.

"I'm sure people will help you if you follow the rules, which means going away, right now. Don't you want Elladaire to be safe and healthy? She is, now, I swear."

"Dumb-ass name. I call her Ellie. Mary hates it. And who says the kid's safe with a bunch of freaks like you and your family?"

Now those were fighting words. I might have fear sweat dripping down my spine, but that spine was damned stiff. My grandmother was scary, my mother talked to dogs, and I— Well, we were not freaks! "Go away, Roy, before I have to call the police."

"Not until I've seen my kid!"

He pushed me aside and stumbled up the path. Piet had the light on the porch on by now and he came forward to meet the troublemaker. "You lay one hand on her and you're a dead man."

"I'm not here for your girlfriend. I want to see my kid."

"I cannot let you go inside."

"You're going to stop me, scarface? You and who else?"

Roy was bigger and broader than Piet and primed with Dutch courage, if not Columbian cojones. I really wished the plot went the way I wrote it, with the pyrophage wizard casting flames at his enemies. Piet couldn't cast a shadow if it was on fire. I wasn't sure about punches.

I tried to distract Roy. "The police are on the way."

"I want the kid. I paid for her, didn't I?"

Despite wishing I could run the other way, I hurried up the path to get between him and Piet. This wasn't Piet's town, or his fight. "It doesn't work that way," I tried to reason with Roy, "and you know it. A child needs more than food and clothes. She needs love and affection and someone to protect her. Do you want Ella-daire to remember her father as a mean, cowardly con-vict?"

"Who are you calling a coward?" He pulled back his arm, but I ducked away. Piet roared and took the first step down from the porch.

"Stop!" I shouted before the testosterone started to boil over. "This is no way to get what you want."

"I deserve to see her, don't I?"

"Yes, but with the court's permission, under their su-pervision. You know that. Not at night, barging into someone else's house."

"I want to see her!" he roared. Little Red must be frenzied by now. The big dogs were barking too, deaf as they were. And Elladaire was crying.

"That's enough," Piet said. "Go home."

"I hear the kid. My kid. You lied, both of you. Now get out of my way."

Piet stood firm. "You're not getting past me."

"Oh, yeah?"

"Yeah."

Roy charged. He threw the first punch, too.

Piet staggered back against the front door. Roy came at him, but Piet landed a blow to Roy's stomach that had him go "ooph," and fall back, onto the porch railing.

"Stop," I shouted again. No one listened this time ei-ther.

They exchanged more blows, back and forth. The rail-ing cracked, the screen door ripped, the dogs barked, the baby cried, flesh smacked into flesh. And sirens sounded from the main road heading to Garland Drive.

"Roy, the police are coming. You'll be arrested and sent away for life." I had no idea how long they could keep him, but life wasn't long enough. "Go on now and we won't press charges."

He swung at Piet instead. Piet's lip was split, but

Roy's nose was bleeding. They weren't going to stop and who knew how much damage the bastard could do to Piet's healing burns before the cops got here? What were the police going to do, anyway, shoot them?

I did the only thing I could. I hefted up that big mosaic pot of my mother's, petunias and all, and heaved it at Roy's bare skull, shiny under the porch light. The pot landed right where I aimed. Unfortunately, Roy wasn't standing there. Piet was. He got in a strong right to Roy's jaw at the same time I pitched the petunias. Roy went down. The pot sailed over his head. Uh-oh.

I screamed. Suddenly the sky was filled with floodlights. No, the police cars had not arrived yet. The fireflies were overhead, as bright as a million shooting stars.

Holy shit! That meant Piet was unconscious.

Roy dragged himself to his feet by hanging onto the porch upright. "What the hell . . . ?"

"Emergency flares. My grandmother or my aunt must have set them off to get the police here faster. I bet my uncle's on the way across the road, with a pitchfork in his hand, and you do not want to know what Grandma Eve will be carrying."

He turned and left, heading for his truck.

He was going to get away before the police arrived, and Uncle Roger was away at an agricultural symposium. Grandma Eve was too far away to have heard anything and if she saw the fire in the sky, she'd only blame me.

"You better keep going, Roy Ruskin, because the police know where you live. And so does Grandma Eve."

"You can't keep my girl from me, bitch. I'll get her back, see if I don't. I love the kid."

He was almost to the truck when a contingent of fireflies dived at him. They gave new meaning to the old saying, "Liar, liar, pants on fire."

CHAPTER 14

"**D**ON'T TOUCH ME!"

"Stop being such a baby. It's only ice for your head. And I said I was sorry, about ten times."

"Yeah, but you're sorry for missing Roy. You don't seem to give a rat's ass for beaning me or breaking my rib when you stepped on me to get inside."

"I didn't step on you on purpose. I tried to jump over you but slipped on the wet dirt from the flowerpot. And your rib isn't broken. That's what the EMT thought."

"He said he couldn't tell without an X-ray."

"Which you refused to go have, so it couldn't hurt that much. And what was I supposed to do, anyway? You were unconscious. You're the one who told me that's when your power quits. I had to stop Elladaire from crying before she set the house on fire."

"She didn't, did she?"

"No, and she went right back to sleep as soon as the shouting and barking ended. But how could I know that would happen? Who'd believe she was cured after so short a time?"

"When I put out a fire, it stays out."

"She's a baby, not a casserole left in the oven too long. Don't ask. And she's not a fire; she causes fires, like the fireflies. They proved you're not infallible. They burst back into flames the second the pot hit your head, bigger and brighter."

"I told you, they're otherworld creatures. They don't just have magic; they are magic. The rules of earthly logic—Royce logic—do not apply."

"And a good thing, too, or Roy might have gotten away without a trace when he abandoned Frankie's truck. Thanks to the glow beetles, the police will know if he stops at the hospital or the immediate care center. The lightning bugs put him on the hot seat, all right."

"You're sure the police didn't see your friends form a fireball?"

"You woke up seconds before the first car arrived, thank goodness. The beetles turned off and disappeared from sight right on cue. God only knows what kind of acid reflux I'd cause Chief Haversmith if I tried to lie my way out of a lightning bolt chasing his suspect or hovering in the sky over my house. The truth would give him an ulcer."

"Your flying pals knew Roy was bad, though, didn't they? How do you suppose they figured that out?"

"I have no idea unless they picked vibes up from me when we were getting attuned, or they sensed hostility in his voice. Beings from Unity are supposedly all tele-pathic with each other, across species and families. That's how they communicate, the people from Royce believe. The horses could. I've seen it myself. I don't know if anyone's ever studied insects or fish or birds, or if they have xenozoologists at all. I think not, or they would have sent someone."

"Instead of a firefighter. Go on and say it, I'm not much help."

"You saved me from trying to stop Roy Ruskin on my own, and stopped him from carrying off the baby. I'd say you were just what I needed." I quickly amended: "At the time."

"Sounds like they didn't like him picking on you, that's for sure."

"Unless they were protecting Elladaire as one of their own."

"She's not one of them!" Piet sat up suddenly, then groaned.

"Are you sure you don't want to go to the emergency room? The EMTs said you didn't have a concussion, and the split lip doesn't need stitches. But if you are in agony ..."

"I have my own pain pills."

"They thought you'd be fine except for a headache."

"Yeah, and her name is Willow Tate. What the hell had you going after Roy Ruskin in the first place? I was winning!"

"That's not what it looked like from my angle."

"I could have put him down anytime. I was stalling to let the cops get here, so he couldn't claim I attacked him."

"Good thing I am no lie detector. He was bigger and meaner. Anyway, they set up roadblocks and have Roy's room staked out. They'll get him. If not tonight, Big Eddie and Ranger will track him through the woods to-morrow. There's a lot of open space, but he'll have to surface sometime."

"Unless he steals a boat and crosses to Connecticut or Rhode Island."

"Good riddance to him. He didn't get Elladaire, and that's all that matters. The chief says the town's got con-tingency funds to help Mary out with whatever Social Services won't pay. No one will hire Roy whether he goes to jail or not, so she won't be getting money from him. She won't be living in fear, either."

He held the glass of iced tea up to his sore lip. "At least something good came from tonight."

"And we made some kind of contact with the fireflies.

I know they can recognize my pictures, and I know they are concerned about a creature with six limbs." I started to sketch the figure I'd seen while it was fresh in my mind.

"But we don't know if it's a fish or an insect, if it's a friend or a foe, if it came with them or keeps them here. So we have more questions than we had before. And not a lot of answers."

"I have a question for you. You instantly extinguished the fires in the entire swarm, but then they all started to glow. I can understand when they were high up, out of your range, but they kept that warm half-light when they landed right on us, too. I thought your knack was all or nothing."

"So did I. I'd love to sit near embers in a fireplace, or have one tiny birthday candle, but it's never worked that way."

"So when I told you to tone it down, you weren't controlling the dampening effect?"

"I tried. I've never had to put out half a fire. Never saw a reason for it, never thought I could. For that matter, I've never had to consciously think about snuffing flames. It was always get there, get it done, get out. As if all that was required was my presence, not my brain. Tonight was different. I didn't want to hurt your bugs. They made me feel, I don't know, peaceful? Content? Protective, too. I wanted to help them, and you. I tried my damnedest to find a way to let them keep the light. Maybe I did have something to do with it, or else it's the alien magic thing again."

"This is important, so we know for next time. If you *were* in control, not the pyrates, how did you do it? How did you negate or minimize the fire dousing?"

He took the cold glass away from his lip and smiled, which made the hurt worse. "Ouch." But he kept smiling. "I thought about something else."

"You what?"

"I directed my thoughts elsewhere, to not be thinking of fire. It worked."

"Great. What did you think about, so you can use it next time we try to converse with winged matches?"

He grinned, and a drop of blood formed on his cut lip. "I thought about making love to you by candlelight."

There were seven of us in the living room: Elladaire all snug in her canvas mesh crib, three sleeping dogs, Piet at his computer, me with the library books and my sketch pad, and the eight-hundred-pound gorilla of sexual tension.

I was attracted to Piet of course. Who wouldn't be, despite the scars? And I liked him, which naturally made the attraction stronger. My heart almost stopped when I thought I'd killed him with the petunias. And I was flattered that he reciprocated. I was not, under any circumstances, going to act on that mutual attraction and admiration. He'd be leaving. He'd be in constant danger. He was a confirmed bachelor. If I wanted a man, I'd choose someone like the nice, reliable vet. But I'd sworn off men. All men. So there.

I had to get back to my career, not go gaga every time a handsome, hero-type dude smiled and said he wanted me. But, oh, tell that to the parts of me that hummed and vibrated and glowed.

I opened the book to close my mind to opening that can of worms. Scary, slimy, stomach-turning worms.

The insect book was extensive, indexed, and not much help. It was better than the Internet, because I could flip pages and skim and look at hundreds of color plates without having to open new windows or hit the go-back button every time a new link petered out. What wasn't helpful was the fact that my bugs weren't in it, of course.

I kept reading, anyway. A lot of stuff I already knew

from quick Google searches, like how the entire order of beetles was called Coleoptera, which had over half a million separate species. The fireflies belonged to the family of Lampyridae, and there were hundreds of different ones, commonly called Luminaries, spread around the globe. They'd been called Lucifers, not for the devil, but for early matches and the chemical Luciferin that caused them to glow. Mythology had them minions of Vulcan, a god of fire. The English called them Lantern Beetles, which I found charming and more accurate, since they were neither flies nor bugs.

After that, the book got technical about what was common knowledge, that the iridescent flashes came from a chemical reaction, not any kind of flame. Right. Tell that to the German shepherd, or Barry, or Roy. My beetles had real sparks. I didn't care about the chemicals' names or how they got extracted for use in warfare and medicine, which may benefit mankind but didn't do much for the beetles. Now that I had friends in the field, or in the sky, my attitude toward the bugs took a turn toward compassion.

I read about how those chemicals made fireflies poisonous to a lot of species, which was why the beetles had few predators. Which didn't tell me if anything tried to prey on Lucifers.

Nor did the book provide any guidance about my bunch's lives or behavior.

Some fireflies lived underground, I read, some in trees. Some ate other insects; some ate plants, carrion, or wood. Others ate everything and a few ate nothing after the larval stage. Some were short-lived, dying in days after laying eggs for the next generation, others lived long, for insects. Mine could be eternal for all I knew, in their own environment.

According to the experts who wrote the book, all fireflies used the illumination to signal, attract, and identify a mate of their own species, depending on how long they flashed, with what frequency. In some varieties, only the males flew or glowed, in others both sexes hit the sky, like an open-air pickup bar with strobes.

I skipped the parts about larvae and pupal stage and metamorphosis and went to the pictures. Some of the insects were brightly colored, some dull. Some big, some small, some striped, spotted, or solid colored. None had blue eyes. None looked like mine. How could they, when my bugs didn't exist in this world?

Magic. I needed a book of magic right out of Hogwarts to tell me what I was seeing and how to get them home. DUE's arcane library at the Royce Institute was my only hope.

"Are you having any luck?" I asked Piet, who was hunched over his laptop.

"It's taken me an hour simply to get clearance to view the site."

Security had to be tight for a secret section of a public university. This one had more firewalls and passcodes and encryptions than the government had. Heck, the FBI, the Army, and the White House had been hacked; DUE couldn't be. Not when they recruited computer geeks with extrasensory capabilities. An attempted unauthorized entry to one of their sites, the hidden library included, got the web thief tracked, arrested, his memory erased. His computer's memory chip didn't matter, because the whole computer blew up the instant it tried to trespass. Big psychic Brother wasn't watching, but he sure as hell was defending his territory. One could only hope that the DUE crew had more honor and less evil intent than the usual hacker. Imagine what a cyberwizard could destroy. Or steal.

Piet sent my sketch of the fishy creature to the researcher he finally reached, plus my drawings of the lightning bugs themselves, blue eyes and all.

U kidding me? he got back in IM. U I these?

A friend did, Piet typed back. Just search the archives. Maybe some bard centuries ago told a tale about a flying fish, or beetles that caused fires.

Paumanok Harbor, USA, right? :)

Where else?

Piet typed in his cell number, then asked for mine.

Hurry.

He signed off, shut down his computer, and leaned his head against the sofa back. "One hell of a day. I'm ready for bed. You?"

Not his bed. "I have to get the dogs out and tidy up around here. You go on upstairs."

"What about Edie?"

"She'll be fine. You said so. When you put out a fire, it stays out, right?"

He got up and tucked a blanket around her, then came over and kissed me good night: A light kiss, because of his sore lip, but sweet and stirring, and it left both of us wanting more.

I thought he was supposed to put out fires, not start them.

CHAPTER 15

PIET AND ELLADAIRE took a nap the next morning. I called my father.

"Did you get my message, baby girl?"

"Yes, Dad, and my rear end is fine. What worries me is some kind of strange creature. It might be a fish, but it has too many fins. It might be an insect, but it has no wings. Do you have any feelings about something like that?"

"A creature! That must be it! I've had a niggling fret about something, not strong enough to be truly worrisome, but troubling all the same. You know how it is, something in the back of your mind that won't go away, like a sore tooth. I thought I was glimpsing a preacher, but this makes more sense."

When I heard "preacher," I thought of tents and televangelists, not the minister of our tiny local church where I attended weddings and funerals, nothing else. Quiet, gray-haired Reverend Shankman offered no threat to anyone, except possibly boring his congregation to death.

"So you don't think the creature is a big danger?"

"Oh, no. I'd have called right away. As I told you, it feels more troublesome than perilous."

"Okay. Nothing about bugs either?"

"They've got termites in the next condo unit. Everyone has to get out while they fumigate the place. A nice widowed woman from Jericho is going to stay at my place temporarily, but don't tell your mother."

"Then Mom isn't in Florida now?"

"I don't know. She's not talking to me. At least she's not nagging anymore."

I hadn't actually counted on my parents getting back together, not after all these years and all the arguments. Still, I loved them both and wanted to see them happy. "What happened this time?"

"Gotta go, baby. Golf game in fifteen minutes. You take care of yourself, okay?"

In other words, none of my business, and business as usual. "You, too, Dad. Love you."

I left a message for my mother on her cell phone. "Hi, Mom. How are you? Where are you and are you coming home soon? Do you know any entomologists? The dogs are all fine, now. Call me. Oh, and do you think Dad is strong enough to be playing golf so soon after the heart surgery?"

When I got back from walking the dogs, she'd left me a message: "Do you know the number of puppy mills they have in Arkansas? And organized dog fights, too. Do you think I have time to worry about that womanizer? If he's well enough to entertain his bimbos, he is well enough to play golf. I took care of him after the surgery, that's more than generous, isn't it? And all you care about is some bugs? No, you also care about when I am coming home so you can use my room with its king-size bed. Did you think I didn't hear about the new man you have staying at the house? What does that make? Three different men in three months?"

She didn't remember Arlen, the stockbroker in Manhattan I'd been seeing before Grant and Ty Farraday and now Piet. Thank goodness. Four for four. Yikes.

I heard her unmistakable sniff of disapproval, then the message continued: "What are you turning into, a slut like your cousin Susan? I didn't raise you to be a floozy. Maybe your father did, when you spent weekends with him. Now you can't be happy with one—"

I pressed erase.

Susan herself came home after four days in the city, at my apartment.

"Don't worry, I'll replace the lamp. And the rug. Mrs. Abbottini remembers where you got your glasses, so they won't be hard to match."

I slammed down the jar of peanut butter I was opening. "What the hell have you done?"

She looked out the kitchen window and saw barechested Piet—Edie's diaper had leaked—and the bare-assed baby in his arms in the backyard. "The better question is what have you done? Did you kidnap a guy with a kid to make your mother happy in one shot? It won't work, you know. No handing down the genes."

"The child is neither mine nor Piet's. We are babysitting."

"And you're trying to kill the kid by feeding it peanut butter? That I can believe."

"What's wrong with peanut butter? I was raised on it."

"They don't give it to kids that young, in case they're allergic to it. Parents of kids your age didn't know about allergies. Her throat could close up, she could die."

"Wouldn't someone have told me?"

"Anyone crazy enough to let you babysit their kid mightn't have known."

The peanut butter went back on the shelf. "So what

am I supposed to feed her? We're out of yogurt, she won't eat the jars of baby food—"

"I can't blame her. Have you seen that crap? Or what they put into it? You're supposed to make your own if you want the best for your kid, or buy organic."

I looked at her, trying to appear helpless. I didn't have to try real hard. "Will you . . ."

"No way. I have to cook for seventy finicky paying customers tonight. That's enough."

"What about my lamp and my glasses? You owe me."

"And your rug. They're not worth it. They were ugly, anyway. Besides, you're better off with less stuff. That's what all the articles and interview shows are saying now. Getting rid of clutter clears your mind."

My mind didn't need clearing. It was empty enough. And I liked my stuff. I felt comfortable surrounded by things I'd chosen, like I was among old friends. "You could still help, you know. You're better at this baby thing than I am."

"Medea was better than you, and she cooked up her kids for dinner, didn't she? I'd only be in the way here. I'll go on back to my parents' house. Now that school's open and Mom's got all those brats to whip into shape, she'll go easier on me."

"You're leaving me? With a baby and a strange creature?"

Susan was staring through the back door. "He looks good to me. What did you do to his lip?"

Sometimes I wished I could press the erase button on my relatives.

Uncle Henry Hammersmith, our police chief, arrived next. He glared at the rings in Susan's eyebrow, I swear there was one more than when she left, then glared at me.

"I didn't do it."

Susan kissed the chief's cheek, asked if he and his

wife wanted a reservation at the restaurant tonight, then breezed out the door.

"I don't know what the hell the world is coming to," the chief said. "Can you imagine what kind of kids that one will produce?"

They said Susan might never get pregnant, after chemo and radiation. Maybe that's why she didn't want to stay around Edie, to be reminded of what she couldn't have. I could sympathize, but I couldn't relate. In fact, I'd give her Elladaire in a second, so she could see exactly what she was missing.

Piet had on a clean shirt, Elladaire had on a clean diaper and a sundress and half a jelly sandwich all over her face. I wore the rest of the jelly sandwich.

Uncle Henry didn't care. His world was awry, and not because of body piercings, although he took that as an indication of the deterioration of civilization. I seemed to be another harbinger of the downward trend. He glared at me over his bushy eyebrows, but accepted a glass of iced tea.

He reported that the police hadn't found Roy Ruskin, not at his rented room, at any medical facility, or at the homes of whatever friends and relatives they located. Big Eddie could go sniff around where they found Frankie's truck, but the chief figured Roy was long gone, and inclined to leave it that way. Uncle Henry couldn't spare any of his men, not with everything else going on in town, and Roy had no real charges against him. He hadn't taken Elladaire. He hadn't disobeyed any injunction against me. His lawyer could claim Roy was merely a concerned parent asking about his daughter's safety, unsure where she was. He hadn't carried a weapon.

"He hit Piet," I said.

"And got hit back," the chief answered, "if you're thinking he'd need the emergency room."

I'd rather not mention how Roy might be burned, not broken.

"You could press charges," Uncle Henry said to Piet, who shook his head. He was counting plastic spoons with Elladaire, but I knew he was listening carefully.

"Or you could, Willy, for damages to your porch and door. Then I'd have to send men looking for him."

Piet had repaired the screen door and nailed the porch railing back in place. I'd swept up the broken pot.

"I guess not. But if he comes near here again—"

"You call me. Don't go wrecking the house, or getting your boyfriends bashed up."

"He's not my—"

The chief set his glass down. "What I really came to tell you is that boats spotted strange lights over the wetlands late last night. Moving lights. Moving sideways like a missile, not up and down like fireworks. The Harbor Patrol cruised by early this morning, but they didn't see anything. I'm sending the Bay Constable out there. He can walk some, or take the rescue dory, but it's miles to cover."

"He won't see anything, not by day."

Uncle Henry gave me a look of disgust. "I was afraid you'd say that, and I don't want to hear how you know. Just tell me it's not a missile, so I can reassure folks we're not under a terrorist attack."

"It's not a missile."

He swallowed, then waited. When his stomach didn't protest the way it would have if I'd been lying, he nodded. "Good. We'll tell folks it's St. Elmo's fire or swamp gas." Now he reached in his pocket for his bottle of antacid tablets and took three, in case he had to do the telling. "Get rid of them."

"The officials, the boaters, or the beetles?"

"All three if you can."

"I am working on it."

He watched Elladaire crawl over to the sink cabinet and pull herself up by the handle. "You need baby locks before she gets into the cleaning supplies. They can kill a child, you know."

Like peanut butter, electric cords, and playing in the street. How did they survive until school age, when they became someone else's problem? I picked her up and handed her to Piet.

Uncle Henry was telling him how Paumanok Harbor used to be such a peaceful place. "Worst thing we had was some kids breaking into vacant houses, a few DUIs, a couple of domestic situations." He bent his head toward Elladaire, remembering her case. "Then Willow got here."

Piet laughed. Some partner he was.

"I said I am working on it."

The chief hauled himself out of his chair. "Work harder. Faster."

"You didn't have a lot to say," I said to Piet when we were alone. "You could have helped, you know."

"How? By telling him I can get your fireflies to go to half-power if I get a hard-on? He'd love to hear that, being your Uncle Henry and all."

"He's not a real uncle, just a good friend of the family. He and my father had a poker game every week in the summers, and no, you should not have discussed your, ah, personal issues with him."

"I didn't intend to. Of course I could tell him how the bugs come to your backyard and draw pictures in the sky for you. That'll help him calm the civilians."

I bit my lip. "No, that'll only get people over here with nets and flyswatters and bug spray."

"Oh, then I should have told Chief Hammersmith about some monster you thought the bugs were show-ing you?"

"You saw it, too!"

"No, I'm not so sure now that it was anything but a haphazard blur, like when they put a brush in an elephant's trunk. You're the one who saw it as a flying fish."

I was dismayed. I thought we were partners, friends, working together. "Then you don't believe me that the creature is the problem, not the beetles? That the fireflies don't set out to start fires?"

"Willy, I don't not believe you. I can't feel it like you do, is all. I came to put out fires, not interpret flight patterns. There were no fires last night. No calls to nine-one-one, nothing. Then, when I do see your guys, I can't extinguish them entirely."

I gasped. "You wouldn't kill them, would you?"

"Not unless they were setting people on fire, I guess. Not even you could let them burn down the town. Killing them mightn't work, 'cause the others might retaliate. Or there could be consequences we have no grasp of."

"Like more coming from the otherworld."

"Exactly. I'll give it a couple more days, but then I've got to be going. People will start to notice when their cigarettes go out when I walk past, or how the candles in the restaurants won't stay lit if I eat dinner out. I can do more good somewhere else."

"You're still mad I hit you with the flowerpot."

"And stepped on me. Don't forget that. But no, I'm not mad. Just frustrated, about the fires, about staying in the house with a female who kept me up all night long."

"Elladaire slept through the night."

"Not Edie."

"I didn't make a peep."

"In my dreams you moaned damn loud."

CHAPTER 16

BEFORE I COULD THINK of how to respond to that without stuttering, running out of the house, or throwing myself into his arms, the phone rang. Saved by the bell.

Or not. Barry wanted to come over. At least he'd called before showing up on my doorstep, but I said I was busy. His anger last time made me uneasy.

"Okay, how about later? I need one more picture of you to put up at the webzine site."

"I still have the baby here."

"And the fireman, I suppose. Leave the kid with him and come out for dinner. I heard there's a great new place in Montauk that won't be so busy now that Labor Day is past."

He was wrong about that, too. Montauk stayed busy on weekends through the fall. Some people came for the fishing, others knew enough to come when the beaches and roads weren't so crowded and the water was still warm. Nor did I want to spend time alone with him at a cozy, secluded table in a half-empty restaurant. "No, I don't think that's fair to Piet."

Barry did not suggest Piet and Elladaire come along.

I did not suggest he come to my place for dinner. I was out of bread and jelly.

"I know, how about I pick you up just before sunset? The fireman can put the kid to sleep, can't he? We can go out to that swampy place where people saw lights. That'll make a great background for the picture. Kind of spooky, like some of your stories, and kind of diffuse in the dusk, 'cause you said you wanted to stay enough incognito to be unrecognizable. We can get the tail end of the sunset for color, and wait to see if the weird lights appear. Then we can get a late supper or a couple of drinks. What do you think?"

I thought I'd rather crawl through glass than be anywhere near the wetlands in the dark. Or let him see the lights. On the other hand, it was kind of a kick having two men interested in me. Three if I read Matt's parting smile right. Okay, one wanted a story; one wanted a quickie; one wanted to keep on my mother's good side. They were all good for my ego.

"You know, right now might be better after all. Why don't you come over here. We can get great pictures in my grandmother's gardens, or go to the beach down the block. That's a better image of Paumanok Harbor anyway."

It wasn't what he wanted, but he agreed. Piet agreed to watch Elladaire while I changed my clothes.

There was no way I could keep my writing identity androgynous in a photograph. I wasn't as well-endowed as Susan, but I was womanly enough that only a space-suit or chain mail could hide my shape. So I went the other way, toward femininity. I'd have to put my summer clothes away soon, but I could wear one of my favorites a last time. The yellow jersey tank dress was comfortable, the patch pockets were convenient, and the color always made me happy. I thought it was perfect for a picture in a garden or on the beach. Very Hamptons chic. And it looked good with my straw sun-shielding hat which helped hide my face for that ounce of anonymity, and hid those dratted darker roots, for my vanity.

Piet thought it was revealing.

"Way less than a bikini," I said.

"You're not wearing a bra," he said.

"I don't need one under this dress."

"Like hell you don't."

He huffed about needing another roll of mesh from the hardware store to repair the window in Mother's bedroom. Mosquitoes came in.

"What about Elladaire?"

"She could get bitten, too. I read they carry West Nile virus."

Add mosquitoes to the peanut butter on the list of things a surrogate mother had to worry about. "I mean what about taking her with you?"

"No car seat in the camper."

"You can take my car."

"You want to be alone with Barry that badly?"

"No. I don't want to be alone with Elladaire. Badly."

"You have to test it sometime. I'll be gone for fifteen minutes. Play outside if you're nervous."

Who, me? Nervous to tend a baby who might go up in flames—in front of a man writing about my books?

I tried to stay away from Elladaire while I waited, to stay clean. She didn't cry, which was a relief, but no good test of her return to normalcy outside Piet's range. Be-sides, she'd spent every minute with him. What if his magic wore off when he was gone, not just for fifteen minutes, but a week or a month? What if there was no permanent cure? How could anyone trust her, ever? Poor baby.

I felt so sorry for her I picked her up, and got muddy

footprints and animal cracker fingerprints all over my yellow dress. I took her inside and changed into a Paumanok Harbor shirt, over a bra, and cut-offs with frayed hems. Hamptons shlep.

Maybe Elladaire could stay with my grandmother during Barry's photo shoot. Sure. And maybe I'd ask Granny to lend me a cup of eye of newt while I was at it.

There was no need; Piet rumbled down the dirt road before Barry arrived, late. That pissed me off. I could have gone with Piet to town, maybe had an ice cream, maybe found root dye at the drugstore. I could have changed my clothes again. Or worked on my book in progress, whichever story I dared to use.

He didn't apologize for being late, or for grimacing when I said Elladaire and Piet were coming along on the photo shoot. I wanted an objective opinion, I told Barry, if my picture was going to be broadcast across the Internet.

"Beach or gardens?" I asked him.

I thought I heard him mutter, "What effing difference does it make?" but that had to be wrong.

Grandmother Eve's old Jeep was in her driveway, which meant she was home. "Let's go to the beach."

Which meant Elladaire needed sunscreen and a hat and the stroller.

"Can't you stay here with her, man?" Barry asked Piet.

"I could. But I'm not going to, man."

Maybe having more than one man interested in me at the same time wasn't such a good idea. I made it all better by bringing Little Red and the two big dogs. "You want to show an accurate portrait of how I live? This is it. Muddy footprints, dog hair and . . . low tide?"

Something stank at the beach. We didn't see any swath of rotting seaweed, dead fish, or empty shells, but the putrid odor was enough to gag on. Sometimes we

got the dreaded red or brown tides that killed the sea
life and put the bay fishermen out of business, but I
didn't know if they smelled. The shallow water looked
clear enough and the pebbly beach appeared clean.

Piet and Elladaire started home.

Barry took a few hurried pictures, and I didn't bother
to look at the playback screen on the digital camera. I
did ask if I could see the article before he sent it in, to
check for facts.

"That's not how it works. If the subject of an interview gets to rewrite the piece, it's not an honest opinion."

I didn't know this was a review. I thought he was
doing a bio, which was not a matter of opinion. "Can you
at least show me the article before it's online, so I'm prepared? And I'll need the name of the ezine so I can tell
people about it."

"Sure. I'll send you a link."

Good. If I hated the picture or what he wrote, I didn't
have to forward it to anyone. "I suppose you'll be going
now that your car is fixed and you're done with the article?"

"No, I paid for two weeks at the motel after I left
Martin's place. He was too fussy. No smoking. No one
needs me in the city, and I like the area. You can say it
inspires me to write more. I might do another piece
about the off-season, or side trips, out-of-the-way loca-
tions no one knows about. You know the kind of thing."

"For side trips, there's the aquarium in Riverhead."
Where I was thinking of taking Elladaire and my picture
of the mysterious creature to show their marine biolo-
gists. "For off the beaten path, there's an incredible garden in East Hampton that's open to the public a couple
of days a week. Or you could write about the hidden
army bunkers along the shore all the way to Montauk."

"I was thinking more of those wetlands right here. I

could do a fascinating environmental piece on what changes manmade ditches bring."

The smell wasn't the only thing that caught in my throat.

"Have you heard about West Nile fever? The place must be overrun with mosquitoes. And ticks. There's not much to see, either, just an expanse of sea grass. You can't walk on much of it except at low tide, and if you think this stinks, you don't want to go to the salt marshes then."

"I'd like to see them anyway. And the lights. When are you getting rid of the kid and the smoke eater?"

The smoke eater was sitting at his computer when the dogs and I got back, without Barry. I hadn't invited him in, claiming an urgent need to go grocery shopping, which was no lie. I hadn't planned on company, much less a baby. In fact, I usually counted on Susan to cook or bring leftovers home from the restaurant. We were low on dog food, too.

Elladaire sat on the couch, rapt attention on one of Louisa's videos and a sippy cup of apple juice. "Want to go bye-bye car?" I asked. She didn't look at me. Little Red ran to the door, ready.

Piet said he needed a few more minutes.

"Find anything we can use?"

"It's what I didn't find that's the problem. There's no website for a Barry Jensen. No Facebook account. A freelance writer looking for work has to have a way for people to find him, doesn't he?"

I didn't have Barry's email address either, now that I thought about it, or the name of the ezine he worked for, only a cell phone number. "Maybe you spelled his name wrong. Try Jenson. Or Jenssen."

"I tried all of them. None are writers."

"That's odd."

Piet looked up, with the expression I usually saw on my grandmother's face. "Odd is that you didn't think to look him up before you went out with him the first time. Odd is your being the only single woman I know not to do a Google search before letting a stranger in your house."

Barry wasn't exactly a stranger. Susan knew him, didn't she? She'd brought him home when his car died. Susan brought home a lot of men, though, which didn't make Barry an automatic friend.

I found a nearly empty bag of chocolate kisses. I needed one. Piet needed an answer. "He must write under a pen name. That's not altogether unheard of, you know."

"When he doesn't give it to people he meets? People he's trying to impress with his writing?"

"You don't like him, that's all. I can take care of this in a minute." I called Kelvin at the garage and asked what name was on Barry's credit card when he picked up his car. And if he had left an address or anything.

"You know I'm not supposed to give out that kind of information, Willy."

"Do you want me to lie and say he left his sunglasses at my house and I lost his phone number?"

"Hell, no. I don't need that aggravating itch now. Hang on."

When he came back to the phone, Kelvin reported that Barry'd paid cash. No numbers or addresses.

Getting more anxious by the minute, I repeated the lack of information to Piet, who asked if Kelvin had a license plate number.

He did, right on the copy of the paid bill. "What'd the guy do, anyway? I thought you liked him?"

"Want me to lie?"

He hung up.

Piet pushed a button on his cell phone and read the

license number into it. Most likely he called the Department of Unexplained Events, whose people had access to a staggering amount of personal information.

He set his phone down. "They're going to call back. What kind of guy pays cash for a car repair?"

"Someone on vacation who took a lot of money with him?"

"With an ATM on every street corner? No one carries a fat wallet anymore. It's too dangerous. I can't believe you didn't ask to see his credentials."

"Like what? He said he was just starting out writing, sold a couple of pieces, that's all."

"What did he do before?"

"I have no idea. I didn't think to ask."

"Well, you should have. Or did you let his flattery flatten your common sense?"

"That's not fair. I didn't ask to see your birth certificate or your driver's license either."

"You asked for a demonstration. Did you ask to see anything he'd written?"

"It was free publicity! And there wasn't time. The lanterns appeared and I—"

His phone rang. The ring tone was "Come on Baby, Light My Fire." Piet wrote something down, thanked the person at the other end, and went directly to hitting the computer keys. I looked over his shoulder.

"Barton Jenner?"

"The Third. Got him. Website and all. And the scandal sheet he writes for."

I put another kiss in my mouth. With its little paper tag. Yeck. "You must be wrong."

He tapped the screen, and I leaned closer.

Piet enlarged the picture. "That's your pretty boy, isn't it, in the picture beside his father, Barton Jenner the Second. The owner of the sleaziest dirt rag to hit a supermarket checkout counter. You know what they specialize in? Alien babies, UFO abductions, and demon possessions. You couldn't have picked a worse tabloid for ruining Paumanok Harbor if you tried. You screwed up big time, Tate."

So did my father.

No old table.

A tabloid.

And a shitload of trouble.

CHAPTER 17

IN SOME TOWNS, the whisper of a pervert was a call to arms. In Paumanok Harbor a child molester was child's play. Between Grandma Eve and the town council, he'd never harm another victim, not in the Harbor, not anywhere. Here the worst villain, the evil-doer unspoken, was a reporter. Like the Grim Reaper, a nosy journalist could bring life as we knew it to an end. Tourists, Paumanok Harbor could handle. Demon hunters, paranormal fanatics, federal investigators, and curious, jealous, demanding mobs, not so well. Publicity was the last thing a village of espers wanted or could afford.

Word went out. We'd meet at Town Hall.

Elladaire didn't want to leave her movie. "This is important, kid, and you're not going to set anything on fire, so don't waste the effort of crying." I ate the last kiss but gave her the tippy-top of it.

"Nice parenting skills." Piet was grabbing up her stuff, his laptop, and the fake "experimental" fire retardant canister.

"She stopped crying, didn't she?" I gave the dogs wait-here cookies.

I drove too fast, my mind racing, too. How could we

stop Barry, whatever he called himself, short of tossing him and his camera and computer into the bay? The picture of me was no problem, and I knew nothing otherworldly left an image, but what else had he shot and speculated about? Worse, had he transferred his story and photos to the magazine yet?

We left the baby with Mrs. Ralston, the town clerk and gatekeeper to the inner offices.

"Is she safe?"

"She is now."

"Thank you, Mr. Doorn," she said to Piet, ignoring my part in keeping Elladaire from burning down the town, or eating mushrooms from the lawn.

We headed toward the police side of the building, where Uncle Henry was waiting for us. The Chief of Police gave me that Grandma Eve look, filled with disdain, disgust, and disappointment. But not surprise.

"I didn't—" I shut my mouth. Maybe I did.

Uncle Henry refused to arrest Barry/Barton, even if he'd given me a fake name. He wanted to lock me up instead.

This time Piet stood up for me, kind of. "Come on, Chief, there must be a way we can keep him from writing that story."

"I wish I could keep you from writing your damn stories and painting your blasted pictures, too, Willow," said the man who used to brag to everyone he knew how he'd encouraged me when I was just a kid, coloring outside the lines.

I ignored his wishes. "I know what we can do. You can bring the mayor to his room and wipe out Barry's memory of everything he learned about us."

"I already called the mayor. He's in Albany trying to get the state to cough up more money for the school programs they insist we have. He'll be home tomorrow, if he doesn't forget what time his plane leaves."

"Jensen—Jenner—will have the article written by then, unless he's waiting to see the fire lights tonight," Piet said. "We need to act now."

I offered to go to the motel where he was staying and divert Barry. I'd say I forgot to tell him about my new book, which was the purpose he gave for writing the damn article, the lying slug. While I had him outside, someone—I looked at Piet—could go around back and smash his equipment.

Piet refused. He was no criminal. "And I'm not going to jail because you trusted a good-looking slimeball."

The fire captain, who was also the building inspector, hurried into the chief's office. If Barry was at the Harbor Inn, Mac swore, there'd be sprinklers. Mac had insisted on them himself. All we had to do was hold up a match to set them off and flood him and his equipment.

Mac looked at the pipe in his hand—the suddenly cold, dead tobacco—then at Piet. "Guess that won't work."

The next suggestion came from Micky, the firehouse maintenance man. He wanted me to call in a fake fire alarm so the volunteers came with hoses pumping.

The village finance director tried to crowd into the small office. We didn't need a fire alarm, he said, a bomb scare would do. Evacuate the motel, confiscate the equipment as an agent of terror.

As if that would hold up in court, where we had to move, to fit in more people, including Mrs. Ralston and the baby. Everyone shouted their ideas, from giving Barry a bottle of drugged wine to feeding him laxative-laced brownies. The chief held up his hand for quiet. He didn't want to hear any more. There'd be no breaking and entering. No false fire alarms, no damned bomb scares, no damage to private property, no poisoning the perp either. He'd go to the motel himself and tell Barry we don't like our visitors operating under false pretenses and ask him to leave.

That wouldn't work and we all knew it. Barry'd only move to Montauk's motel strip and spy on us from there. We had to destroy his equipment—flash drives and external hard drives, iPads or smart phones, even yellow legal notepads—then keep him from rewriting the story another time, on another computer. Or calling it in, the way newsmen used to. If he hadn't sent it in yet.

We needed the mayor, and a miracle.

No, offered the tech guy, Russ, who'd been updating the juror rolls. We needed a cone.

This was not the time for ice cream, but I'd take it.

He meant a cone of electronic silence. Russ was middle-aged now, but he made legends as the kid who shut down the stock market on a school trip to the Exchange. And he wreaked havoc with the power grid at the high school when he failed the computer class he could have taught. They'd shipped him out to Royce University to get control, and a conscience. Score one for the freaks in London. Now Russ volunteered to shut down the motel—the electricity, the wi-fi, the cable—to keep Barry from filing his story.

Piet raised his eyebrows and whispered to me: "He can do that?"

I raised mine back. "You can put out fires, can't you?"

Judge Chemleki banged his gavel. "What about the first amendment, you know, freedom of speech and all that?"

Everyone shouted him down. Homeland security overrode the constitution, didn't it? The Feds thought so. If it was good enough for them, it was good enough for us, wasn't it?

Mr. Graystone, the village lawyer, timidly raised his hand—the only one to do so—and in a quavery voice noted that the police could arrest the intruder if he was registered at the motel under a fake name. He'd be out on bail by morning, of course, but they'd have a little more time for the mayor to get home and to keep Barry from going public with his suspicions.

Unless he already had. Maybe that's why Barry was here in the first place. Lord knew there were plenty of rumors about Paumanok Harbor after the spate of murders and drug raids, the mysterious mares and the un-identified mayhem while the unseen—except by me—troll wandered the streets. Yeah, the place just might interest a sensationalist rag sheet and its nepotic columnist. I bet he was a lousy writer.

Piet had his phone out. "Shutting it off at the other end," was all he said until he completed the call. "Some-one at DUE will close down the magazine, for libel or something. Or they'll simply do what they do to hackers. That's what DUE is for, to protect its people and keep their secrets."

Barry and his father would only start another scandal sheet, if they didn't already own a bunch. That's what they did. Everyone knew it. And Barry'd write another story, under another name.

Unless the mayor got to him.

Even the mayor's gift wasn't infallible. The problem with wiping out a memory was it left room for new memories. The mayor couldn't follow Barry around, de-stroying every conversation he had with the nontalented residents and visitors. He couldn't keep Barry from see-ing something strange and wanting to write about it.

"I say we drown the guy once and for all," came from the back of the room.

The judge banged his gavel again. Uncle Henry put his hand on his revolver. "None of that talk, now. We are a peaceable town. And we don't need any more bad publicity."

What we had to do, everyone seemed to think, was

keep Barry busy so he couldn't compose another story or see anything worth investigating.

They looked at me. "No, I am not going to entertain that rat bastard. If you are suggesting anything more, you should be ashamed of yourselves."

A few of the men looked at their shoes. Mrs. Ralston clapped. So did Elladaire, mimicking her.

"It's poker night tonight, isn't it?" I asked. A handful of heads nodded sheepishly, as if it were another secret. "So invite Barry. Russ can interrupt cell phone transmissions, so he can't get a message that his story got lost. And try to get Mayor Applebaum on an earlier flight."

More nods, but mutters that the shithead most likely cheated. And how could Tom levitate the cards, or Bunny keep the room free of smoke when a stranger sat in? More importantly, they didn't play all night. Barry was still going to want to look at the lights in the salt marshes.

Once more I was the focus of every eye in the room, and George Washington's, from the painting over the judge's bench.

I bit my lip. Gulped twice. Then said, "I guess I'll have to try to keep the lights away until the mayor gets back or Barry leaves."

Piet took my hand. "And I'll put them out if he comes too close. We work together."

Sure. I drew pictures for bugs and he pictured me naked. What a pair! We were partners in a situation we didn't understand, didn't know how to resolve, and didn't have an inkling where to begin. And we were all the town had. My heart sank.

"And no more fires, you hear?"

"No fires," we chorused. My heart sank lower.

They looked relieved. I wasn't. How the hell were we supposed to make good on that promise?

*   *   *

The problem with working with self-assured, talented, independent-minded people in authority was that they were self-assured, talented, and used to giving orders, not taking them. Put a couple of big dogs together, you get a pissing contest. Put a bunch of wizards together, you get a clash of power. We had a police chief, a fire captain, a judge, a lawyer, the woman who actually ran Town Hall, a technical engineer, and handfuls of other psionic experts. In other words, too many chiefs, not enough Indians.

Good thing Barry did most of the work himself.

I knocked on his door. When he answered and I saw the computer plugged in, I asked him to come out for a short walk with me and Elladaire.

He said he was busy writing.

I said I'd remembered something important for the story.

He came with me out to the motel's front lawn, his room out of sight. Before I set the baby down to play in the grass, I smelled her diaper, to check if it needed changing. It did. Barry wrinkled his perfect nose and curled his luscious lips.

Now I truly intended to tell him I'd changed my mind about the story. The sneer and the sniff—and knowing what a dick he was—changed my mind again. "How dare you," I started. Then I shouted and stamped my foot and tossed Elladaire's dirty diaper onto his sandal-shod foot.

"You are a cheater and a liar and a user and a dirt bag, Barton Jenner the Turd!"

"And what are you, if not using me for publicity for your stupid picture books?"

I gasped. "You—"

People came out of the motel, yelling. "The power's out! Someone call the electric company."

Barry cursed. "I didn't shut off my computer."

He ran back around the building to his room. I followed with naked Elladaire. Barry had the laptop and his phone in his hands when I got there. "Shit, both batteries must be dead, too."

He rushed past me to the motel's lobby, where the desk clerk was lighting candles. "No telling how long the power'll be off this time." The candles caught, which meant either Piet was too far away, or he was thinking really, really dirty thoughts.

Barry cursed some more, then shouted, "Does anyone have a phone that can text?"

Half the people in the lobby had no idea what he was talking about. The other half were having trouble with their own phones. "Must be trouble at the cell tower."

Barry pounded his fist on the registration desk, which sent one of the candles off its dish, onto the stack of Chamber of Commerce brochures, which caught on fire, which had people pushing and screaming, which jostled another candle that ignited the curtains.

The sprinklers went off, the automatic call went out to the fire department, and everyone fled outside. The fire engines arrived—miraculously, two of the motel guests noted—in minutes.

"We were training nearby," Mac shouted, running past us. While half his men went around back, to check the rooms for guests or smoke, Mac directed his hose at the office. And at Barry, whose pant leg had caught a spark. His cell phone got drowned.

In seconds the fires were out. Piet appeared. Or vice versa, but no one noticed.

The police chief and the motel owner arrived at the same time. Mr. Hinkley wanted Barry arrested for starting the fire and causing all the damage. The clerk and I both saw him knock over the first candle in a rage.

"Bullshit. I'll sue you for negligence if your fucking sprinklers damaged my computer."

"You'll do it from some other motel," Mr. Hinkley told him. "Or a jail cell. And I just heard you might have used a false name at registration." He turned to the judge, who'd ridden on one of the fire trucks. "Isn't that illegal? It ought to be."

Piet, Chief Hammersmith, and I followed Barry to his room. The place was dripping, so was his camera, but his computer didn't look bad, still plugged into the wall. Then the lights came back on, the TV and the clock and the air-conditioning. They came on in a burst. Smoke came from the computer, then a sizzling noise. Then it went black and Barry wailed in anguish as if he'd been the one electrocuted by the power surge.

"Sorry about that," Piet said. "You should always unplug them in a power outage. Or use a surge suppressor."

Barry was storming around, kicking the bed, knocking the chair across the room, dumping his suitcase full of soggy clothes onto the floor.

"You don't want to be causing more damage here, son," Uncle Henry told him. He put his arm around the younger man and led him out of the room. "I'd hate to have to lock you up, this being my poker night and all. In fact, I think you ought to go cool off a bit."

Mac came in then, and apologized for soaking Barry's phone. "To make up for it, here's my cousin's card. He has a nice little bar on the road to Springs. Tell him I sent you, and drinks are on me."

One of the firemen said he was going there, too. Could he have a ride?

They called the fireman Tank because he could drink more than anyone in town and never get drunk or passed out. He winked at me as he passed by. He'd keep

Barry busy for a long, long time, right into tomorrow morning. He'd be in no condition to write anything, not even his name, whatever it was. Then the mayor could join him for lunch.

So we'd dodged a bullet, temporarily. Now we had to face the flying firing squad.

CHAPTER 18

THE OTHER PROBLEM with having a lot of alpha dogs on a team was they all wanted credit for the success. Everyone who didn't have to go back to work wanted to go celebrate, at a nicer bar where Barry wasn't. They invited Piet, who looked to me like he wanted to go. Here were people with talents almost as oddball as his, who didn't ask questions, who didn't consider him a freak. Besides, he'd had nothing but female company for a couple of days now, me and Elladaire and dinner at Grandma Eve's, so I told him he should go talk boy talk: fire engines and computers and poker. Edie and I would go food shopping.

"Without me?" He nodded toward the baby, who was giggling at Mrs. Ralston's funny faces. The town clerk had arrived in time to get Edie into a fresh diaper, more securely than I'd ever managed. She didn't want to give her back.

"Yes, without you. You said she'd be safe and I trust you."

He smiled. Mrs. Ralston didn't. "You weren't sure when you handed her to me both times?" Now she was eager to get rid of the baby.

"I was fairly sure." I went to lift the kid into her

stroller, but she decided she wanted to walk now that she half knew how. "No, baby, we have to go to the store. You know, bananas and cereal and dog food."

"You're feeding her dog food?"

Piet laughed and left in the fire captain's car. He'd be home—at my home—in time for dinner. I wanted to make a decent meal for him. Or get one from the deli section of the supermarket in Amagansett.

Then Elladaire unbalanced and fell and started to cry. Everyone stopped what they were doing to see what would happen, from a safe distance. I held my breath. "Come on, Edie, you're not hurt." I was getting used to Piet's nickname for her, and Elladaire started using it herself, or close to. She was Deedee, Piet was Pipi, and I was Lo. Figured. Except when she was tired or hungry or hurt or frightened, like now. Then I was Mama, no matter how many times I told her I wasn't her mother. I have to admit it felt nice. Until miscellaneous firemen and cops started snickering.

"Looks good on you, Willy."

"You ought to get one of your own. Keep you out of trouble, kiddo."

"Your mother'll be thrilled, Will."

I gathered Edie and my dignity and drove off. Then I backed up to pick up the stroller.

Anyone considering parenthood should be forced to experience the horror of a cranky toddler in a store. That cute little cherub in their minds? Uh-uh. Ugly, scrunch-faced devil's spawn, more like. Edie didn't want to get in the cart. She didn't want the safety belt on. What she did want was to walk, to grab everything she could reach, and she wanted it now, in her mouth, immediately, or else. At least she didn't set the place on fire. Or embarrass me too much with her upset "mama" cries. I didn't know anyone in the store, so I didn't care. I was afraid if

I kept saying I wasn't her mother people might wonder why I had someone else's crying baby, when I was so obviously inept at childcare. I waited for someone to call the cops.

Her plaintive cries tore at what little confidence I'd developed by conquering the baby seat harness contraption. So I hurried through the shopping to get out of the place as quickly as possible.

I found raisins and bananas and cereal and the baby aisle, but what could she eat after that? I had no idea, so I followed a woman with a little kid in her wagon and another one holding on alongside. Both of them were better behaved than Edie. Hell, Little Red would have been better behaved.

I bought whatever the Good Mother ahead of me did, apple juice and watermelon and blueberries and sweet potatoes that I knew how to cook and baby carrots. She ordered turkey wraps at the deli, so I figured they were okay. And I got an already roasted chicken fresh off their barbeque machine. I added a bag of prewashed salad, chocolate pudding pie, and some ice cream. A fine dinner, if I said so myself. I got some broccoli, too, because it was healthy and looked good in macaroni and cheese. More chocolate kisses, more pretzels, and dog food. I got the dogs some new biscuits too, because I felt guilty giving Edie so much attention and leaving them alone so much. Damn, I was a neglectful dog surrogate mother, too; I'd forgotten to bring Buddy back to Dr. Matt to have his burned lip checked. It looked fine to me when I put the salve on it, but I know my mother demanded the best for her rescues. And Matt Spenser really was a nice man. I'd take care of it soon. Crises and catastrophes had to come first.

On the way home I gave Edie a little box of raisins. Mom's car was never going to be the same.

*   *   *

Piet loved the dinner. "You cooked all this yourself?"

"Most. Some. The sweet potatoes."

"They were my favorite part."

My favorite part was watching him enjoy the meal, cutting tiny pieces of chicken for Edie, laughing at her efforts to feed herself. Sure, he didn't have to swab the table and the chair and the baby. (The dogs cleaned the floor.)

Piet already looked better after the few days of Grandma Eve's burn potion. Not that he wasn't attractive before, in a rough, wounded-hero kind of way, but now you could see where he'd be drop-dead gorgeous without the angry red marks, when his sandy hair grew a little longer and the scraggly, scar-hiding beard either got trimmed or shaved off. I couldn't decide if he'd look better with it or without.

I wondered if he'd stay long enough for me to find out.

When he carefully wiped his chin to make sure no crumbs stuck to the hairs, I also wondered if I'd like kissing a man with a beard. That was a rhetorical question, of course. I did not intend to find out.

But he smiled across the table at me, laugh lines crinkling around his green eyes. Maybe the question wasn't so rhetorical. I gave myself a mental kick and ate another forkful of chocolate pudding pie. One decadent pleasure was as good as another, right?

We were partners. I couldn't let hormones ruin our working relationship. We were growing into friends, which sex usually destroyed. Love affairs disordered one's brain, too, which I couldn't afford right now.

Tonight we felt like family. Not my family, of course, with its sniping and faultfinding and unmet expectations, but a warm, cozy, loving family. Did I say love? I had more pie.

Maybe I'd have a family like this one day now that I

saw how it could be. Not with this baby, of course, and not with this man. Edie belonged to Mary Brown; Piet belonged to DUE. And I? Tonight I belonged to the bugs I might have brought into this world.

While Piet got Edie ready for bed, I changed my clothes. I wanted to see the flyboys tonight, to try again to communicate with them. No matter what the mayor convinced Barry he hadn't seen, there'd be more sightings and more fires, if I couldn't get the Lucifers to go home. If not Barry, other reporters would come. If not reporters, government investigators, which was just as bad.

To make sure I saw the lightning bugs, in their full glory and no confusion, I put on a skimpy ribbed white long-sleeved jersey. Yup, you could see my nipples, and yup, it had the effect I wanted. Not on the bugs, but on Piet.

"What are you trying to do, kill me?"

"Just trying to keep your mind occupied so the bugs won't be afraid to come."

"You're playing with fire, woman."

I reached over and stroked his cheek. The whiskers weren't coarse at all. "No, I'm not. The bugs won't hurt me."

"I'm not talking about the bugs."

"I know." I smiled and turned away, making sure he could see the back of my tight jeans. After the chocolate pudding pie, they were so tight I couldn't bend over, but Piet groaned, so the discomfort was worth it.

The fireflies came, lighting up the backyard. Then they disappeared.

"What are you doing?" I asked Piet. "You are turning them off."

"Thinking about your grandmother, what she'd look like in your clothes."

Talk about a turnoff.

In the interest of saving the world, I grabbed his shoulder, pulled him close, and kissed him.

He cursed. The sky lights came on.

Piet went back in the house. "You talk to your friends. I need a cold shower."

He came back before I could finish a scratchboard picture of an angry man stomping on sparks. This time he had Elladaire in his arms.

"She wasn't asleep yet, and she should see this."

Except the lights instantly dimmed. The beetles were still visible, so they didn't panic about finding each other. They knew to gain altitude, to gain more fire power, but most of them flew off, leaving a comet's tail across the night. The remaining swarm came down, closer, dimmer, perhaps curious.

"What if they remember Edie biting one of their kin?"

"They cannot hurt her with such low strength. And they don't appear aggressive at all."

I don't know if Elladaire remembered them, or what happened afterward, the flames, the fire, her mother being taken away in an ambulance, but she was frightened now.

She cried in Piet's arms, struggling to get away. No, she wasn't trying to get away from the bugs, she was trying to get to me.

"Mama!"

She held those little arms out to me. Her lip quivered, and a tear rolled down her cheek. "Mama."

If she didn't have my heart before, she had it now. "Poor sweet baby. I'm here." I took her from Piet and held her close, rocking. She hid her face in my chest, pulling my shirt down. Like magic, the fireflies got brighter.

They came closer. So did Piet. I felt warmer, especially when he rubbed the back of my neck.

"Stop that!"

"Then stop the peep show. You're confusing all of us with your mixed messages." He came closer still and leaned toward me.

I started to lean forward, but then I remembered I had a kission. That is, a mission. I stepped away, out of danger. The fireflies went back to quarter-power. Piet was on the job.

I couldn't use the scratchboards, not with Elladaire in my arms, so I tried to reach out with my mind even though I was not a telepath and did not know their language. I gathered pictures, emotions, sensations in my head: flying, happy, safe, the beauty of the fireworks display, the fear of my neighbors, the burnt cottage, anger, dread, trespassing, breaking vows, flowers and fish and fire.

And words unspoken: *Please go home, please don't stay where people might hurt you. Please don't start any fires. Please.*

I closed my eyes and imagined them bright in the sky, over a different world, with elves and trolls and halflings waving to them. *My friends. Your friends.*

I desperately tried to *feel* my thoughts, my images, so they could sense what I wanted to tell them, see the pictures. I felt Piet's hand on my back, supportive, caring, trying to help when he didn't understand what I was doing. *And don't let me fall for a fire wizard.*

Nothing.

I felt like crying. Instead, I shouted out loud, "Talk to me, Lucifers. Show me. Give me a hint."

The few bugs over our heads formed a rough fishlike sketch, smaller than before, naturally, with fewer glimmers making up the outline.

"I got that already. What is it?"

All I heard in my head was an echo of Elladaire's woebegone "Mama."

She was asleep and getting heavy. I handed her to Piet.

Mama.

"Did you hear that?"

"Hear what?"

Oh, boy. The sound came again, right when I was looking at him and the baby. Her lips never moved. Besides, the plaintive sound seemed to come from up, above me. I pointed up. "What do you see? Right now."

"Fireflies, I guess. Bigger than I've ever seen. Not as many as before."

"What color are they?"

"Plain brown, with a greenish glow except near the tail, where something looks like an ember."

"No green wings, no blue eyes or iridescent luster?"

"That's what you see?"

"Yes, and I think they are finally trying to talk to me."

"I didn't know you could communicate. I thought you were a Visualizer."

I thought I was crazy.

CHAPTER 19

"**Y**OU ARE NOT CRAZY," Piet said. He must have read the expression on my face.

I knew he would have reached out for me if his arms weren't already full of the baby. "But no one sees what I see."

"That's because you are so damn special no one else can do what you can. We see big beetles or small flares. Some of us can feel their magic while ordinary folks only see the strange. I can put out the flames, but, hell, Tate, you can see what's hidden behind ancient spells and alien sorcery."

Just what a woman needs in life, insight into a world that doesn't exist for most people. "Why couldn't I be a weather magi or a truth-seer? That might have been fun, especially on first dates. No need for a Google search."

He smiled, a rare flash of white teeth in the dark. "But now you can communicate with them, without your fancy-dancy linguist or a celebrity animal trainer. Your talent is growing, adapting. And not simply because someone handed you a custom-tailored gift. You are the one who is learning."

"So are you, learning to control your power."

"I think the bugs are letting me affect them, to a point, after their initial surprise."

"And I suspect it is the luminaries who are learning to talk to me, not the other way around. The elf king spoke our language. So did the lord stallion. We did not learn their tongues."

"Either way, you are expanding your abilities, which is great. Now tell them to go home."

We both looked up, high, to see a tiny meteor shower streaking away. I didn't have a feeling of success, that they'd listened to me and left for good. They had somewhere else better to be, that was all. "That's what I've been trying to do, but they don't understand. Or don't want to. I think they want their mo—"

My cell chirped.

Uncle Henry called from the police station. His voice was a near growl, he was so mad at having to leave the poker party. He was in pain, too, I could tell, from the lies he'd had to spout.

The Harbor Patrol intercepted a complaint from a boat headed east, he told me. I held the phone away from my ear so Piet could listen in, too. The yachters stopped to watch a fireworks display off the area east of Paumanok Harbor, but a spark hit their teak deck and started a fire.

"Did the boat sink?"

"They killed it."

"The firefly?"

"They couldn't catch your freaking fly. They killed the flames. Then they turned around and headed back to Shelter Island. They intend to lodge complaints of negligence with the Coast Guard, though, as well as NOAA, the DEC and whoever else will listen. The area wasn't marked, patrolled, or on any alerts they should have received. And it wasn't the Fourth of July."

"So they got too close to some fireworks. That's not so bad, is it?"

"Not so bad?" He shouted loudly enough for Piet to wince from beside me. "When there was no firecracker barge, no rocket booms when they went off, and no one standing on shore with a lighter?"

"Don't tell me, the salt marshes?"

He didn't tell me. He didn't have to. "Do you know how many people listen to the ship-to-shores and the police scanners? Do you have any idea how many people are headed out there now, in the dark, in kayaks and canoes and traipsing across those sand-spit causeways, to see the show?"

"We're on our way, Chief," Piet called over my shoulder. "But maybe you want to put up roadblocks to keep any more spectators away."

"What I want is to go back to my poker game. You fix this, you hear?"

Elladaire heard, too, and woke up disoriented and distressed. That was bad enough, but what did we do with her now? She wasn't a puppy we could lock in the kitchen or a dog that would be content with a good-bye cookie.

"Your cousin?"

Susan worked until the kitchen at the Breakaway closed, then stayed to shut the bar. Her mother and Uncle Roger kept farmers' hours, so they'd be asleep by now.

"Mrs. Garland?"

I shuddered at the thought. "Do you know what trouble I'd be in if Edie's not one hundred percent flame-free out of your range for what could be hours? Or what Eve Garland could do to her? She'll have to come with us. She'll go back to sleep in the car, and then we can leave her with one of the cops at a roadblock, or dragoon a local who gets turned back from the shoreline into sitting with her. We'll have to walk into the wetlands."

"No problem."

"Yes, there is a problem. You don't understand. We'll have to *walk* into the wetlands."

"I have high boots."

And I had a bogeyman from my childhood nightmares hiding out there. My father'd warned me about the creature when I was five. And again now, when I was thirty-five. My stomach was already doing somersaults and my knees were locked, shouting, "Hell, no, we won't go." I'd say we had a big problem.

Big Eddie blocked one of the access roads with his K-9 patrol partner and squad car. The dog wore an orange vest. Big Eddie wore a gas mask and an oxygen tank on his back. As soon as we got out of our car, I understood why. The same stench from the beach near my house filled the air here, only stronger. Poor Eddie with his incredibly sensitive nose had to be suffering. The dog, with no training and no urge to exert himself by finding or detecting anything, ever, slept in the back seat of Big Eddie's car, unaffected. Good thing Main Street and the developed areas of the Harbor were so far away.

The young policeman almost snatched Elladaire from Piet's arms, removed the gas mask and inhaled deeply. "Ah, baby lotion and urine and, um, chocolate kisses? A touch of perfume. Chanel, I think."

That would be mine.

"And dog."

Mine, too.

"Maybe a smidgeon of smoke and aftershave. Something English. And beer, Sam Adams."

Piet.

"Thank you, thank you. I really need this. Can I keep the kid to clear my head?"

I handed him the diaper bag. "She gets worse."

"Can't be worse than this."

"So what is the awful smell?"

Big Eddie didn't know, and that hurt him worse. He spent hours every week studying new scents sent from laboratories all over the country, via DUE, of course, to learn to identify them. This wasn't from any lab. It wasn't something easy, either, like low tide, a dead dolphin, or decomposing deer carcass. He knew what those smelled like, and this was different, which made it more painful.

"It's a lot of everything," he said, inhaling the eau de bebé. "Chemicals, botanicals, organics."

"Like the old twenty questions."

Eddie looked blank.

"You know, animal, vegetable, and mineral."

"Yeah, but none from around here, that's for sure."

I didn't need his nose to tell me that. I did not want Big Eddie and his big nose telling me some huge slavering beast lurked in the marsh, either. On the other hand, I'd welcome a name, an identification of what waited there.

"Isn't there such a thing as swamp gas?"

"We're telling people that's what this is. It isn't." He held up two sealed bottles. "I've got samples ready to be analyzed, and the Harbor Patrol is bringing up water specimens." He sniffed at Elladaire's hair, not looking at us. For the first time in memory, our psychic sniffer couldn't do his job.

I patted his slumped shoulder. "Don't worry. It's not your fault. It's most likely something new."

"Oh, I know that, Willy. Everyone knows you brought it here."

"I didn't—"

Piet pulled me away. "We'll figure it out."

We left Eddie with a bottle of organic baby milk and

our cell numbers. Then we started away from the car's headlights. Into the dark. Off the road. Oh, hell.

"You could have stuck up for me, you know," I sniped at Piet rather than think about what else was on the deer path ahead of us. "Partners and all that."

"And let the kid think he failed at his job? Besides, you're not going to change anyone's mind no matter what you do."

"I could explain how I don't create the aliens, I just sense their presence. Once they come and find me." Of course that meant I wasn't half the imaginative artist I thought I was. "You're right. No one will believe me."

"But they trust you to fix the mess."

I don't know if trust was the right word. Demand, insist, and blame defined the locals' attitude better. I trudged on, feeling as if the weight of the world rested on my shoulders.

No, that was the backpack I wore, with everything I could think of to bring: flashlights, fresh water, clean socks, cookies, a hammer, bug spray, a little field guide book of fishes, another of insects, nets, Reese's Pieces, a small first aid kit, duct tape, a steak knife, and an extra cell phone in case mine went dead.

We didn't need a flashlight. The moon was out and bright. Except the golden orb in the distance wasn't the moon, unless blue cheese caught on fire.

We didn't need cell phones. Nothing worked this far from a tower.

We didn't need a map, either. We just followed the not-moon and the dreadful scent.

I put the hammer in my hand.

"What are you going to hit with that?" Piet asked. I could hear the smile in his voice.

"You if you don't shut up. This is serious. We don't know what's ahead. All you've got to protect us is a canister of nothing."

"Very official looking nothing, though. And I thought you felt the bugs didn't mean us any harm."

"They don't. It's who or what else is out there that might be dangerous."

"I have a pocketknife."

"How big?" I wanted to know.

"Not big. But it's got a bottle opener and a nail file."

"That's not funny. Heaven knows what we'll find."

He held a low branch of some pricker bush out of my way. "What's the worst you can think of?"

Oh, he didn't want to know the worst I could imagine. Eight-headed monsters, eight-foot ogres, gore-dripping fiends, unattached hands that played piano. And those weren't real. Vampire bats, black widow spiders, quicksand, collapsing sides of the ditches, so you fell in the water and your boots filled up so you couldn't get out and drowned and your body got swept out to sea to be scavenged by crabs and seagulls.

"Okay, give me the hammer."

I started to hand it over. "Why?"

"So you don't sink so fast in the quicksand."

I thought I showed great restraint in not hitting him over the head with my weapon. Or throwing it at him when he got too far ahead. I ran to catch up and tripped on a root I hadn't seen. He came back and helped me up. Then he unbuckled my backpack and slung it over his shoulder as it were no heavier than his empty canister. "We're wasting time."

Yeah, like I was in a hurry to meet Dad's creature.

We didn't see anyone else as we walked toward the fireball, the stink, and the shoreline. We didn't see any snakes, ticks, or spiders either, but I knew they were out there. If those were the worst we encountered, I'd consider myself lucky. And lucky I didn't faint when a raccoon burst out of the reeds and humped across our path.

I thought I was in good shape from walking the dogs

all summer, but I was out of breath after the first half hour, maybe from holding it to lessen the smell. Maybe from getting ready to scream.

At least the ground was level. It had to be, to serve as a flood plain. Unfortunately, it was about three miles of level deep to the bay, and maybe five miles wide. If our path ran out, we'd be forging through tall Phragmites, jumping ditches where anything could be lurking.

The path held, and was pretty dry considering how much water flowed around it, reflecting the light in silvery bands. I thought I heard an owl, then small things in the reeds, but nothing bothered us.

As we got closer to where the ditches opened onto the bay, we could see boats in the distance, their lights bobbing on the water.

We could also see what they'd come to view: a shimmering ball of fire hovering over a section of the wetlands about half a mile west of where we stood.

I tugged on his arm. "Turn them off before they start any fancy acrobatics. Don't you dare think about my body now. Full power, Piet, full concentration. Shut them down."

He chuckled, but took my hand and picked up the pace toward the swarm. "Do you actually have a body under all that armor?"

My mother's yellow rain slicker reached to the tops of her rubber boots, which were a size too big for me, but better too big than too small, I figured. I had on a baseball cap under the slicker's hood, to keep bats out of my hair, and thick gardening gloves to protect me from poison ivy and thorns and those piano-playing severed hands. I was hot and sweaty and not at my fashionable best. Or bravest. I clutched Piet's hand so tightly he'd lose circulation in his fingers soon. He, of course, looked calm, cool, and macho in high leather boots, tight jeans, and a long-sleeved work shirt. Then he looked pissed.

"We're too far away. You try."

"Try what?"

"Talk to them, damn it. Distance doesn't matter for telepathy."

While he searched for a path going in the direction of the light, I concentrated on telling the lightning bugs to pretend to be lightning, and leave.

Instead, *Mama* echoed in my head and the fireball flattened into a streaking rocket, headed toward us.

"No, don't let anyone see you!"

They tried to look like a cloud in front of a sliver of a moon, but still coming in our direction.

Then we heard voices—both of us heard them this time—ahead of us where the ditches emptied into the bay along a narrow muddy beach. "Hide!"

How do you visualize the concept of hiding? A kid behind a tree? A burglar in an alley? Nothing I thought of made any sense to beetles in a beeline for their friends. Besides, I was distracted by emoting that I wasn't their mama, either.

The smell got worse as we got near the beach. The voices got louder. The swarm got brighter, and closer. Crap.

There were five or six boats, kayaks, canoes, and small outboards pulled up to the reeds, and a bunch of kids who looked to be high school or college age sitting around a driftwood fire, watching the light show. I could hear one of them wondering if they were under attack. "Should we duck?"

Piet left me and ran ahead. By the time I huffed and puffed onto the mudflats, the fire was extinguished. So were the fireflies. And about fifteen adolescent a-holes were staring at their joints and bongs, wondering where the lights went.

CHAPTER 20

"HEY, DUDE, WHAT HAPPENED to the fires?" Piet dropped my knapsack, pulled out a flashlight, and shined it in their faces. He held up the canister with Fire Retardant written on it and some kind of official-looking badge. "Shut down by order of the Commissioner for Public Safety. You know that smell out here? It's flammable. The swamp gas can ignite any second and blow up the whole salt marsh. And the vapors are noxious. Our man at the blockades is already suffering the effects. We're evacuating the area." He pulled my two water bottles out of the backpack. "We only have this much antidote, so you are in danger. And liable for any damage if your fire ignites the protected area."

The kids were already scrambling to gather up their gear and shove their boats into the water.

"Don't start your engines until you're fifty feet or more away. Paddle or get out and swim, but don't chance any sparks."

They splashed off, by the light of a nimbus around the moon.

Piet paced around, kicking the charred driftwood apart and picking up a six-pack the kids had left. "See? The bottle opener will come in handy."

I couldn't joke. Where were the lanterns? What was the smell? Could we go home now?

I heard engines start, then saw floodlights out on the water. The voice on the bullhorn from the Harbor Patrol boat would be Elgin, harbormaster and the best weatherman in Paumanok Harbor. He could forecast better than the Weather Channel, keep storms away from the Fourth of July parade, and make it rain when the fields and underbrush got dry. I bet Al Roker couldn't do any of that.

"Return to port," Elgin was shouting to the boats that had come to see the fireworks. "There has been a chemical spill. The vapors are noxious. Repeat, leave this area. Do not breathe."

Piet laughed. I had to smile, despite being alone out on a five-foot-wide patch of muddy sand, in the dark, miles away from the car, with a foul monster somewhere in the marsh. Then Piet took my hand. I wasn't alone.

He led me to a fallen log where the kids had been sitting, pushed the hood of my raincoat back, and kissed me.

The fireworks were back.

No, those were the stars I was seeing. And the heat I was feeling. And that feeling that I was safe, wanted, lo—No, I was not going there. Or here, not on a damp log with the smell of swamp and beer and grass, the illegal kind.

I pulled back. "What was that for?"

"For wanting to all night. For seeing if you tasted as good as you look in your clown costume. For scaring off your monsters."

"I don't think we scared anybody but some stoned kids and some curious boaters." But I wasn't half as fearful now, so maybe he was right. He was definitely a great distracter, and a great kisser. "Now what?"

"Now we wait to see if your friends come back and tell you what they want. If not, we call for the Harbor Patrol boat to come get us so we don't have to trudge those miles back to the car. He'll be standing by in the bay waiting to lower the life raft."

I could definitely get to love this guy who thought of everything, if I let myself. Since that wasn't in my best interest, I scooted over on the log so we weren't touching. I drank some water. Piet had a beer.

"Call them," he said.

Easier said than done. I tried picturing a meteor shower headed our way, or a rocket, or the aurora borealis. This wasn't the right time of year for an already rare sighting of the Northern Lights in our area, but they were beautiful, and not so paradoxical if anyone saw them. I thought high, higher than Piet's magic.

He was humming. "Damn, I wish I'd thought of that." So we both sang, "Glow little glow worm, glow and glimmer." Neither of us could remember the next line so we hummed. And laughed, since neither of us could carry a tune in a bucket, either.

There they were. That glowing nimbus separated from the moon and drifted our way in shimmering bands of color, high overhead.

"Ooh." That's all I could say.

Piet stopped singing and let out a long breath of awe. Me, too.

"Well, hello, gorgeous," I whispered, standing to welcome them, to thank them for putting on a display that almost made me weep for its beauty.

The colors came closer, flickering now like a million tiny candles. "No, don't get any near—"

The lights went out, and I felt like my best friend kicked me. I kicked Piet instead.

"Dial it down. You can do it, I know you can. And without thinking dirty thoughts."

He closed his eyes and lowered his brow in concentration.

The sky stayed dark. "I tried. It won't work."

Damn it, I had to take one for the team. I pulled him toward me and locked my mouth to his, and teased his lips with my tongue. I felt warm and tingly and damp. Must be the raincoat, the swamp, and the muddy log. Or the fireflies. They were back, dimmer but still visible, and dancing.

Sure, they loved a good mating ritual.

Piet had his hand on the back of my neck, stroking, caressing, asking for more. Too bad I had more important things to do. "Hold the thought while I try to talk to them."

To make sure he did, I held his upper thigh, not touching anything crucial, but close enough to have him suck in a breath, knowing I could.

"Okay, guys, talk to me. What's going on here, and what's the smell?"

Mama.

Oh, boy. Was that the only word they knew? "I am not your mama. I'll be your friend and try to help you get home, but I am not adopting you like a litter of kittens."

Mama.

Persistent devils. And trying to tell me what I already suspected. "Your mama is here?"

The bands of color shifted again, this time into wiggly lines and intersecting rows.

"Plaid? A chain-link fence? Is she caught in a fishing net?"

The lights got dimmer as Piet's mind switched to the new puzzle. I squeezed his thigh and moved my hand an inch. Now I could see that one square of the grid was filled with the soft flames. "A map of the drainage ditches! That's what it is, isn't it? And she is there?"

The lines danced across the sky.

"But how will we find her? Show me where we are now, in relation."

Another box in the map grew brighter, then they all went out.

Damn, my firefighter had the attention span of a flea. I tried to move my hand, but he grabbed it with his. His other hand was holding a stick, drawing the map in the mud at our feet. He kept looking up, as if to check his accuracy, but the more he looked at where the Lucifers were, the less chance they had of being seen. I could hear the whirring of their wings and almost inaudible chitters . . . and Piet's teeth grinding.

"Fly high," I called, and thought and projected. "He can't help himself."

And I didn't dare kiss him again or we'd be naked in the mud, putting on a peepshow for the pyro-opters. And maybe Elgin, too.

"It's okay. I think I got it." Piet had his phone out and switched it to camera mode. The flash went off a couple of times as he changed position. He checked the play-back, checked our location.

"It's that way." He pointed up the beach. "And inland, about a mile, I'd guess, judging from the number of drainage ditches."

"If the guys can count."

"They didn't have to count, just copy the pattern they saw below them. They got here, didn't they? So they had the map in their heads."

"Unless they followed the smell."

He looked up. "Can insects follow a scent like a bloodhound?"

I had no idea. Bees found flowers, mosquitoes found fresh blood in the dark. "But I think the map points to where we first saw the fireball."

"Me, too. It should be easy enough to find whatever they've got out there."

"I think it's their mother." I didn't want to tell him I heard the word in my head. That was too weird, even for me.

"Bugs have mothers? I know bees have a queen who lays all the eggs, but I never heard of any other colony as big as this"—he pointed up—"with one matriarch. And don't fireflies flash to attract mates?"

"These seem to flash to get our attention. I don't know much else about their social system, but I'm pretty sure their mother is out there, in trouble. Maybe the big fish thing has her, or the swamp creature."

"We'll know when we follow the map. I think we ought to wait until morning to go looking."

He'd considered the alternative? Hiking another mile of smelly salt marsh in search of something that could eat us, in the dark? Maybe he'd breathed too much smoke after all. "That sounds good to me. We can get Chief Haversmith to send in the cops and the fire volunteers. Maybe the road crews and the Harbor Patrol guys. They can fan out and—"

"And find the lightning bugs' mother? See what no person on Earth is supposed to? If you call out that many people, the rest of the village will know, besides. They'll want to come see what's lost in the swamp. If you turn them back, they'll want to know more. People like your reporter friend."

"He's not my friend. And maybe he'll leave."

"And maybe there won't be anything out there in the daylight. Did you think of that? We never see the fireflies during the day."

I hadn't thought of anything except getting out of here.

"So what you are saying is . . . ?"

"You and me, kiddo. You and me. By boat, so we can count the openings to the bay. By daylight because it's easier. By night if we don't find anything."

"I vote for daylight."

"Good, because I have other plans for tonight."

Me, too, a hot shower being first on the list. "What are your plans?"

He started to pack up everything we'd brought, plus what the kids had left. "To finish what we started here."

"To map the wetlands?"

He raised an eyebrow. "To do what we both want."

"Have an ice cream on the way home?"

He pulled me up off the log and tipped my head back so he could kiss my neck and my eyelids and my cheeks. "This." He kissed my lips. "And this." His tongue flirted with mine while his hands left a heated path on my back, my ribs, my breasts. Oh, my.

"And a lot more."

I thought about it—especially the lot more part—on the way home, and while I got Elladaire settled in her crib and took that hot shower. Why not? The whole town assumed we were sleeping together, so why not live down to their expectations? It's not as if I am a virgin or anything, or committed to another man. It's not like I sleep with every chance-met stranger, either, like my cousin. Piet was a partner, a friend. We shared secret knowledge and a trek through the wilderness and really, really hot kisses. Most of all, he made me feel good. I knew he could make me feel a lot better.

Now I had to figure a way to tell him I was willing, without having to say the words. Maybe if I paraded around in my sexiest nightgown he'd get the idea. Which was a great idea, except I didn't have any sexy negligees. I gave them to Susan when I decided not to marry Grant or run off with Ty. Wrap my shower towel around me and ask him to check my back for ticks?

Or maybe I shouldn't go down that path. Not the one with the ticks and spiders and poison ivy, but the one that could leave me aching and hurt and twice as alone.

I didn't have to decide. His beeper sounded, his cell phone chimed, my mother's phone rang, and sirens came tearing up our dirt road.

"I came to get you on my way to town," Mac shouted from the fire captain's car. "The bowling alley's on fire."

CHAPTER 21

PIET RAN TO HIS TRUCK to get his gear.

I couldn't go, not dragging Elladaire out of bed again and into a fire. I couldn't help them anyway, and I might even be a hindrance. No one suggested I come, either.

I could tell Piet about the old building and the apartment upstairs, though, so I raced after him in my towel. While he grabbed a heavy fire jacket and helmet and gloves from a hook on the back door of his camper, I shouted that Joey Danvers lived over the bowling alley by himself now, and he used crutches. Piet didn't need to know that his wife was in jail. Maureen actually resided in a hospital for the criminally insane after running Joey over in a fit of madness. She backed up and ran him over again. I guess she was really mad.

"The captain will fill me in on the way." He gave me a quick kiss on the cheek and ran for the fire department's SUV.

"Joey has a dog!" I yelled after Piet. "Be careful." I didn't mean be careful of the dog, who was one of my mother's rescues, a sweet hound mix. I meant don't run into the burning building. Don't think of me in nothing but a towel in case you lose concentration. Don't get hurt.

I watched the dust from the dirt road billow up as they tore off. Piet waved his hand out the passenger window.

The house felt cold, though I knew it wasn't. I put on warm pajamas and wrapped up in the dog quilt from the living room but still felt chilled. Elladaire's cheeks were warm, but I tucked another blanket around her anyway. I made a pot of tea. Now that Piet was gone, I could use the top of the stove.

Now that Piet was gone, I felt like an old-time whaler's wife, watching my man sail away for years, if he returned at all. How did soldiers' wives do it? How could firemen's wives watch their husbands speed off to infernos? What about cops' families, when the police got shot at every other day in the news?

They sucked it up, I supposed. Stiff upper lip, the show must go on, no pain, no gain. Bullshit. I wasn't that brave or stoical or altruistic. I wanted to call Piet on the phone and tell him to come back. His last burns weren't all healed. This wasn't his town. Let the volunteers do their thing.

Little Red jumped in my lap. Dogs understood when their humans needed comfort. Or that they usually had a cookie with their tea.

I hugged the Pomeranian and regretted telling Piet about Joey's dog or his crutches. The dog was old, and Joey'd thrown a bowling pin at Maureen. They weren't worth dying for.

Little Red growled. I was squeezing too hard and not sharing enough. And I was a rotten person.

Sherry was a sweet dog, and both Joey and his wife had been hit with the psychic nightmares that stormed across the whole village. They all deserved rescuing.

"Just don't outrun your magic," I whispered into Little Red's soft fur, as if Piet could hear my prayers. "Come back. I lo—" No. I could not go through this every time a siren blew. "Come back. I want to make love with you."

And what about the Coleoptera? The fireflies needed him, too. I couldn't read maps for the life of me, but I had the feeling their mama's life depended on it. On me and Piet.

"Don't be stupid," I whispered again.

So Little Red stopped looking for crumbs and charged at the whole bag of cookies. Smart dog. Smart fire meister. He'd be back.

He didn't get home until nearly six in the morning and sank onto the sofa, exhausted.

"I'm filthy."

"So are Mother's dogs, but they sit there, too."

I pulled his boots off, hung his jacket over a chair, and brought him coffee and what was left of the cookies. "Tell me."

Yes, the fire was out. No, no one got hurt. Joey and the dog were waiting outside when the fire engines pulled up.

The building was big. Piet had to circle around it twice to put out all the flames, avoiding the volunteer firemen with their ladders and hoses. Then he went inside to extinguish any embers. He let the locals think their efforts worked, which took him longer. The hardwood lanes were destroyed by the water, the apartment upstairs only had smoke damage. Yes, it was definitely arson.

"And?"

He rested his head on the back of the sofa, leaving his coffee untouched. He took a plastic sandwich bag out of his pocket.

Oh, hell.

Five charred carcasses sank to the bottom of the bag. I shook them, to get a better look.

"Yes, they're your guys."

"But they're flat, as if—"

"Someone stepped on them," he finished. "I think I got them all, so no one else gets any ideas. That's what took me so long, waiting for the fire squad to leave. I want to send them to the labs at DUE for analysis."

"But they were with us, out in the wetlands."

"Not the ones who visited here first, remember? Maybe they stopped off in town before joining the others at the ditches. Hell, maybe they wanted to bowl a frame or two. Mac thinks it's the same guy who torched that cottage." He yawned. "Could be. You've got to get them out of here."

He was in no condition right now to go looking in the salt flats. "You go on to bed."

"Mmm."

"By yourself."

"Okay."

"I decided I can't have sex with you."

"Hmm?"

"I take things too seriously, that's all, not that I don't want to or don't find you attractive, because I do. But if we make love, I am going to want to do it again, and spend more time with you. Then I'll get used to having you around and maybe fall in love with you." If I hadn't already. "And then I'll be heartbroken when you leave."

"Uhm?"

"And I can't fall in love with someone so much in harm's way. I couldn't sleep all night, worrying about you, and you were right here with the entire fire department, and most likely the neighboring villages, too, from all the sirens. I know you can put out fires, but you're brave and kind and noble and you might do something heroic and get yourself killed. I couldn't stand that, especially if we made love because to me that's like sharing part of yourself, so part of myself would die a little, too. Every time you went out on an emergency call. No, every time the phone rang. So we better not make love, okay?"

He snored. I could never love a man who snored.

I wished I could sleep while Piet did. Sure he'd been fighting the fire, but I'd been fighting incipient panic all night. I couldn't nap; Edie was awake.

To keep Piet's rest undisturbed, I took Elladaire and Little Red into town. I wanted to hear what people were saying about the fire.

Some thought we had a pyromaniac among us. Some thought Joey'd set the blaze to collect the insurance, rather than buy out his wife's share. Or Maureen had hired a hit man. Janie at the beauty salon, after hugging and kissing Elladaire, whispered: "It's your bugs, isn't it?"

"They're not my—" Why waste my breath? "Someone's been catching them and using them to start the fires. They're not doing it themselves, not on purpose. I'm putting up more posters telling people not to harm them."

After a few more stops, I wheeled the stroller out to the more residential blocks. Little Red couldn't go so far, or so fast, not with three legs that were short to begin with. I didn't trust him in the stroller with Elladaire, or her with him for that matter, but he was content to ride in the mesh bag behind the seat, on top of the extra diapers and animal crackers.

I asked Mr. Merriwether if he had any numbers for me. He and his wife had four cars, three houses, two cabin cruisers, and heaven knew how many offshore bank accounts, all from picking the right numbers on sweepstakes, lotteries, roulette wheels, and bingo cards. He scratched his head.

"I'm thinking the number you want is 3,549, but that

makes no sense. You don't want to play Pick Four or anything like that in the lottery, do you?"

"No."

"Forget a password? Lock combination?"

"Neither. I'm not sure what I'm looking for, but I'll keep that number in mind. Thanks."

Mrs. Desmond next door cooed over the baby and offered the Pomeranian a biscuit. Little Red ignored her. A dog biscuit when he'd finished off a bag of animal crackers? Sheesh.

The elderly widow set a pot of water on to boil for me, but she wasn't happy with the alphabet noodle letters I wanted her to use.

"You don't think something terrible has happened to your mother, do you?"

"No, she's fine. Someone would have called me, otherwise. It's m-a-m-a anyway. I always call my mother Mom."

"Gracious, not you-know-who's mother?" She shifted her gaze to Elladaire. "I heard she was recovering nicely."

"Mary's fine. Janie just told me."

"But you want to know if this mama person is alive? If the letters float, that's a good sign."

That putrid smell of the swamp was a bad sign, to my thinking. I wanted to check. "She's not exactly a person."

"Oh, dear."

Despite Mrs. Desmond's misgivings, an M and an A popped right up to the top of the saucepan. That was good enough.

My next stop was at Margaret's house and her wool shop. I loved it there, all the colors and textures, the big looms, the vats of dyes in the back. Edie stared around, wide-eyed. Margaret handed her a felted wool teddy bear with button eyes.

"Is it okay if she puts it in her mouth?"

Margaret laughed. "Better than the animal cracker she took away from your dog. So you are looking for something again?"

She didn't mean a woven shawl or a hand-dyed hank of wool. Margaret made finding bracelets, with all kinds of wishes and hopes braided into them. If the wish was honest and heartfelt, the bracelet stayed on until the seeker found the one he or she sought.

Margaret cut a lock of my hair—dark roots and all—and one of Elladaire's curls, then she picked colors and strands from her shelves and baskets. But she needed something from the person who was missing. "It doesn't have to be hair."

That was good, because all I had was one burnt wing, from the box I was going to mail for Piet.

Margaret carefully picked up the wing that looked like a blackened, shriveled leaf and clucked her tongue.

"It was beautiful, once."

"And will be again," she assured me.

She crumpled the wing and sprinkled the ashes over the yarns and hairs she'd collected, then started to spin them together on a drop spindle. When she deemed she had a long enough strand, she cut it into even lengths and braided them together, her fingers flying every which way and her lips moving in some silent chant or prayer or incantation. I didn't ask which.

When Margaret put the finished bracelet around my wrist, I simply stared in awe. There was the aurora borealis, right on my arm, gleaming and glowing and changing colors when I turned my arm. "It's gorgeous."

"And it will stay on until you find . . . ?"

"Mama," Edie and I both answered. Only the kid

held her hands up to be carried, or to have her diaper changed.

"Good luck."

I tracked our local plumber—and scryer—down at the rental house where he was working that morning. He scratched his head when I explained what I wanted, but he filled a sink with water and stared into it.

"Nope, all I see is clogged drains. Looks like someone flushed down something big. I sure hope they call a plumber from up the Island."

My last stop was at the post office. The blind postmaster wasn't sure he could legally send the little box.

"What about with extra postage?"

He shook the box. "Hazardous materials. Illegal. Where did you say you were sending it?"

I read him off the address in Virginia.

He cocked his head toward his guide dog, listening. "Oh, them. That's all right, then."

I was sure it would be. I didn't know about the rest of us.

CHAPTER 22

PIET LOOKED A LOT BETTER than I felt. Ella-daire and I were both tired and dirty and needed fresh clothes. Little Red was out in the fenced yard, pooping lions and tigers and bears, oh my. "He is not sleeping in my bed tonight."

But I had news.

"Mama is alive," I told Piet. "But she's stuck, so we have to find her and get her out. She might be in the 3549 area of the grid, if the ditches are numbered. Or maybe that many feet inland from shore. I hope that's not her weight. Can you imagine a lightning bug that size? I'm not sure about the number, but the rest is al-most positive."

"Positive because . . . ?"

"Because this is Paumanok Harbor and I have a bracelet."

He looked at the bracelet, looked at me, then at the door. A lesser man might have made a run for it. Piet rubbed at his whiskery chin and nodded. Then he started to massage my shoulders. I let him, because they were sore from toting the baby around all morning. She had to weigh three times as much as the Pomeranian I was used to.

"Oh, and I saw Barry and the mayor and Chief

Haversmith having lunch at the deli. Barry kept his sunglasses on and looked like he had trouble holding his head up. So we should be okay there."

Piet kept his hands kneading my strained muscles, but he started kissing the back of my neck too, nibbling, licking, rubbing. Funny, I felt it down to my toes.

"Uh, do you remember our conversation when you got back this morning?"

"Nope. I do recall you in that towel, though, before I left last night. The image helped me leave a spark here and there for your volunteers to put out. That kept them from asking any awkward questions. I had no idea which firefighters were safe."

By that I knew he meant who could be trusted to accept his talent without amazement or disbelief, who could be trusted to keep their mouths shut.

"So what did you tell me this morning?"

"That you're not sleeping in my bed either."

His hands dropped away. "I never agreed to that."

"You didn't have to. It's my bed."

"But I thought we were good together. Partners."

"We were. We are. I really like you. That's the problem. Remember what you first said? You wouldn't marry me to please Royce, or any other reason?"

"You're talking marriage?" Now he did take a couple of steps toward the door. I thought his scars showed more vividly with color draining from his complexion.

"No, I'm talking lovemaking. But then I'd want more. More sex, more closeness, more of your time. I'd want you to stay, to be safe here. I'd try to make you happy so you wouldn't want to leave. I already bought stuff to make you a nice dinner. But I'm selfish. I don't want to turn myself into someone I never wanted to be, to be what you might want. And I hate what you do."

"Whew. For a minute there I thought you were serious. It's only sex. I'll change your mind."

Now I left the house. Little Red needed me.

The good thing was I got out before I could change my mind, again. The bad thing was Barry got out of his car in front of my house.

"Hello," he said, flashing that cover-model smile, dimples and all. "You're Willow Tate, aren't you? I was hoping to do a story about your books for a webzine I'm working for, until I can write my novel. I was hoping you'd give me some pointers."

"Sorry, I don't give interviews."

"But it would be good publicity for you and—"

"Sorry. I like my privacy."

The smile slipped. "Well, how about if I wrote about Paumanok Harbor, maybe drum up some tourist business for the place. Seems like a nice friendly town."

"You'll have to talk to the Chamber of Commerce about that." They closed up after Labor Day.

"Then maybe you can tell me about the fires here? That's public knowledge, isn't it?"

"Yes, and the fire department can give you all the information you need. Good day, Mr. Jenner."

He knit his brows together. "I didn't give you that na . . . that is, my name."

"Oh, but it's such a friendly little town, we find out about our visitors. We know all about your magazine and your style of journalism."

His voice got louder, and a snarl replaced the smile altogether. "Then maybe you can tell me what happened to my equipment? I had to go buy a new Blackberry, camera, and laptop, to start. And pay five times as much as I would in Manhattan."

"Then maybe you should go back to Manhattan. We have a lot of power outages here. I think I heard that's what fried a lot of electronics this week. Oh, and I do believe you started a riot at the motel that set off the sprinkler system, so you have no one else to blame for the water damage. I recall the manager asking you to leave. Do you remember that part?"

"I wouldn't stay in that rattrap if they paid me. I have friends with houses in East Hampton."

"I'm sure you do." That wasn't a compliment either. Posh Hampton housed herds of celebrity hunters, hangers-on, and wannabes.

"One way or another, I am going to get a story, no matter what anyone in this shithole thinks."

Piet put his hand on my shoulder, holding me back. "We think you should leave now."

Barry turned and stomped down the path. But not before Little Red puked on his foot.

We watched him leave, but both of us knew he'd be back. The mayor'd done a fine job, but he couldn't erase someone's entire history or his rotten personality. Which meant we had to put out the fires and get the fireflies out of the Harbor quickly. Piet, too, before the sleazeball figured out his role.

He put an arm around my shoulder. "Ready for a walk along the shore? Maybe 3, 549 steps?"

I was as ready as I was ever going to be. Except we couldn't go. Elladaire was throwing up, too.

"What did you feed her?"

"I didn't—" Well, maybe I didn't, but I let everyone else feed her. I bought the animal crackers, but Janie gave her a banana, Mr. Merriwether gave us tomatoes and string beans from his garden, Mrs. Desmond offered a bowl of blackberries and biscotti, and Margaret had fresh figs from a tree in her yard. Even the plumber had a bag of chocolate chip cookies. "Do you think she needs a doctor? The nearest pediatrician is in East Hampton."

He touched her forehead. "She doesn't have a fever. We should wait a little."

"Yeah, but I think I should take Little Red to the vet. Mom told me that with a dog that small, you can't wait too long. They get dehydrated and lose their appetite, and the blood sugar drops. I have to take Buddy back there anyway, to have his burn checked and—"

"And you're going to leave me here with a sick kid?"

As fast as my feet would carry me.

On the way to the vet's, I wondered when we could give Elladaire back to her great-aunt. Janie worked half days on Saturday, not at all on Sunday or Monday. Maybe she could take Elladaire with her one of those days if she went to visit Mary. Mary must be missing her baby and Edie shouldn't forget what her mother looked like. No, Mary wouldn't want her daughter to see the bandages and IV tubes, and Janie would be afraid of driving Elladaire so far away from Piet. I hardly thought about it this morning, but I had the comfort of knowing he was nearby.

Still, Janie ought to have the child she so obviously adored. Lord knew she'd be a better stand-in mom than me. Even Piet was a better surrogate. Neither of them would abandon a kid with an upset stomach. Guilt rode in the backseat with Buddy, but relief dangled from the rearview mirror like lucky dice.

I'd miss Edie when she went back to her family, the drooly smiles and silly giggles and the clean smell after a bath. Then I thought about the rest of being a babysitter so I wouldn't get depressed. Who wanted the sick, smelly parts? Then there was the responsibility, the complete dependency, and the overriding feeling of inadequacy. If I wanted to feel like a failure, I could call my mother.

Little Red started trembling three blocks away from Matt Spenser's house and office. Buddy might be half blind and deaf, but he started whining, too. They'd both been here often enough to recognize the turns or the smells.

Matt's receptionist looked about twenty, with a fresh diploma from junior college above her desk. She had long hair, long legs, and a short, short skirt. She was pretty, if you liked almost-anorexics with attitude. I wondered if she took the job because of Matt, or whether he'd hired her because of her looks. Not that it was any of my business, of course, just natural curiosity.

She was extremely protective of Dr. Spenser for an employee most likely earning minimum wage and no benefits, scowling because I'd arrived without an appointment. "This is not a walk-in clinic," she announced with a sniff. "The doctor is fully booked."

I'd been scorn-sniffed by experts. My mother and grandmother wore out their sinuses showing disdain. "Dr. Spenser will understand. Why don't you tell him Willow Tate is here."

In five minutes I got another sniff. "The doctor will fit you in after his next patient."

When I got to the examining room, I complimented Matt on his efficient office staff. Okay, I was fishing for information, but he didn't know that.

"Yes, my niece is working out great."

"Your niece? How nice." Not that it was any of my business, still. Or how good he looked in his white lab coat, or how his light brown hair fell over his forehead. Not my affair, at all.

"I was lucky to hire her before she goes on to regular college next January. She's great at the computers and the billing."

I apologized about not calling ahead. The waiting room hadn't been wall-to-wall cat carriers or canines, but he was busy enough. "I should have made an appointment, I know, but I worried about Little Red."

He put the Pom up on the metal table and took his temperature, to the dog's snarling indignation. Then he listened to his heart, looked at his teeth and mouth, and felt his stomach. "Don't worry about it. Or Red. He'll be fine in a couple of hours."

He was great with the bad-tempered monster. Or else Little Red was too sick to snap at him. He handed him to me and lifted Buddy to the table. I couldn't help noticing how easily he managed the big dog, and how gentle he was with the old guy. I thanked him again for seeing me.

"Any time. I know you're really busy right now, helping the police and fire department stop the arson attempts. Can I help at all?"

Aside from giving Little Red a shot to calm his stomach and Buddy a clean bill of health and soothing my own jittery nerves? "Do you know anything about entomology?"

He washed his hands at the sink and smiled at me. "So the bugs really are connected to the fires. I heard that at the deli but couldn't see how. I'd still like to see one up close."

I bet he wouldn't, if it weighed over three thousand pounds. If the little buggers could set the bowling alley on fire, Mama could wipe out half the continent.

"I had a course in invertebrates, but it was a long time ago. I could make some phone calls if you need an expert."

There was no such person, not for these bugs. DUE would have had him or her on their list. Matt didn't seem in that big a hurry, and Little Red was limp in my arms, so I asked, "Do you think it's possible for an insect to know its own mother?"

He thought for a minute, kneeling to stroke Buddy's ears. "Egg, larva, pupa, imago. I doubt the bugs ever see their parent, much less recognize her, if she's still alive and in the vicinity. And that's without considering if an insect has any kind of memory or rational thought process as we know it."

"That's what I thought."

He looked up, at me. "But now you think differently?"

His brown eyes seemed so open, so honest, so trustworthy. I wanted to tell him yes, to explain about the lantern beetles, the light shows, the baby, the mangled bodies, and Mama, but I couldn't. What a relief it would be to share my concerns with an objective, intelligent person, but I daren't.

Instead of getting angry like I expected, Matt smiled. "I know, in Paumanok Harbor anything is possible, but nothing is spoken aloud. If it was, the mayor would pay me a visit with his perfectly healthy cat and I'd have a blank space in my mind. But then something else would happen, something totally unexpected and inexplicable, that no one wants to talk about. I wouldn't, you know."

I did know, deep down, where it mattered. "Thank you." I gathered up my pocketbook and the leashes and the pills for Little Red. "But you know my question about the insects and their mothers? It's for one of the books I'm writing."

He grinned. "Of course it is."

CHAPTER 23

W HEN I GOT HOME, Susan was blowing soap
bubbles with Elladaire. It was one of those perfect
family photo album pictures, full of rainbows and laughter. It should have made me happy, but it didn't.

Susan said that Piet had gone to the firehouse to meet
with Mac and the arson investigators. That was his job,
but I was annoyed that he'd gone off and foisted the
baby on my cousin. I admit that I'd done the same to
him, but he was better at the kid thing than either me or
my cousin, and safer. Decades of family lectures and her
recent history kept me protective of Susan.

He should have called me. It's not as if I'd run off to
Ronkonkoma or something. We were partners.

Then there was that protective thing again. He could
have shown more sensitivity to Susan's feelings about
babies.

Which I realized I did not know. Everyone was so
careful around her, no one brought up any delicate subjects. We all figured that if she wanted to talk about her
possible infertility, she would.

Now she gave me the opportunity to find out by
bringing up the subject of children herself: "You better
give the kid back soon before you get attached to her."

"I already adore the brat, especially when she's happy."

"She is a cutie."

We both watched her bumbling chase of the bubbles across the yard. Edie didn't fall once this time, and I did feel like a proud mother. Susan noticed. "That's how you ended up with Little Red, you know."

I did know. Care for him for a week or two, my mother'd said. That's all. But the little terror sank his teeth into my heart as well as my ankles. He loved me in his own way. He needed me. Now I wouldn't part with him for a *New York Times* bestseller. Well, maybe I would if my mother got back to take over his care.

"That's how she gets all those dogs adopted," Susan reminded me. "By asking people to foster them for a couple of days so the poor abandoned animals are not locked in a pen, frightened and lonely. They look up at you with those big blue eyes—"

"The dogs have brown eyes. It's Elladaire who has blue eyes."

"Whatever. And you're sunk."

"Would you want to keep her if— No, Mary is going to be fine, Janie said. Would you want one of your own?"

"Now, when I'm making my way up the restaurant ladder? When I'm not sure if I'm cured or in remission? When I'm having a good time coming and going when I choose? Hell, no. Someday? Yes. Two or three. If I can't have my own, then I'll adopt. Sometimes I think of adopting three different nationalities, start my own UN peacekeeping force. Show the world we're all the same under our skin."

My crazy cousin had her head on straight. Even if it had eyebrow hoops and three colors of hair. Sometimes I admired her.

Sometimes I hated her. She looked straight at me for

the first time and shook her head. "You did something bad again, didn't you?"

That depends on how you define bad. What crime did she read in my face this afternoon? Showing jealousy over the veterinarian, lusting after a fireman and then rejecting him, leaving Piet with the baby, or inviting the bugs to town?

"I swear I didn't— How is Edie anyway? She was a little peaky when I left for the vet." Okay, she was pukey. "Little Red was sick. I had to go."

He was sleeping on my foot now, wiped out from the trip and the shot, I guessed. Otherwise he'd be fighting Elladaire for the soap bubbles.

"Piet said her stomach was bothering her, so I took her over to Grandma's. Gran gave her some special concoction mixed in honey. She's fine now."

I checked Edie for a tail or rabbit's ears or crossed eyes. You never knew with Eve Garland's potions. Sure, she'd never changed anyone into a toad that I heard of, but I swear she could if she wanted to.

Elladaire was fine, and cute as a kitten—not cute as a bug, not these days— chasing the pretty bubbles. Instead of scooping her up and twirling her around just to hear her baby laughter, I decided Susan was right: I had to get her back to Janie's.

Jane could send her to day care while she worked, where Edie'd have other kids to play with and professional attention. The other children would be safe, I was sure. Safer than she'd be here or handed off to the nearest person when I had to go back to the marshes.

"Are you working this afternoon? Tonight?"

"Yes, I have to leave soon. My mother said she'd take Elladaire when she gets home from school. Everyone wants you to concentrate on the fireflies."

If everyone did, why wasn't Piet here? Whatever horror was in the drainage ditches had to be the key to getting the lanterns home. Searching during the day was bound to be hot, smelly, sticky, and scary. Going again at night was unthinkable.

Susan left. Of course Edie was tired of the bubbles by now—it had been all of twenty minutes, some kind of record for her pea-sized attention span except for the TV.

I put it on for her. I'm sure day care sang and danced and read books and played games. I started Edie's favorite video.

My own work hadn't been touched in days, it seemed. I needed to get back to it before I lost too much time, continuity, and confidence. I dropped the creature-in-the-dark-lagoon idea. Hell, that was too close to reality for me. I wanted to draw something clean, graceful, and strong, not frightful and ugly. The story line could come later.

My sketch pad quickly filled with fish—no, intelligent, mammalian dolphins, leaping out of clear waters, playing in the sun.

Except some of them had six flippers.

I turned the page. This time I drew a large dolphin, the king of the dolphins, who could transform himself into a sea god, fighting to clean up the oceans so his people were not threatened. I liked it. I liked him. He was noble and caring and dedicated, like Piet. Like Matt Spenser, too, it occurred to me. I gave him Matt's clean-shaven look, but Piet's short hair. I could almost feel the water dripping off him as he rose as a man in muscular glory from the surf— No, that was Elladaire spilling my iced tea on my notes and drawings.

I really had to get her back to her aunt.

I left a message there, then thought about calling Piet to ask if he'd be home for dinner, or did he want us to meet him in town and get pizza. Blech. That was too damned domestic. Let him worry about his own dinner.

Let him come and go when he wanted. So would I. Except pizza sounded good.

Meantime, I called my mother. She was in the middle of a meeting. "I am busy. What do you want?"

"I want you to come home and help with this baby. You're always saying you want grandchildren. Here's your chance."

"I want grandchildren with my DNA. Ones I can love, not babysit every day. I did that for you. It was enough."

"You left me with Grandma Eve every summer."

"So?"

"I am babysitting your dogs."

"So?"

"So I need help here."

"So do the poor dogs at the puppy mills. You can take care of yourself. They can't. You're a big girl, Willow. Figure it out."

I figured I'd get at least a smidgeon of sympathy from my father. Not that I expected him to fly north to care for a baby. I didn't remember if he was any good at it when I was young. He worked a lot. He worried a lot, too.

He still worried. "You've got to be careful, baby girl," he told me. "There's something rotten in that ridiculous town."

That would be Mama, judging from the smell.

"Or maybe in the family."

Definitely Mama. "Everyone's okay here, Dad."

"No, sweetheart, there's danger. I feel it. It's been keeping me awake nights. Well, last night Karin and I went out dancing, so that doesn't count, but I felt it. Rot."

Rats. I wasn't surprised. I knew the salt marsh was dangerous; maybe Mama was, too. I didn't want to frighten both of us any more than we already were, though, so I said I'd stay away from Grandma Eve's extensive compost piles in case something poisonous or rabid lived there. "I'll warn Uncle Roger and his workers at the farm, too. Okay?"

"Good, but you be careful, hear? Remember to wear sunscreen, even though the sun isn't as strong up there now."

"I always do, Dad. So who is Karin?"

"Got to go, Willy. It's half-price day for the early show at the movie theater."

Just when I started to get annoyed that Piet didn't call—damned if I'd call him—I heard a squawk from the scanner box the fire department lent him. I didn't know what the number codes meant. It could have been a traffic accident, a fire, an ambulance call, or a school of bluefish off the shore. Either way, it gave a location: Rick Stamfield's marina.

Rick is one of my favorite Paumanok Harbor residents, and he'd had enough bad luck in the past, with a fancy yacht sinking suspiciously right at the dock. He was one of the few people in the village who didn't blame me for that.

Now he was in trouble, and I couldn't go. Not that I'd be much help, but that's what friends did. They showed support by getting in the way. Elladaire couldn't see me stick my tongue out at her.

Then came the sirens and the volunteer alert klaxon. Damn. I called Uncle Roger on his cell. He managed the family farm, but he'd be going to whatever emergency called for every member of the force to respond. "Fire at Rick's," he shouted over the siren on his car. "Bad."

Piet had his camper, so he had his protective gear with him. I believed in his magic, I truly did, but a fireproof jacket couldn't hurt. If he remembered to put it on.

And I couldn't go. I had a baby. I didn't want a baby. Didn't need a baby. Damn, damn, damn.

She looked up from the TV with those baby-blue eyes and four-tooth grin. "Go bye-bye car?"

Shit. I loved a baby. Maybe I loved a dedicated fireman used to flying solo. It was a good thing I'd sworn off men, or I'd be dragging him to my bed to make a baby in the age-old method for keeping a man. Not keeping him happy, mind, but keeping him from leaving.

Wrong. Everything I was thinking was wrong, mean, and immoral, and I'd regret it tomorrow. I sat down to do some serious thinking about my priorities and my intentions. What I came up with was something rotten in the family.

I called Piet's cell and prayed he'd answer.

"It's Roy Ruskin," I shouted when he picked up. "It's Roy, not Rot, and kin, not family. Rick fired him when he got arrested for wife-beating. And the Danverses let him go before that for drinking at the bowling alley. He's the one setting the fires!"

"The chief made that deduction, too. He's got everyone he can spare out looking for the bastard, along with the East Hampton town police and the county sheriff's office. They're setting up roadblocks, but there are a million places he could hide. I'm on my way back to your house now."

"Great." That meant the fire was out. "How are things at the boatyard? Is Rick okay?"

"Rick's fine. His own boat and a couple of others aren't. We got the fires out before they could spread to the whole marina, and only one fuel tank exploded. Part of a dock is gone. One guy got cut by flying glass, but everyone else is all right."

"Thank goodness for that. Did you find any . . . ?"

"Dead bugs? No, but Rick's boat got towed out of the harbor before I could look, to keep sparks away from the dock. It sank before they could get the arson squad aboard. Big Eddie smelled kerosene, though, so maybe Ruskin couldn't capture any more of your friends."

I'd tried to tell them to stay away from bad guys with

evil intentions. Maybe they understood me after all. "So no one suspects them?"

"They're positive it was Ruskin. He'd been spotted earlier. They'll get him sooner or later. The other problem is that Jensen, or whatever he's calling himself these days, was at the fire. Taking pictures and watching me. I had to step back so the fires did more damage than needed. Then he wanted to know what new experimental chemicals I was testing, that worked so well, for a book he's going to write. I heard him tell one of the firemen. He's going to call it *Hell Harbor in the Hamptons*, about all the weird disasters here."

"I don't suppose the mayor can—"

"They're on public record."

In a way, Barry was more dangerous than Roy. And more unstoppable. "What do you think we should do?"

"First we get rid of Ruskin, then the fireflies, then worry about the reporter. Meantime, I'm going through town. Do you want me to pick up a pizza?"

That would be the next best thing to getting rid of all the plagues. "Great, then I can leave Elladaire with my aunt Jas, and we can track down Mama in the ditches."

He was so quiet I thought we'd lost the connection. "Piet?"

"I thought you understood."

"I do. We need to get the bugs gone."

"We need to keep the people safe from a vicious arsonist. The chief sent messages to the Coast Guard, because one of the commercial fishing boats in Montauk fired Ruskin, too. And Joe the plumber went to bring Jane to his house, in case Ruskin goes after her."

"They've been seeing each other recently, ever since she helped him after the accident."

"The chief told me she's the one who called the police on Ruskin the first time, and who paid for Mary's divorce lawyer."

I thought about it a minute. "Which leaves me in danger?"

"We think so."

"He'd never hurt the baby. Would he?"

"Who knows what's in the mind of a sociopath? He blames the whole town for his troubles. I told the chief I'd stay close, in case they need me in the village, but I think he'll come after you for keeping the baby from him. God only knows what he'll do if he finds you gone."

He could torch my mother's house. Or my grandmother's. I sank to the floor and held Little Red with one hand and Elladaire with the other, the phone tucked against my shoulder. "How soon before you get here?"

CHAPTER 24

WHILE I WAITED FOR PIET and the pizza, I thought about all the places Roy could hole up. Squatters—homeless, adventurous or cheap—were always building illegal tent sites in the woods, but we also had a lot of vacant houses and beach cottages now that the summer rentals were over. Neighbors were fewer, farther apart. A lot of boats sat empty and unattended at docks from here to Montauk, easy pickings for thieves and fugitives. The water was Roy's best bet for avoiding the roadblocks on the few roads leading out of the Harbor. Who knew what he was thinking, though? Trying to figure out the thought processes of a bitter, hate-filled, and vengeful man was a waste of time.

Time that the fireflies did not have. Could they survive the cooler nights? Were they finding food? How long before people realized they were out of this world, literally? No one else was going to help them. I understood that well enough. But how was I supposed to do it? I couldn't leave the house or Elladaire or my grandmother unprotected, but how could I let the Lucifers down? Maybe if they came to my backyard tonight, they'd give me better directions to whatever was stuck in a ditch. Maybe they could tell me why it—she—was so important. So far our communication had been in pictures and feelings and one word. I had to hope for more.

The more I thought about it, though, the less sense my staying here made. It was Piet who could protect my family's houses and the baby. On my own, I couldn't do anything but wait for a Molotov cocktail to come flying through a window or a murdered firefly to land on my wooden porch.

So once Piet came back here I could go to the salt marsh. By myself. At night. To look for a dangerous creature.

And pigs would fly.

I flew into Piet's arms when he drove up, almost squashing the pizza between us and imperiling the six-pack he had in his other hand.

"Now that's what I call a welcome. And here I thought I'd have to spend at least a couple of hours trying to change your mind."

"I can't do it, not without you."

"I sure hope not."

I took the pizza from him. "I thought you were going to try to convince me to go alone."

"Now where's the fun in that?" He set down the Sam Adams and opened a bottle. I disliked the smell of beer, and the grin on his face.

"Fun? Going into the marsh and the mud?"

The smile faded. "Is that what we're talking about? Hell, woman, do you think I'd let you go off by yourself into that no-man's land? What kind of guy have you been seeing? It's no wonder you're so skittish if that's how your boyfriends treat you."

"Then what were you thinking—Oh. That."

"I s'pose we could try it in the mud."

"That's disgusting. Here you are, back from firefighting, facing a night of uncertainty, and you're thinking about dirty sex?"

He held up his bottle in a mock toast. "The finest kind. Maybe the only kind." Then he took another swallow of beer. "Hey, I'm a guy. What else am I supposed to think about, especially after fighting a fire? Adrenaline is an aphrodisiac, you know."

No, I didn't. Danger had me quaking and limp afterward. I was exhausted merely from worrying about him at the boat fire.

He wasn't finished. "And if the future is so uncertain, why not enjoy it while we can?"

He had a point and, for heaven's sake, a bulge in his jeans. "Not in front of the baby," I whispered, as if Elladaire could understand sexual tension. She barely understood the danger of pulling a dog's tail.

"So far I'd guess her only view of an adult relationship was full of violence and cruelty. We better give her a better memory, before she gets ruined for life."

Then he kissed me. He tasted of beer, which I did not like. He smelled of smoke and soap. He must have showered and changed his clothes at the firehouse, but the smoke stayed with him. I pulled back, very aware of the baby.

Both of us noticed she was playing with the spoons I'd given her, not watching.

"We better do it again."

This time he pulled me closer so I could feel his hardness, feel his heat. His kiss was deep and long and suddenly it was like a conversation with the mayor. You forgot where you were and why you'd come there. I was here, in Piet's arms, and that's where I belonged, for now. What beer? What baby?

"Okay, she's seen enough," he said. "The pizza's getting cold."

Man, he really knew how to put out a fire.

"But we'll continue this after Edie goes to sleep."

I was afraid we would. And afraid we wouldn't.

I slid pieces of pizza onto paper plates. It tasted better that way. "I thought we'd put her in the backpack carrier and kind of patrol the block together, in case Roy decides to take his revenge on the whole family, not just me."

He chewed on a slice of pizza while I debated giving some to Elladaire. The sausage and peppers looked deadly, but the crust couldn't hurt her, could it?

"Not a bad idea, except you need to have a talk with the flying matchsticks. I'll make the circuits of the houses. You set up your teleconferencing in the backyard."

"What about the baby? If Roy gets her . . ." That was too terrible to contemplate.

"He won't. Everyone knows what he looks like, so the cops should have him in custody soon. Unless Rick gets hold of him, or Danvers from the bowling alley. His chances of seeing a jail cell sounded pretty slim to me from what I heard. Meantime, Edie goes with me."

Lucky kid. I got to hang out with alien insects. She got a piggyback ride.

Plans changed, right in the middle of the pizza.

We got company. It wasn't Roy Ruskin, but the unexpected guests were almost as dangerous.

I'd forgotten my friend Ellen was coming back out to Paumanok Harbor on the weekend to spend more time with Martin, the science teacher. I'd forgotten it was Friday, besides.

She tried to call, Ellen said, but the answering machine didn't pick up. I must have been on the phone with my mother or father and didn't hear the call-waiting beep. So she and Martin decided to come by and see if I wanted to go out to dinner with them.

I pointed to the baby and the pizza, two easy outs. Piet offered them beers, though, so they sat down. Martin took a slice of pizza and a beer, but Ellen leaned close to me and whispered that she was embarrassed for intruding, but they'd thought Barry would be here.

"Not a chance," I told her. "He lied about his name and his job and his reasons for being here."

"But you have so much in common, your writing and all. And he's gorgeous."

So was Piet, in his own, better way. After sharing his beer, he ignored the company and concentrated on feeding Edie tiny slivers of pizza she could chew or gum. She loved it.

I hated having to explain about Barry to Ellen, one of my oldest friends, without telling her how threatening he was to Paumanok Harbor.

She shrugged. "This new guy isn't half as hot."

She'd never guess how hot.

"He's real quiet, too, and not as friendly as Barry. He's a fireman, for Pete's sake. You have nothing in common with him."

She'd never guess how much we shared, either, not that I cared. I forgot how much of a snob Ellen was, when it came to men. I tried to keep the sharpness out of my voice when I told her, "Barry was using us. Piet is helping."

She should have noticed the pizza getting cold, Martin having another beer, the baby getting tired, and me getting snippy, but she didn't. Or that I didn't offer coffee or dessert.

Instead they got down to the real reason for the visit, not my company, not my pizza: Martin wanted my bugs.

"I know you were offering a reward for them," he said. "I'll double it."

"I stopped doing that. They were getting hurt. People were getting hurt. You saw what happened to Barry when he swatted at one. Their, ah, bites are poisonous."

"I can be careful. I have nets and jars in the car, along with thick gloves and a beekeeper's head cover. If that works, I thought I'd bring my science class here to gather some. Word is they like your neighborhood."

Ellen started to say how she'd bring a couple of her own honors science students next weekend, so they had the same experience.

Piet slammed his bottle down.

I shouted, "No."

They both looked surprised. "Why not? They're disturbing the village and causing fires."

"They wouldn't if people left them alone." Speaking of leaving alone, Piet got up and took Edie away for her bath and pajamas. Feet of clay, fire boy, I muttered to myself.

Martin was adamant, enthused, excited. "But they are obviously a new species. Someone needs to do research on them. It's a great opportunity for my students. Think of the discovery!"

"And think of you getting your name in some journal?"

Martin was oblivious, but Ellen got offended. "Willy, that's mean. Science is all about uncovering new things. Why are you being so defensive anyway? They are beetles that could prove valuable."

"Exactly. They are too valuable to endanger in any way."

Ellen leaned forward. "But we wouldn't want to harm them, just see how they can be used."

I leaned back. "Used?"

Now Martin took over. "Think about it. Cheap cook fires for undeveloped countries, instead of chopping down every tree. Portable heat for cold climates. Why, it's the renewable energy everyone's been searching for. If we can breed them and harness their capability to create a spark, we can eliminate the dependency on foreign oil, on polluting coal, on nuclear reactors with disposal issues."

Ellen added, "Once we establish their breeding habits and a suitable controlled environment, we can have an unlimited supply."

Captive breeding in a laboratory? For the creatures who could make an aurora borealis? "You don't know anything about the bugs!"

"I know they are neither flies nor bugs," Martin said in condescending tones, while he reached for another bottle of beer.

"I know what they are. They are beetles, which have hard outer wings." Except mine had gossamer wings. "They are still called fireflies or lightning bugs."

"But different, larger, out of season, burning stuff, which is all the more reason to gather some up and examine them, to see how they create heat and fire."

I was horrified. "They don't make fires unless they're hurt! You'd be torturing innocent creatures!"

Martin dismissed my argument with a tutting sound. "To serve mankind. That's what we do, what we've always done."

Ellen looked at the sausage on the pizza. "You eat meat, don't you? And fish and chicken."

Not anymore, I didn't.

"We wear wool and leather. Where do you think they come from if not innocent creatures. It's the way of the world."

I was an instant vegetarian. And I'd wear—yeck—polyester if I had to.

Martin's face turned red, and the comb-over came loose as he insisted: "You cannot withhold such a discovery from the world, from science. Just think, if we're the first to study them, we'll be famous. Why, we can patent them."

If I were drawing Martin, I'd put dollar signs in his eyes. "But they—" How could I say they were from another world? "They communicate."

Martin went tut-tut again. I wanted to smack his patronizing puss. "We know certain insects communicate with each other, but that's limited to finding mates and food. They have no intelligence."

My insects—beetles— did! More than these two imbeciles hiding greed in the name of science. "You've seen them, Ellen, at the fireworks, how they formed patterns and pictures."

"I saw abnormally big and bright lightning bugs gather in a swarm and mimic some of the rockets."

"What if they weren't imitating what they saw, but planning new designs? What if they have the intelligence of a dolphin? We don't eat them, do we?"

"Some people do, hungry people. And our government has been known to train them as weapons bearers or weapons detectors. To say nothing of how many are captured for marine shows. Because they are intelligent and can be trained to perform. For people."

"And these are just beetles, Willy," my former friend Ellen said. "You hate all bugs. Remember how you left the dorm when a wasp made its nest outside our window? And screamed every time a daddy longlegs got in the shower?"

"These are different, and you cannot have them." I got up, indicating the conversation was over. And our friendship, too. How did I miss her coldhearted, calculating ways? By not seeing so much of her since she moved to Connecticut.

Martin smirked. "How will you stop us?"

"I'll stop you from here. This is private property, and you are not welcome."

Ellen gasped. "What's got into you, Willy? You're acting crazy. I bet it's the fireman. He wants to keep them for himself, doesn't he?"

"He puts out fires, he doesn't start them. I think you should leave."

Martin was determined to seek his fame and fortune. "Then I'll have to organize a school trip out to the salt marshes. I hear the beetles have been seen there."

I was on safer, muddier ground here. "No, that's swamp gas."

He didn't believe me. "Then they'll study swamp gas."

"No, it's too dangerous. The smell there is overwhelming. The police, the Harbor Patrol, and the Bay Constable have the entire area shut down anyway."

"Not anymore they don't. They're all too busy beating the bushes for Roy Ruskin. And I'll equip the kids with face masks."

"You'll do no such thing. I'll explain to Aunt Jasmine." His boss. "She'll never give permission for you to take a kid out there."

He knew I could do it.

"We'll stay here, then. I'll park at the end of your road—on the public right-of-way—and wait for them to come. You can't stop me."

Piet came back without Elladaire. "No one wants to stop you. I can use the help patrolling the block. The police think Ruskin might show up here." He jerked a thumb toward the stairs. "That's his kid I just put to bed. The man's dangerous."

Martin and Ellen looked at each other, then at the door.

"Besides," Piet went on, "you're too late to have any claim on the fireflies. They've already been sent to a government lab in Virginia. I am certain they'll be rushed to the endangered species list."

Not as fast as Martin, if DUE decided to act on his threat.

I could smile again. "Yes, Martin, why don't you keep guard with Piet? Ellen, you can stay here to protect the baby if her father comes. That way you'll both see the fireflies if they show up."

Piet sighed, but he nodded. They wouldn't see anything burning that night. And he wasn't getting lucky.

CHAPTER 25

THEY LEFT. I KNEW THEY WOULD, the sniveling cowards. What I didn't know was if they'd stay gone, or continue their "research" in other ways. Like trapping the beetles from his boat, or creeping back to my yard under the cover of the trees. Chances are those two selfish sadists saw nothing wrong with using beagles for brain-damage experiments.

I called Aunt Jas, telling her of her science teacher's plans to have kids mutilate the bugs to see what happened. She sounded as upset as I felt. Not for the beetles but for the repercussions from the rest of the swarm. If they communicated, which I knew they did, we'd be toast, literally. She said she'd call the school board and the principal tomorrow to discuss policy. They stopped dissecting live frogs years ago. Now they'd stop Martin from maiming insects. Everyone knew that animal cruelty in children often presaged adult violent behavior. Paumanok Harbor should not be desensitizing its kids to the pain of anyone. They shouldn't be endangering the kids by exposing them to stagnant swamps or unexplained phenomenon. She never liked Martin anyway.

Meanwhile Piet called the police chief. Good citizen that he was, he reported that Martin Armbruster'd just had three beers—Piet's beers—in less than an hour, while he planned on capturing enough fireflies to burn down the school. Chief Haversmith said he'd take care of it. A failed breathalyzer test could put Martin in the drunk tank for the night. By tomorrow his boat wouldn't start, so the teacher couldn't spend the weekend looking for bugs on the shore.

"How do you know his boat won't start?"

"I'm sending a man to make sure."

"You take the law kind of casually around here, don't you?"

"Hell no, we're dead serious about keeping the peace. A schoolteacher BUI, that's Boating Under the Influence, would be a bad example for our kids, besides. We're spread pretty thin, though. You see anything your way?"

Piet wouldn't look at me. I wore baggy sweatpants and one of my father's old shirts. "Nothing to get excited about. Damn it."

Little Red wanted to go out, but all I could think of was Roy Ruskin lurking in the bushes with a can of kerosene. Or Barry hiding behind a tree with a camera. Or Martin and Ellen creeping back up the street with butterfly nets.

Martin was a greedy, self-important, pompous hypocrite. I was more disappointed in my friend Ellen than in any local science teacher. "Teacher!" I shouted toward Piet. Little Red snapped at my flip-flop. I ignored him. "My father was right. Almost. He didn't mean a preacher, or a creature. That prig Martin is the danger!"

One of the dangers. If he was the source of my father's unease, though, that meant Mama, the creature I feared, wasn't a threat. Not to me, anyway. That's the way my father's talent worked.

That meant I could go look for her myself. Were those pigs sprouting wings yet? I was having a hard enough time facing the backyard by myself now that the sun had set.

Piet took Elladaire in a baby backpack on rounds of the neighborhood. She didn't wake up, not even when he leaned over to kiss me good-bye and good hunting.

I did *not* want him to find Roy Ruskin. For all we knew, Roy had a gun or a knife or a hatchet or—I reined in my imagination. Roy liked using fire, which made Piet invincible. I just said, "Stay safe."

I went outside around the house with a flashlight and another pile of drawing supplies. I held up a blank black scratchboard first, not a mark on it. "Dark skies," I said aloud, but hoped I sent a mental image across the ether. For about the umpteenth time, I wished I were a telepath. Nah. With my luck, I'd only get to talk to dead people. Talking to blazing beetles had to be better. You are the Visualizer, I told myself. So visualize what you want.

"No shooting stars, no fireworks." But how to show the absence of something? I waved the black board over my head, like an airplane traffic handler.

My arms got sore. Then my neck got stiff from looking up. "And no rings around the moon, either. People will notice. Come on, guys, but fly down low where you can't be spotted from any distance."

It worked! Damn, I was good. Or else they were on their way anyhow. No matter, there they were, a carpet of diamonds a foot or so off the grass. They were far fewer than before, maybe thirty or forty, and I worried where the rest were. With Mama? Or in bottles somewhere, or out getting into more trouble? Either way, some had answered my call. Once more I felt familiar warmth. The temperature rose, but a sense of fellowship settled over me, too, the opposite of fear.

From what I'd learned about their world, every being of Unity was both a telepath and an empath. The luminaries must be trying to project that comfort to me, but I could not understand their unspoken mental language, only the sense that we were in this together.

That was it! Together! I got a white sheet of paper and a big marker and drew the symbols from my pendant, the one supposed to say "One life, One heart, I and Thou, One forever." I held it up and tried to think the words Grant the Linguist had taught me. I said them aloud and in my head and tried to emote the intention, along with the inscription. That old bumper sticker, "Visualize world peace," had nothing on my efforts.

The tiny lights rose up another foot, bobbed in synch, then settled down again. Was that a bow? An acknowledgment? Or part of their mating ritual? I had no way of knowing, but now that I had their attention, I tried again to explain the dangers of my world.

My second drawing showed men—one with a combover—chasing sparks with nets and bottles. "Danger, danger!"

The next had a good likeness of Roy, tattoos and shaved head and all, stomping on a bug, with fire spouting under his foot. "More danger!"

As fast as I could sketch, I held up another: Handsome Barry swatting at a bug. "Danger of too much publicity." How could they understand that concept? I added more people, and more, standing on top of each other with cameras and nets and flashbulbs— No, they might think those were relatives. I flipped to a new page and put hordes of people on foot, in boats, heading toward the drainage ditches that made the marsh. Instead of trying to show water and grasses and muddy banks, I drew the grid they'd flashed for Piet and me.

The lantern beetles singed my mother's lawn.

Fear? Anger? I couldn't tell, only that the grass looked like a sloppy smokers' break room. They didn't set any fires, though. I was glad we were friends. "You see? Danger all around."

They hovered closer to me. "No, not to me. To you. I cannot protect you from everyone. You have to leave."

Mama in my head.

"Couldn't you dudes learn another word?" Getting snarky was no help. I took a deep breath. "Okay, you're not leaving without Mama. So tell me what's wrong with her that she can't leave?"

I kind of expected them to fly a formation showing the grid of ditches blocked somehow. Instead they flew closer to me. They were not threatening, but trying to communicate, I sensed. They must be as desperate to be understood as I was, but all I got was a feeling that the time was wrong.

"Wrong to talk to me? Wrong for Mama to leave? What could you or she be waiting for?"

Maybe they knew tonight was the wrong time to be in my backyard. I heard it then, what they must have seen or sensed: a car slowly pulling up the dirt road.

There was no time to call Piet to come extinguish the tiny flames. I held up the first black board. "Dark sky, dark sky!"

They clustered together, which made them more conspicuous.

"No, hide. Hide." I didn't have time to figure how to draw the concept of hiding, so I pulled my shirt over my head. "Hide."

They strung themselves on a big scrub oak, like Christmas tree lights.

Hmm. Sometimes restaurants hung those tiny twinkle lights out to draw attention. Sometimes hostesses strung them up when they were having a fashionable summer lawn party. I heard the car door slam. No time. "Okay, we'll be fashionable. But no fires! Decorations only."

That's what Officer Keys saw when he came around the front of my house with his flashlight. "Nice touch. My wife wants me to do that for the backyard next summer."

"And they look nice for the holidays, too," I said, "so you don't have to take them down." I wasn't worried about lying to Eric Kenton. Truth detecting wasn't his talent. Opening locks was, thus the nickname of Keys. They'd hired him onto the police force before he could put his gift to profitable but illegal use.

He directed his light around the yard, looking for whomever I'd been talking to, that led him to find me. He shined the light on my art supplies and shrugged. The whole town knew I was nuts enough for anything. Talking to myself and drawing outside in the dark were the least of my craziness. "The chief sent me to give you the all clear. He's got your teacher friend under lock and key, yelling something fierce, but the judge doesn't hold night court, so no one can set bail."

"Gee, that's too bad. Can he arrest that reporter, too?"

"He thought about it when the bastard showed up back in the Harbor, but he didn't want the two of them talking in the jail cell. They deputized Jensen instead, to help look for Roy Ruskin at one of the roadblocks. The one the mayor is manning. Problem is, the mayor forgot what Ruskin looks like."

"Then Roy can get off the Island?" I started walking back to where the village police car was parked, to get Keys away from the fireflies.

He never looked back to see them head for the barbeque grill on the rear deck, thank goodness. I did not need him asking what I was cooking or what happened to the lights in the tree.

"Too late," he said. "They found Roy's bike at the Amagansett train station."

"So he got away?

"Chief's got state cops waiting at every station, and a couple of train security guys are walking the cars. They'll find him unless he's already off. Another theory is that he could have stolen a car at the station, where people leave their rides long-term when they go into Manhattan. If the owners don't come back tonight, it could be days before we know if a vehicle is missing. Either way, the chief is notifying that hospital where they took Mary Brown to be on the alert."

I thanked Keys for bringing the message, then I called Piet to come home. When I looked back, the grill was dark and empty, the trees were bare of lights, and the moon was hidden behind clouds. Dumb insects? Hah! The guys were creative, intelligent, and quick-thinking. They were a whole lot smarter than Farty Marty.

Except they were gone. "How can I help you if you don't talk to me?" I shouted into the cold, dark, empty night.

CHAPTER 26

"RUSKIN WILL BE BACK." Piet laid Elladaire carefully in her crib, without waking her.

I agreed, but hoped it wasn't true. "Why do you say that?"

"Because his life is in the toilet and he can't blame himself. So he blames Paumanok Harbor. He's got nothing but revenge to look forward to."

"But he knows everyone is looking for him."

"And he knows this area as well as any one of them. The chief said he was born somewhere nearby called Springs, but he lived and worked up and down the South Fork."

"And got thrown out of every bar in every town. What I don't understand is why he didn't keep going, why he decided to burn the place down."

"Pride and power, that's what drives a lot of twisted people. If Ruskin outwits us, he's regained his pride. He can use the beetles to regain power over his environment. Destruction is the only power he has left. The insects are a sign of what's different about this place, and how he doesn't fit in. I've seen it, how the espers hang together, and I've only been here a couple of days. Ruskin sees himself on the other side of inside informa-

tion, surrounded by weird goings-on he cannot understand. I think he snapped at the new oddities. He was
already miserable, his ex-wife in the hospital, his kid
taken away, cops on his back, no money, maybe no job.
He had no chance of reclaiming the life he thinks he
deserves. Now he's scared." He looked at Little Red,
curled asleep on the sofa cushions, looking like a sweet
little fox kit. "You know how dangerous animals can be
when they are frightened."

I knew Little Red. He wasn't sweet at the best of
times, but when he was scared, he turned into a six-
pound pit bull, when he didn't pee on people's legs.

I was scared, too. "What do you think will happen?"

"Nothing good. Ruskin knows he's gone too far.
What more has he got to lose?" Piet opened the last
bottle of beer and relaxed on the opposite end of the
couch. "I almost feel sorry for the bastard."

I didn't. He beat his wife. He tortured my beetles. He
could have killed people in the fires he started. And he
threatened me. "Have you known a lot of arsonists?"

"More than my share, I'd guess. They're all warped
inside, even the ones who do it for money. Most like the
attention. Pride and power, all over again. They feed on
it until the fire consumes them, like an addiction or an
obsession. Ruskin started as a bully and graduated to a
would-be killer. Who knows where he'll end?"

I was too restless to sit still. I kept checking the windows, looking for fireflies or fire-starters, hoping neither
of them appeared. "So what are we going to do about
him?"

He sighed. "Wait for the police to find him, or wait for
another blaze. Meantime we need to get rid of his arse-
nal. No one is going to sell him kerosene or lighter fluid,
but he can catch his own flame-throwers as long as they
hang around."

Getting rid of the winged matches wasn't going to be

easy. I explained how I'd tried again tonight to talk to the guys, how they seemed to understand and showed surprising intelligence, but they wouldn't go away. "I got the feeling they are worried about the time."

Piet thought about that for a minute, rubbing his fingers along the moisture on his beer bottle. "It's September, the nights get cooler. Do we know if the beetles can survive in the cold? And what about the fall rain and windstorms? Even without bad weather, do we know how long they live under optimum conditions?"

"We know next to nothing except they can think, and they can recognize a friend. Nice, but not helpful in getting them back to their own home."

"Maybe they are afraid they can't free their queen, if that's what the creature in the marsh is, before they expire."

Just what I needed—more pressure. Now I had to worry about a deadline, too. I hated deadlines in my work. Some writers did better under the gun, but I wasn't one of them. Panic is not conducive to creativity, I've found. I much preferred to work steadily, on schedule, without rushing at the last minute. Who knew how long the beetles had, or which tomorrow was their last minute? I started pacing, which was better than chewing my fingernails. "So you think we ought to go looking in the salt marsh tonight?"

He considered that. "I don't know if we can search well enough in the dark."

Thank you, night. "And we have no one to watch Elladaire." Thank you, baby.

"And if that creep Barry is still around, we don't want to draw attention to the wetlands."

Thank you, Barry? Nah. My pacing led me to the kitchen, where I accidentally happened to open the freezer. What do you know; Ben and Jerry had paid me a visit. "Do you want some New York Super Fudge Chunk?"

"With beer?"

Maybe that's why I didn't like beer. It didn't go with ice cream. I put a tiny bit in three dog bowls, and a big bit in mine.

Piet watched me eat, his eyelids half closed. I watched him, watching me. Just to see his reaction, I took extra time licking the spoon, licking my lips. Unfair maybe, but I never said I was perfect.

He groaned.

Power and pride. I was doing it right.

"It's early."

"Want me to see if there's anything decent on television?"

He kept watching me. "I can think of better things to fill the time."

More pressure.

Somehow my gut had decided Yes, no matter that my mind shouted No. What mind? My ice cream was gone; Piet was still here, looking delicious and cool and just what I wanted. He didn't say anything, but I knew one bowl was not going to be enough for either of us. The problem was, what now? The moral—or immoral and imbecilic—decision to have a one-night stand for however many nights he stayed was easy compared to the logistics of the thing. I was okay with taking our partnership to another level on his terms: good times, no commitment. That's exactly what I needed right now, like the ice cream. I'd worry about the calories and the heartbreak later.

Where to start, though? What should I do, take his hand and lead him to my bedroom? I tried to recall if the bed was made, or if I'd left my dirty clothes on the floor. Or should I tell him I needed a shower and hope he'd be in his bed with the lights out when I got done? Maybe I should just jump him, right there on the couch.

Teasing was one thing, taking the lead was another, and the infuriatingly closemouthed man kept waiting. I knew he was waiting for me to make a move, to be sure. I'd been the one to declare I wasn't interested in an affair, but he was the one who swore he'd change my mind. Get up and convince me, I wanted to shout. Don't make me do all the work. I wanted to be sweet-talked and seduced, swept off my feet. Instead, Piet did his strong, silent, sexy thing. He stared.

Equality between the sexes was a great, important thing. I believed in it implicitly. I just didn't like being the aggressor. Not that women shouldn't be, if that's what they wanted. They could go to the moon if they wished, with my blessings. I didn't want to do that either. I was afraid of planes, heights, and closed spaces, among other things. And I was afraid of making an ass of myself in Piet's hooded eyes.

So I decided to check my phone messages. I put the answering machine on speaker phone, to be polite. Chances are all the calls had something to do with Roy or the fireflies anyway. This way he could hear, without my having to repeat everything.

The first recording was from my father. As usual these days, he was in a hurry. "I'm on my way to the clubhouse for comedy club night. Annie and her sister are picking me up in five minutes, but I had a chill run up my spine. Baby girl, don't go near Saks. Love you. Dad."

Yeah, like I was going to go spend my next advance on a ball gown or something. Or head to Fifth Avenue in the morning for a makeup consultation. "Saks has a store in Southampton," I told Piet. "Maybe Dad means I shouldn't drive there because of the weekend traffic." Easy enough. I had too much to do right here. I pressed erase, and wondered who Annie was, and if my father's heart could handle sisters.

My mother's informants never slept. "I want to know about this fire person. I hear he's good with children. You could do wo . . ."

I pressed erase.

Ellen's voice came next, strident and shouting about how mean I was, how embarrassing to be taken to the police station, and what if word got back to the private school where she taught? Had I thought about Martin's reputation? She knew I'd set him up, me and my new lover and this inbred, insane town.

"Doesn't our friendship count for anything?" she finished.

No, it didn't, not if she shared Martin's attitude toward the beetles, except for regret over times past. I looked at Piet and tried to make light of losing an old friend. "At least I don't have to invite her out to the Harbor again."

Janie's message said she had to work in the morning, as I suspected, but if Piet thought it was safe, she'd come get Elladaire after her last appointment. Joe the plumber said he'd rig a sprinkler system in her house, and Mary really wanted to see the baby. Joe was going to drive them to the hospital, and maybe they would all stay out of town where Roy couldn't find them.

She added that they were planning a benefit fundraiser at the firehouse to help Mary pay her medical bills. Would I make a poster?

Of course I would, once I had the details. I paused the message replay to explain to Piet. "That's what we do in a little town like this, we help each other. Sometimes it's a spaghetti dinner at the firehouse, a pancake breakfast at the church, a potluck supper at the school, or a barbecue on the village green. I guess the fire department offered this time, because of the burns. They'll take the trucks out and set up tables in the empty bays. Restaurants provide some of the food, and the firemen cook the rest. Liquor stores get their distributors to donate wine, local bands agree to play for free, and stores give prizes for raffles. After the meal they move the tables away for dancing. Everyone buys tickets, gets drunk, and has a good time." Except people like me who hated crowds, didn't drink, and couldn't eat the usual hamburgers and hot dogs now that I was a vegetarian. I had to go anyway. "You'll enjoy it."

"Afraid not."

"Why? You already know the firemen and the police. Everyone else wants to meet you."

"They have gas stoves, not electric ranges. If they decide to use those outdoor grills? You'll have a lot of hungry people demanding their money back. They won't work, nor those Sterno things they put under casseroles to keep food hot. I'm not exactly the life of the party, you know."

I thought of all he'd missed in his life. He wouldn't miss this one. "We'll work something out. Maybe change it to a dance." I was a self-conscious, clumsy dancer, but he had to be there. He came to help the town; the town owed him a pleasant evening.

I pushed the Play Messages button on the machine again.

"Hello. Is this Willow Tate's residence? My name is Barry Jensen and I wonder if I could do an interview for a webzine. It'll be great publicity for your books, which I've admired for years. I met your cousin Susan last week and was excited when I realized you live here in Paumanok Harbor. Please call me."

There was a long pause while he tried to find the number of his new cell phone.

"I hope to hear from you soon."

Piet wore a half-smile. "Groundhog Day?"

I laughed. "Courtesy of Mayor Applebaum."

The next message was from Matt Spenser, the vet, and he sounded worried. "Please call me back, Willow, no matter what time."

"Something must be wrong," I told Piet. I started pacing again. "Maybe more dogs have been burned. Or he's spotted Roy Ruskin in the woods behind his house. Or else he wants me to take in another stray. What if he gave Little Red the wrong shot? Or—"

Piet pointed to the phone. "Call him."

Matt picked up at the second ring. "Spenser here."

I switched to the handset, not the speaker phone. "This is Willow. Is everything all right?"

"That's what I wanted to know. I heard about all the trouble with Roy Ruskin, and how the police thought he might come for his daughter. I worried about you, alone with the child out there."

I walked to the end of the phone cord, away from Piet. "That's really nice of you to be concerned, but they think he's on a train. We're fine."

He cleared his throat, then said, "I thought if you were anxious or anything, I could come keep you company. You know, keep an eye on things with you."

I turned my back on the man on the sofa, who already had his eyes on me. "I appreciate that, I really do. And I might have taken you up on it, but . . ."

"But you already have company?"

"Yes, I do."

"The fireman?"

I wasn't surprised he knew. Everyone knew everybody's business here, which was one of the reasons I wanted to get back to the city. "Yes."

Matt could tell from my short replies that I wasn't alone, in private. "He's there right now. I'm sorry. I guess I shouldn't have butted in."

"No, it's fine. I'm glad you called."

"Well, I'm glad you're not by yourself. Now I can go to sleep without feeling I was letting your mother down."

"My mother?"

"She told me to look after her kids. I figure you're one of them."

I laughed, forgetting Piet across the room. "Only a friend of my mother's could lump her daughter in with the dogs."

He laughed, too. "I'm sure you're her favorite."

"Then you don't know her all that well."

I heard the amusement fade from in his voice when he asked, "Maybe I could call after the firefighter leaves . . . ?"

So everyone knew Piet Doorn wasn't staying.

"Maybe. No, yes. That sounds good." It did.

We said good-bye and I turned to look at Piet. He had turned the TV on, out of politeness, I guessed, so he didn't have to overhear my side of the conversation. The Yankees were playing, and winning.

"That was the dogs' vet."

"Yeah, I got that."

"He was worried that I was alone."

"Got that, too. He offer to come bodyguard?"

"Yes. He sounded glad you were here, though."

Piet turned the TV volume down. "I'm sure he was." Sarcasm dripped like the condensation on his empty beer bottle. "He's kicking his desk right now."

"It's not like that."

"He's a man. Trust me, it's exactly like that." He clicked the TV off. "Now where were we?"

Top of the ninth inning, two outs. "You were sipping your beer and I was listening to my messages."

"Not there. Before."

Before I heard Matt's voice, I was considering taking my clothes off in the living room, under Piet's watchful eyes. Swinging for the bleachers.

That moment was gone. I couldn't talk to Matt one minute, then jump into bed with Piet the next.

Strike out.

CHAPTER 27

WOULD HE STILL STAY AND HELP? That was the question. He looked pissed, and I couldn't blame him. He wasn't getting paid. Now he wasn't getting laid. He came to put out fires, besides, not babysit or locate a missing matriarch. Definitely not to have his libido squashed.

"I'll make another loop around your grandmother's house, then go to bed. If you hear or see anything suspicious, call me, or beep your car horn with the remote."

So he wasn't going to leave tonight. Relief washed through me. I could be brave when I had to be. I felt better when I didn't have to.

He kissed me gently on his way out the door. He did not push nor show aggravation that I'd messed with his head for an hour. I liked him more for that. I did not like myself right now.

"I'm sorry," I said.

"Hey, that's life. I'll get over it, in about five years." He smiled, then came back and kissed me again. This time his arms wrapped around me, holding me close, making me feel his strength, his hardness, his desire. "But I don't give up so easily." When he stood back, I leaned against the wall to hold myself up. My knees sure as hell weren't going to do the job.

I'd turned away a man who kissed like that? Who could make me throb down to my toes with one soul-piercing, heart-stopping, blood-warming kiss? A genuine hero who was kind, besides? That was crazier than talking to insects from an alien world.

I couldn't muster up one good reason why I shouldn't be naked in his bed when he came back. This wouldn't be recreational sex, remorse in the morning. I liked Piet. I liked him a lot.

I could hear my cousin saying, "Go for it. Life is too short."

I could hear my mother saying, "I didn't raise a tramp. Show some self-respect."

I could hear my father saying, "Trust your instincts."

I could hear Matt saying, "Maybe when he's gone."

I could hear Elladaire whimpering. Now that I could handle. Less than a week and I had enough confidence that she wouldn't set the place on fire, and that I could solve most of her problems, if none of my own.

Elladaire was sleeping soundly when I got to her crib. "Wait, kiddo, in a few years you'll have to make all kinds of moral decisions. You don't want to cheapen yourself, or hold yourself too high to enjoy what life has to offer. Get your rest now, because you've got decades of second-guessing ahead of you."

I went to bed. With Little Red. In a ratty sleep shirt. And I slept like a baby.

Usually I woke up to dog breath in my face. That morning I woke up to a man's bare, hard chest under my cheek. I jerked up so fast I almost got whiplash.

"Morning, sunshine," Piet drawled.

"What are you doing here? Did we . . . ?"

"Hey, lady, if we did, you would remember, I promise.

Maybe you dreamed about me, though? We could take up where your dream left off."

He wore a half-smile and no shirt. I didn't know what was under the covers. Cross that out. I knew exactly what was under the sheet—I'd been lying right on top of it!—just not why it was here.

"A dog was asleep in my bed, and I thought I could keep a better eye on the house and the baby and you from here. Focused defense, they call it. Not splitting the zone of protection."

I remembered all the threats. "Did you hear anything in the night?"

"A couple of snores, a murmur or two. Not my name, no matter how hard I listened. Speaking of hard . . ."

"Yeah, I've been meaning to get a new mattress."

He smiled and got off the bed, wearing silk boxers with chili peppers on them. Hot.

"C'mon, get up. The kid'll be wanting breakfast and a change, and we've got a lot to do. Ever been on a snipe hunt?"

Half asleep, I was half turned on by the view of his lean, firm body with a strip of pale hair trailing down his chest to the peppers. I liked how he wasn't all muscle-bound like a body-building weight lifter, but didn't have an ounce of fat. He turned to pull on his jeans. Nice butt, too.

"Stop ogling. Snipe, remember."

"I wasn't—"

He cleared his throat.

"Um, never heard of one."

"The relatives used to send us kids on one every summer. To get rid of us, I realized years later. We had to wear boots and hats and carry nets and canteens and whistles to signal if we spotted one, but they never said what it looked like, or if it'd be in the trees or on the ground in the woods near our house. We spent hours searching for a creature I didn't think existed. The whole thing was like something out of *Alice in Wonderland*."

"Did it? Exist, I mean?"

"Snipes do. They're birds, I found out later, but we never caught sight of one. I don't know if they hang out in that part of the country at all."

"Is that what you think about the creature in the ditch? That it doesn't exist? That searching for Mama is a fool's errand?"

"I think we have to go find out. Do you have a whistle?"

"What do we need a whistle for?" Panic stuck a finger in my stomach. "You're not going far away from me out there, are you? What happened to keeping the cone of protection or whatever, together?"

"Cell phones don't work out there. No tower."

No answer, either. My God, what if he took me out there and left me, payback for my leaving him unsatisfied?

Piet would never do such a thing. And if I repeated that enough times, I might believe it.

We couldn't go right away, naturally, not until we made arrangements for Elladaire. I called Janie at the hair salon to find out when her last appointment was. We could wait that long.

We took the three dogs and the baby in her stroller for a walk up to Grandma Eve's farm. The stand was doing good business for an off-season weekend. People still wanted fresh herbs and the sweet pale yellow corn the field workers had just picked that morning.

My grandmother offered us iced tea and muffins spread with the beach plum jelly she'd made this week, a new experience for Piet and Elladaire. I wouldn't touch the stuff, still remembering the head-to-toe poison ivy I got picking the damn things before someone remembered to teach the city kid about leaves of three, let it be.

Janie was waiting for us in front of my house with Joe the plumber in his pickup truck.

"I don't have room for all her stuff in my car," she explained. "And Joe doesn't think the baby and I should be alone right now."

Good guy, Joe. So I asked him to look again for Mama. He looked around, then spotted a dog bowl. He filled it from the garden hose and stared into it. I didn't see anything but dog hair floating on up but Joe said, "Just like before. Whatever it is, it's stuck tight."

I touched the bracelet on my wrist. "But she's still alive?"

He scratched his head. "I've never found a deader. Can't recall looking, though."

Joe and I carried out baby paraphernalia, what Janie'd left with me, what I managed to accumulate afterward. Piet unbuckled the car seat from my Outback, then started to take the portable crib apart.

Janie hugged and kissed the baby as if she hadn't seen her in a week. She also checked her top to bottom in case I'd damaged something.

"Are you sure she won't start any more fires?"

"She hasn't since she's been here."

"Since he's been here, you mean." Janie tilted her head toward Piet, who was bent over the crib.

I stepped into her line of sight. Let her admire Joe's plumber pants and half-moon rising, not Piet's butt. "He thinks she's fine."

"But what if she's not? How will I know?"

"You'll know the first time she cries."

"Then what am I supposed to do when Joe's truck catches on fire or my hair?"

Janie's hair was long and curly this week. I handed her one of my fire extinguishers.

Piet gave her his card. "Call me."

I swear she batted her fake eyelashes at him.

I reminded Piet we were going out to the marshes. "You told me there's no cell reception out there."

Now Janie looked stricken. She glanced at me, then at the baby.

"She'll be fine. And we absolutely have to go."

Piet had the crib all folded up and in its carry case. "We can wait a couple of hours."

No, we could not. I glared at all of them. "We've waited too long as is."

Janie glared back. She picked up Elladaire, but handed her to Piet. She pulled some papers out of her purse. "Maybe you'll have time to make a poster for the benefit for Mary, like you agreed. I brought a picture of her and Elladaire, and all the details. The printer agreed to run them off for us for free. We're aiming for next Saturday, if you can fit that into your busy schedule."

No thank you for taking care of her grandniece; no consideration that my life had been turned upside down, too; no appreciation that I was hurtling into the scary, swampy unknown without a seatbelt—to help her town.

"I'll get to it as soon as we come home."

Now she did take the baby from Piet, which did not sit well with Elladaire. Maybe she'd picked up on the tension in the room, or saw her toys and books being taken away. "Pipi!" she wailed, holding her hands out to him.

I went to kiss her good-bye, and got as much affection as I'd gotten from Janie. "I'll come visit, sweetie, I promise."

She wasn't consoled. Little Red started barking at the uproar. I picked him up before he bit someone, most likely me.

"Well, at least you'll believe she's safe now, as soon as you get to the end of the dirt road."

Joe hitched up his pants and ran his hand over the hood of his truck, as if he was saying good-bye to it.

Jane strapped the baby into her seat. Elladaire was crying, leaving Piet. So was Janie.

I brushed tears off my cheeks, too. I'd miss the kid. And I'd miss Piet when he left.

CHAPTER 28

"LET'S GO.

"I promised her two hours."

I promised the beetles days ago. I remembered how nervous I was with the burning baby at first, though, so I tried to control my impatience. I ate Elladaire's leftover graham crackers that I forgot to pack.

Piet put the TV on to the Weather Channel: forest fires in the west, tinder-dry conditions through the midlands, lightning strikes in Texas. Damnation.

He didn't say anything, but he switched to CNN to read the scrolls along the bottom of the screen.

"Will they want you to go to one of those places?"

He shrugged. "I couldn't get to all of them, no matter what, and some will take weeks to put out entirely, they're so big, with so much kindling. They'll call if they want me. But DUE has its own priorities, like Paumanok Harbor. They also have scores of prognosticators like your father on their staff. They'll know where I'm needed most."

I prayed their seers were better than mine. Heaven knew where Dad would send Piet, if not to Saks. It suddenly occurred to me that ancient soothsayers used entrails to predict the future. Did the people from Royce do that also? The idea of sacrificing a chicken when I was trying to save a swarm of beetles did not make sense. Surely the modern sibyls were wiser than that.

While Piet watched and listened, wondering if he should pack up his truck, for all I knew, I stuffed a sketch pad into a backpack, along with sunscreen, water, a first aid kit, and granola bars. I put the bug spray back on the shelf, with regrets, but found plastic gloves and two carpenter's face masks my mother had for when she refinished furniture. "Is it time?"

"It's been fifteen minutes."

"I'm sorry. I'm being selfish, I know. Janie needs the security of having you nearby. It's just that I'm worried. You heard what Joe said. Mama's stuck."

"I didn't see anything in the dog bowl except a floating leaf. Did you?"

"No, but that doesn't mean anything. Joe saw it."

"If what he saw was your unknown creature stuck in the mud, then she's not going anywhere for the next couple of hours."

"It'll take us almost twenty minutes to get to the marsh. We'll be in cell phone range for most of that."

"Two hours." He flipped back to the Weather Channel.

One hour and forty-five minutes, I calculated, but kept it to myself. To fill the time, I decided to brush the dogs. They'd taken second place to the baby and looked neglected. The two big dogs were no problem. They liked the attention. Little Red had knots the brush pulled on. I took the Band-Aids out of my backpack.

The weather commentator was talking about the lack of rain in New England and the fear of a catastrophic fire season unless a fall hurricane dropped a lot of rain in the area.

"Great, something else to worry about," I said, giving the dogs biscuits and putting away the brush. "A hurricane can flood the whole of the salt marsh. If Mama is trapped there ..." I couldn't complete the thought. "We've really got to go soon."

"There are no hurricanes on the weather map, and you've got to learn to relax. Go with the flow. Take things as they come."

Things like trolls and flaming flies? Or floods and wildfires? If he thought I'd sit back and put my feet up when the world—or my world, anyway—was in danger, he didn't know me at all. I was a worrier. It was in my DNA. Look at Dad. He dreamed of disasters. And my mother fretted over every lost dog in the country.

Or was he still thinking about sex, that I should stop overthinking the issue and accept the current that flew between us? For all I knew, putting out fires and making love were relaxing for him. Why not? There was no pressure involved with either. He was a wizard in at least one of the fields, most likely both. I only stopped worrying when—

Before I could recall the last time I'd been at ease, his phone rang.

I wanted to shout at him not to answer it, that Elladaire didn't cry sparks, that his beeper would go off in a real emergency. Unless the emergency was in California or Texas or at Janie's house. Or his family needed him. I bit my lip.

He let "Come on, Baby, Light My Fire" play through while he checked the caller ID.

"It's Chief Haversmith."

At least it wasn't Joe the plumber, calling from the hospital. "If the police are calling and it's not poker night, you better answer."

He listened, went, "Uh-huh" a couple of times, then asked if they had cell reception there.

My hopes sank.

"I'll meet you at the fire station."

And drowned.

"They didn't sound the alarm or beep the volunteers."

"No, this fire is out. It was a cabin where an old summer camp used to be. Off a place or a road called Three Mile Harbor. I didn't ask which. The chief said he'd drive, so I don't have to know."

Most likely the old Blue Bay property or Boys Harbor. "If the fire is out, why do you have to go?"

"People reported fireworks out there, but the local fire department found no spent shells or evidence of rockets. I need to look for dead bugs. The arson squad wouldn't think to look for them, which is lucky for us. If I find them, we can still keep Paumanok Harbor and the fireflies—and you—out of the investigation. Let's hope your friend Barry isn't checking, too."

I wondered how the lightning bugs got so far away, and why. If their mother was near the Harbor, and they tended to stick near her or me, then maybe someone took them out to Springs. Someone who knew both areas were isolated and untended. Someone like Roy Ruskin.

Piet nodded when I told him my theory, but he wasn't convinced. "If I don't find any beetles, it's plain arson. If I find hurt ones, someone is using them. But if they are setting fires themselves, they've got to be dealt with."

I did not ask how. With dread I imagined the police and the fire department spread out in the marsh and my backyard. Piet could turn the bugs off, the troops could net them or spray them or gas them while they were disoriented and helpless.

"No! It's not them, it's Roy. Or some other freak playing with matches. And we can get them to leave if we free Mama, I'm sure."

"I should be back in a couple of hours. We'll go looking then."

That would be too late if the chief decided the beetles were guilty. He never minded taking the law into his own hands, or a miscreant. Paumanok Harbor was always his first priority, and to hell with civil liberties and endangered species. He'd declare an emergency security risk and worry about the results later.

Piet would side with him, I knew. He lived to put out fires, permanently, if possible. I stepped back before he could kiss me good-bye.

I couldn't stay here safe at home. I couldn't go searching by myself. Aside from the fact that I had a yellow stripe down my back, my front, and everywhere in between, I didn't have a boat. No canoe, kayak, rowboat, or inflatable raft. The reason I didn't have a seaworthy craft was I didn't like the sea. Water had crabs and eels and leeches and undertows and sometimes no ground beneath your feet. And waves. I got seasick.

The alternative, hiking hours and miles through that dismal wet wasteland again, was worse. So I called Rick Stamfield at the marina and asked if he'd ferry me out to the marshes, then lower a dinghy to get ashore. And come with me. Mostly come with me. I had a copy of Piet's map of the grid. "I know where to go."

"That'll be a nice change." Rick wished he could take me out of the harbor and drown me, but that's not what he said. He told me he had to wait for the insurance examiners to come to the marina, again. He also told me to do something, now.

"I'm trying, damn it. I have to get there first."

Martin Armbruster had a boat. And hell would freeze over before I led him to Mama.

My friend Louisa's husband Dante had a couple of boats. He used to live on the big one, but he kept a smaller outboard for fishing in the bay. I called the arts center, but the woman who answered Louisa's phone said the whole family had gone west to visit with Mrs. Rivera's family for the weekend.

Susan knew a lot of guys with boats, but then she'd want to come. I'd rather face ten swamp monsters and a tidal wave than my family's wrath if I dragged Susan into danger.

Her father had a small cabin cruiser. He'd bought it from my father when Dad moved full time to Florida, for day trips when he wasn't working at Grandma Eve's farm. Unfortunately, Uncle Roger told me, the boat never got out of dry dock this year. Uncle Roger'd had Lyme disease so bad he'd spent time in the hospital, time the boat needed. "Next year, Willy."

Next week might be too late. The Lucifers fretted about time. The fire department wanted the flare-ups gone yesterday.

I gave up on private boats and called the Bay Constable. Leonard was too busy keeping boats away from the area. Besides, his orders were to keep anyone from going ashore in the marsh until the water analysis came back and the air quality improved.

I tried the harbormaster next, even though the eastern shore wasn't Elgin's territory. If I'd wanted a breeze to push a sailboat, he could have done something, but he couldn't take me out in his patrol boat. He had the DEC coming to check for environmental damage, and a hazmat crew.

"You can't let them go traipsing around there!"

"I can't stop them, Willow. Your friend Martin tried

to make himself look important by reporting the localized smell, the poor air quality, and a sighting of rare,
dangerous animals. He called the DEC, the EPA, and
the BSA."

"The Boy Scouts?"

"The Beetle Society of America. Can you believe it?
There's an organization for everything. Now we'll have
a lot of geeks out here with nets and microscopes and
reference books. Which will not have pictures of your
beetles."

"They're not my beetles."

He ignored my protest, grumbling.

"It'll be like that time someone spotted an albino al-
batross or something that belonged in the Arctic. They
sent it into the Audubon Society rare bird sighting website and we had traffic jams of telescope toters up and
down the shore roads. They came from New Jersey and
Connecticut, if you can believe it. This could be worse,
because the entomologist types won't be happy with a
sighting or a photograph. They'll want specimens, which
means nets at night, on other people's property."

It also meant the beetle society people could get
burned.

Uncle Henry already knew about the government
meddlers when I called him at the police station. "We've
got enough trouble with the fires now. And the smell in
the wetlands. At least it's staying where it is."

"What are they going to do about it, the Environmental Protection people and everyone else?"

"They decided we need a survey committee to decide
how to protect the shoreline. They cannot act, they say,
before they get a better idea of what they're facing."

"So we have time?"

"They're on the way."

"You have to get rid of them."

"How? Whatever we do will only bring more attention and publicity to the Harbor. The better solution would be to get rid of your bugs, now."

He didn't point a finger over the phone line, but I felt the accusation and the guilt. He might as well have pinned a scarlet letter on my chest. Maybe D for disaster and doom. T for troublemaker. F for you really fucked up this time.

"I'm working on it."

CHAPTER 29

WHO NEEDED JOGGING when they could pace away the graham cracker calories? I'd wear out my mother's carpet soon if I didn't get shin splints or a plan. There had to be someone willing to help, someone who didn't blame me for every misfortune in the village. A lot was at stake here, and you'd think when I sent a call out for help someone in the Harbor would answer. It was their way of life on the line here, too. And not just the espers who ran the place, but the nontalented locals also deserved their privacy from sensational journalists, their safety from arsonists, their clean beaches and water and air. Surely I could find someone who cared enough about the people and the creatures to . . .

Creatures. Great and small. Bright and beautiful. Brilliant, Willy, and the vet worked half days on Saturday, like Janie at the hair salon.

"Are the dogs all right?" was the first thing Matt asked when his snippy receptionist eventually put me through to him. "Did Ruskin come back?"

"We're fine right now, but I need help. You said to call—"

"Sure, I'm almost finished here. What can I do? Move

a refrigerator? Start the lawn mower? Give you a ride somewhere?"

"It's a little more complicated than that. Do you know the coastal area east of Paumanok Harbor where the drainage ditches are? The tidal marshes?"

"Where they've seen the weird lights?"

"That's the place. I have to get there. Can you take me? We can rent an outboard from Rick's Marina."

Dogs barked in the background while there was a pause across the phone line. Matt had to be thinking about my request. I figured he'd want to know why, and I had maybe five seconds to decide what to tell him. He didn't ask why, though, just who.

"Uh, what about the fireman?"

That was easy. And honest. "He's investigating a suspicious blaze outside East Hampton."

"And he's okay with you asking another man to spend the afternoon out in the bay with you?"

Oh, boy, did they ever grow up?

"Listen, Matt, I am not coming on to you or inviting you to a picnic. I need help, that's all."

His "oh" was filled with disappointment, so I guess I owed him more explanation. "Piet's staying at my house, everyone knows that. He's recovering from some bad burns and helping the volunteers with the recent fire epidemic."

"So you're not, um, involved with him?"

I guess I owed him an answer to that, too. "We're partners and friends, with no deeper commitment." Except some deeper kisses. "He'll be leaving as soon as the town is out of danger. Which you can help accomplish."

"Getting him to leave or stopping that maniac Roy Ruskin? I've got to tell you, I've never been great at hand-to-hand combat."

"It's not that kind of help. I have a certain chore I

can't do by myself. I like you and I trust you, so I'm asking you. Isn't that enough?"

"It's more than enough."

"Then you'll come with me?"

I let out a deep breath when he said of course he'd come. How soon did I want to go?

"As soon as possible."

"Uh, I hate to ask, but what are we going to do out there? I need to know what to bring."

"We're looking for something, but I'm not exactly sure of what. High boots for the swampy parts. A shovel, I guess. Maybe you could bring a medical bag?"

"I never go anywhere without it anyway."

"Great. Can you meet me at Rick's Marina? I'll rent the boat." The safest, sturdiest one I could find, with extra life preservers.

"Sure, but I heard the bay was closed in that area. They're not letting anyone go ashore."

"They'll let me." Between Elgin and Leonard and Rick, they'd make certain no one stopped me. They didn't care if I dove headfirst into quicksand, as long as I fixed the problem.

"Does this have anything to do with the fires and the out-of-season, off the astronomy charts Northern lights? Or the strange insects I've been hearing about? You're actually going to let me see them?"

"I don't know if they'll be there or where they go in the daytime." I didn't know if he could see them at all, being a nonsensitive. "I don't know if what we're looking for has anything to do with the burned-out buildings and boats. We have to look, that's all. I have a map, so we won't be wandering around blindly."

"Let me get this straight. We are going to look for an unknown something in illegal waters, with the chance of getting burned by homicidal bugs? And a map makes it better? I guess what people whisper about you is right."

Damn. "That I am crazy?"

"No, that you're neck-deep in the peculiar events that keep happening in Paumanok Harbor. Not all of them, because I've heard stories about this place since I got here last year, before you came out in the spring. I never believed half of them."

"Good, don't. I'll see you at Rick's in half an hour, okay?"

I thought he laughed, but the sound could have been a "hmpf" of frustration. "So I don't get an explanation?"

"It's a long story."

"One I'm never going to hear? Like how come it never rains on the Fourth of July parade, when it pours on the towns on either side? Or how a plane crashed into a boat, but they never found the plane? Then there's the little boy you made lost posters for. He was found, but disappeared that same night. And that's not to mention the missing colt you also made flyers for, the horse show finale that no one remembers, and the baby everyone was afraid of except you and the fireman."

"Any chance you can help me without asking questions?"

Now he definitely laughed. "I can try if that's what it takes for you to take me along. I'm definitely going to enjoy this. You'll see; you can trust me."

And Mayor Applebaum's memory losses.

Rick shook his head when I told him I'd asked Matt to go with me.

"He's a good guy and a fine vet. My dog loves him, but he's not one of us."

"You sound like some exclusive golf club blackballing a new member."

"Come on, Willy, you know what I mean. He could be dangerous. Think about that reporter."

"Matt Spenser is not a reporter. He lives here. He has a right to help protect the place."

"I don't like it."

"Fine. I'll go by myself. How do I start the boat's motor? And where do I sit to steer?"

Rick greeted Matt like his long-lost brother. And he promised to clear our arrival with the EPA, the DEC, and NOAA if he had to, all the agencies Martin alerted, the bastard. It helped that Matt was a veterinarian, with one undergraduate course in marine biology. "I'll say he's our resident expert."

"What about me?"

Rick crammed a life vest over my head. "You're the resident nut case. Get out there and fix it."

Matt didn't comment and he didn't laugh. He took my hand to help me into the boat that looked smaller the closer I got to getting into it. If he felt my hand trembling, he didn't mention that either. He was strong and competent and knew how to run an outboard. Then he asked if I knew how to fix "it" whatever "it" was.

I couldn't fix a split infinitive or a split end half the time. "I'm going to try."

I was going to try not to get seasick, too. Everyone always told me to look at the shoreline or some other fixed, unmoving object. I couldn't look, not knowing what waited there. Talk about a rock and a hard place. Mal de mer or Mama—not a great choice. So I looked at Matt, who made better scenery anyway. His brown hair waved in the wind and he squinted ahead, then down at the map he held. He constantly checked his gauges, the chop on the water, the other boats in the vicinity, and me. He looked cool, calm, competent, and trustworthy. He'd get us there safely. Maybe home, too.

I managed to wave to Leonard in the Bay Constable's boat. He waved back, then gave us a thumbs up. No one was going to stop us.

Too bad.

The closer we got to the salt marsh, the more anxious I felt. I clutched the side of the boat with one hand, my life preserver with the other, and told myself that my father never mentioned death by drowning or a demon in a ditch, only Saks.

This muddy, reedy, malodorous swampland was definitely not Fifth Avenue. I was safe. Now if my heart believed that, it might stop beating loudly enough to drown out the boat's putt-putt as Matt slowed the engine.

"Come look at the map and see what you think."

He wanted me to get up from my bench and walk toward him? Now, while the narrow, shallow, tippy boat was rocking? "I'm not real good at maps."

"I am, but this one isn't matching the shoreline. I counted the cuts where the ditches open to the bay, but I think we missed one. The graph on the map shows them evenly spaced."

"Just follow your nose." As we got closer to the shore, the odor got worse. Thank goodness the area was already uninhabitable, and at least a couple of miles away from the nearest homes.

"I know that smell and it is not healthy."

I handed him a face mask. It didn't help.

"I mean, whatever is making that odor is not in good shape. Are you sure you want to see this?"

I was sure I did not want to be on the same planet as anything that smelled so bad, but I had no choice. "There," I said, pointing at a higher mound of mud and dirt on the narrow beach. "It looks like that canal caved in. Maybe from all the rain we had this summer."

The weather mavens had caused a huge two-day storm before the horse show last month, to head off anything that could ruin the fund-raising event. Roads had flooded and trees got uprooted, so the banks of the ditch might have suffered, too. Maybe that's how Mama got stuck, if she swam or flew or simply materialized on the landward side of one of the ditches. The gates between worlds were open then, with the night mares searching for their missing colt. Or Mama could have come with the eldritch thunder and lightning when we rescued the troll's half brother.

The exit back to the sea must have collapsed, maybe on top of her. Now it looked like the grasses had grown over it, making the channel hard to locate. Except for the smell.

I looked at the two puny shovels in the bottom of the boat. This could be a long afternoon.

Matt grounded the boat, tipped the engine up so the propeller didn't get damaged, and hopped out. He didn't care that his pants got wet, or his boots had water in them, or his feet sank in the muck of the shore. Or that I hadn't budged from my seat.

He pulled the boat higher, closer to the vegetation— and the ticks, snakes, and spiders—and reached back to lift out a small anchor. He tossed that into the reeds and pulled back on the line. "She'll hold."

So would I. To the sides of the boat.

He took out the shovels and his backpack with his medical equipment, laid them on top of the nearest grasses, then took his face mask off. "It's too hot and uncomfortable. You get used to the smell. I don't think it'll kill us."

I took mine off, too. Death by noxious odor might be preferable to what lay ahead. Before I could figure how to get out of the boat without falling on my face in the slime on the shore, Matt reached over, plucked me out of the boat and set me on relatively dry land next to the shovels.

"You didn't have to do that. I'm too heavy to be lifting that way."

He grinned. "Hell, the Vogels' basset hound weighs

more than you." He went back for my backpack while I took off the life vest I didn't need anymore. If I fell in a water-filled ditch, I guess Matt could drag me out before I drowned.

"What the hell is in here?" he asked. "It weighs as much as you do."

"Supplies," I replied, handing him gloves, a water bottle, and a length of rope I thought might come in handy if we had to tow Mama out to sea or, heaven help us, tie her up. I buckled the now lighter pack on, hefted a shovel in one hand, my trusty hammer in the other, and bravely set out for the mound of overgrown mud where the ditch's opening should be.

Strains of "Onward Christian Soldiers" wafted through my mind, which was better than the "Heigh Ho, Heigh Ho, It's Off to Work We Go" Matt was humming. I looked back. The man was grinning.

His longer stride carried him past me, or else he wanted to be the leader. I didn't care which. He tugged on the brim of my baseball cap. "Thanks for bringing me. This is the best adventure I've had in years."

"Tell me that after we have to dig the channel open again."

"Come on, Willy, think positively. Heck, maybe we'll dig up Captain Kidd's missing treasure. Legend has it he buried it somewhere on this coast. Won't that be grand?"

I passed the charred remains of what might have been a seagull, then another burnt carcass. Maybe a rat.

Oh, yeah. Simply grand.

CHAPTER 30

WE FOUND MAMA.
I puked. And cried. My beautiful seeking
bracelet fell off. I took another quick look and puked
some more. And cried some more.

She was huge and dead and covered in quivering
masses of naked, bloated, obscene grubs. Maggots. Eating her.

This time I threw up without looking, only trying to
erase the image from my mind before it got imprinted
there for life. My life, not poor Mama's.

We'd hiked about a half mile along the drainage ditch
that couldn't drain anything from either side, landward
or seaward, it was so congested with weeds and mud and
muck. And scorched bones.

Matt had stopped humming. He'd held the shovel in
front of him like a weapon. I got a firmer grip on my
hammer.

The ditch grew muddier, wetter, and its banks more
intact the farther we walked away from the shore. It was
about five feet wide, jumpable, but easy enough to wade
across with only a trickle of murky water at its base.

Then we'd seen what had the canal blocked from
both sides. Not another cave-in or clogged vegetation,

but a huge lump, maybe fifteen feet long, and filling the entire width of the ditch, like a cork in a bottle.

"What the—" Matt stopped so short I bumped into him. "It looks like a dead dolphin or maybe a juvenile whale. How the hell did it beach itself so far from the water?"

I went around him, got a closer look, and lost my confidence along with my lunch. How was I supposed to tell the luminaries it was too late, I couldn't help them? How was I supposed to get rid of them? How could I explain to Matt?

I hoped he couldn't see the extra appendages, the odd large-headed shape, just a dead animal covered in flesh-eaters, surrounded by incinerated scavengers. I guess the lightning bugs had tried to protect her. They'd failed, the same way I failed her.

Matt walked around the rotting corpse while I rinsed my mouth out with the water from my backpack. He asked if I had any idea what this was, or had been.

Without thinking, I answered: "It's Mama."

"That poor creature is not mother to anything I've ever seen."

I didn't see how she could be the mother to the beetles, either, but this was definitely the figure they'd tried to show me, up in lights. She'd never go sailing in the sky again.

At least the tears kept me from seeing the destruction of a glorious being who'd died for the crime of trespassing into our world.

Matt knelt beside the body. I couldn't look. Instead I tried to judge how far we were from any road, and how we were going to get more people and equipment out here to bury her without alerting the media and attracting sightseers.

"Come look at this, Willow. I think she's alive."

He'd brushed the horrible slugs off a small area on

her side. I forced myself to look and saw smooth, shiny, iridescent skin. The skin appeared to move in a regular rhythm. "She's breathing?"

He was opening his pack to find a stethoscope. I couldn't wait.

"My God, they are eating her alive!" I started scraping the maggots away with my shovel, then worried I'd hurt Mama worse, so I used my hands. I was so desperate, I didn't remember to put on the gloves.

As soon as my bare hands touched an inch of her bare skin, I felt it. Not her heartbeat, but that warmth, that fellowship I shared with the beetles, like being enveloped in a smile.

"Mama?" I whispered.

The skin beneath my hand pulsed in rainbow colors. The smile grew.

"It's me, Willow," I whispered out loud while I tried to project an image of a willow tree, to identify myself. I was the Visualizer, wasn't I?

A picture of the tree covered in the lightning bugs in my backyard flashed through my head. I hadn't put it there.

I replaced that mental picture with one of a flame-lit dolphinlike being with wings.

Yes, I thought I heard in my head. And "Yes," I shouted back, with a quieter, internal *yes* for good measure. We were communicating! Who needed a translator? I knew I didn't have that power. Mama had enough magic for both of us.

"Hurry, Matt, get them off her!" I used both hands to swipe the disgusting worms away. I did not acknowledge his look of disbelief and dismay that I had just introduced myself to a near-dead aberration.

"We cannot save her."

"Yes, we can," I cried, frantically clearing a wider swathe of skin. "It's these leeches that are killing her."

No. The children of light free us to live.

I stopped and sat back on my heels. I didn't need any mental image to understand that the maggots ate through sloughing layers of necrotic blubber to uncover the healthy prismatic skin beneath. I could see it with my own eyes.

Matt was staring at the stethoscope in his hands, shaking his head. "This is not right."

Maybe it was. "Matt, talk to me about maggots."

"They are the larval stage of many different insects. Forensic detection uses them to determine time of death by identifying the particular species. Modern medicine has adopted them for caring for wounds. They eat dead tissue, but leave the healthy. They're voracious, because they need to go into the next stage where they do not eat, but change into the finished product. Metamorphosis, like a caterpillar turning into a butterfly."

The concept took a lot of mind-twisting. These disgusting parasites turning into anything as lovely as the Lucifers? "So the maggots are eating dead skin, but leaving the healthy underneath. Then they'll be reborn as beetles, and she'll emerge as . . . whatever."

"Dolphins are mammals, with live births. Most fish and all birds lay eggs that hatch into tiny replicas of the parents. No larva or pupae or cocoon. No stages, except ones like tadpoles. Only growth to maturity. This is no insect, amphibian, or bird."

Mama was no dolphin, either. But mother to the beetles?

I felt the humor deep in my veins, with a glow of warmth. Mama was an empath extraordinary. And she knew my language, the same wondrous way the elf king and the white stallion had.

Not mother. Male.

Huh?

She showed me a picture of Matt, then one of Piet,

which confirmed for me that Mama and the fireflies also communicated with each other, unless they shared a hive mentality. Either way, they all knew what any one of them knew. "Men?"

Matt looked at me. I forgot to say it to myself.

His curiosity had to wait. I thought I understood what Mama—whatever gender he was—meant. "So you are not the mother of the fireflies, but the host? You have a symbiotic relation? The maggots help you shed or molt or whatever it is that you do, and you nurture the babies?"

The concept was there, not the words. I thought about pulling out my sketch pad and drawing little remora eels suctioned to sharks, cleaning the much larger fish. But I didn't know where the creature's eyes were, under the decomposing flesh, or if he could see. Instead I drew a mental image of a maggot turning into a beautiful shimmery lightning bug. May that be the first and last time I sketched a maggot, on paper or on my brain.

I felt another warm smile in my soul. And envisioned that insect-fish leaping and playing and diving away. *M'ma.*

M'ma, that's your name?

Part.

My mind couldn't put together the string of words, symbols, and feelings that comprised the rest of his name. I moved on, doing my best to project my thoughts his way. *But you can't leave until you're all clean?*

He considered the maggots as cherished offspring, judging by the image I received of me holding Elladaire. *And the children are transformed, too?* I guessed. He did not refute my theory, so I asked, *M'ma, when will you all be ready?*

Soon.

You will be beautiful.

He understood that. *You are beautiful.*

No, I was nuts. I could tell by the look on Matt's face.

I wasn't ready to pretend to act normally for him. I needed to know what I could do for M'ma right now. "Water, shade, food?"

Matt asked for water. I ignored him, listening for the voice in my head.

We rest.

"We? There are more of you?'

Rest, Willow. Rest.

"But how will you get out of here?"

"The same way we got in," Matt answered.

"Hush, I'm not talking to you." I visualized the blocked ditch, the mounded dirt and high grasses. *How can you escape from here?*

A cheerful warmth washed over me again. M'ma echoed Matt: *The same way we got in.*

"Is it safe here?"

Matt grabbed his shovel and spun around, looking for danger. I kept forgetting not to talk out loud, but saying the words made it easier for me to set them clearly in my mind. I pictured a horde of hungry rats gnawing and raucous crows pecking at the decomposing flesh.

In answer scores of beetles rose up from the nearby grasses, ready to do fiery battle.

M'ma sent a message: *Safe for now.* Matt's eyes were huge, but he didn't start swinging his shovel at the fireflies, thank goodness. "What are we supposed to do now?"

Rest.

"Nothing for awhile," I told Matt, convincing myself. "We can't hurry the process." There were tons of blubber left to get through, then the maggots had to build cocoons or whatever they did before turning into full-sized lantern beetles. I couldn't think about what came later, which might be less safe.

*   *   *

Matt wanted to do something, anything. He was not used to standing around when an animal was suffering.

"It's all right," I told him. "He doesn't need anything at this moment."

"He? I thought you called it 'Mama.'"

"M'ma. It's an ancient name for an older god," I prevaricated. I wasn't a storyteller for nothing.

"I never heard of such a name or god or creature."

"It's very rare."

"I bet. And I'm thinking this is some kind of intricate prank you and your friends put together to feed that prick Barry so he'd look like a fool trying to peddle a hoax. I don't appreciate being caught in the middle."

He looked hot and bothered and ready to march out of the vicinity. "It's not a hoax. Listen, I trusted you. You have to trust me now."

"By doing nothing?"

"No, by digging. We have to camouflage the ditch opening better to keep away the worst predators, the Barry Jensens of this world."

Still angry, he started to gather our belongings and stuff them in the backpacks. I took a last look at M'ma and saw the smooth patches we'd uncovered were already barely visible under a fresh blanket of maggots. There must be thousands of the disgusting white worms. 3,549 of them, according to the numerologists in Paumanok Harbor.

Which meant 3,549 new fire-starters.

Heaven help us.

CHAPTER 31

WE HAD TO HURRY, with the officials on the way to inspect the air and the water and the insects. Damn Martin Armbruster and his big mouth and big ambitions. If I could have used my cell phone from here, I'd see if Elgin could get the usual onshore breeze blowing backward. If Elgin and the other weather magis could get wind coming across the grasses, they could blow the stench out to sea so M'ma'd be harder to find. With miles to search, and Piet to extinguish the lightning bugs, there'd be little enough to see.

The phone didn't work, Elgin couldn't come, Piet was out of town, and hardly a blade of grass moved in the still air. So we had to hide our find better, faster.

"Grab the shovel. It's heigh-ho time again, Doc."

Matt seemed to accept that I was in charge, a miracle in a man, in my experience. He took a different path back toward the beach, rather than make our route twice as easy to follow. "I'll be Doc if you'll be Sexy."

"Sexy isn't one of the seven dwarves."

"That's why they needed Sleeping Beauty so badly."

I knew he was teasing to get my mind off the sight and the desperation. "I wish I were asleep and this was all a bad dream."

"Would you rather be Scary?"

"No one's afraid of me. I feel more like Scaredy. As in scaredy cat."

He looked back, but kept going in the right direction, trying to step on drier ground when possible, not leaving footprints. "You're kidding. You scare the hell out of me. I've never known a woman—or a man, for that matter—who can do what you do."

"What, throw up without getting my shoes dirty or talk to bugs and beached whales?"

"No, someone who can face the totally unknown and figure it out."

"I did, didn't I?" And without the hotshots from DUE. "You were pretty great yourself, accepting whatever you saw without asking too many questions. But tell me, what *did* you see?"

He stopped walking to adjust his backpack. "Seriously? You were right there looking at the same thing."

I took the opportunity to have a sip of water to make my interest seem more casual. "I know, but I'd like to hear your impression of what we found back there. Part of your job is figuring what's wrong when your patient can't tell you, by observation."

Matt described a sadly deformed animal—fish or sea mammal—he thought, with inches of dead flesh sloughing off. Instead of the bone and tissue he expected under the rotting layer, he'd discovered smooth, shiny, firm gray skin, which made no sense in a dying animal. When he listened for a heartbeat, he heard something entirely new to him. Maybe two hearts beating. Maybe an echo from the thousands of maggots, or noise from the nearby lightning bugs. Maybe he'd been listening to another organ entirely. "It was more of a concerto than a glub-glub," he said. "Nothing that could keep a creature from expiring. I wish I could have recorded it, or hooked up an EKG. We never did see or hear any breath signs.

Without a more extensive examination, I'd have to assume the animal was in its last hours, at best."

I did not want him turning into Martin of the science experiments. "What about the maggots? What did you think of them?"

"They appeared to be hard workers. Big, white, fat."

"And the beetles?"

"Big, brown, not very impressive, except for a little incandescence in their abdomens. I suppose it shows more brightly in the dark."

I brushed one off my shoulder and willed it back to M'ma before Matt got a better look. But maybe what he saw was all he could ever see, by the laws of the otherworld. Poor Matt did not know what he was missing. For a rare time I was glad I could see the remarkable visitors in their true appearance.

"What was your take on all the creatures?" he wanted to know.

"Just a little bit different." Like the difference between an old black-and-white movie and *Avatar* in 3-D. I'd bet the grubs were a blanket of glowworms at night. Even by daylight, the lantern beetles gleamed like prisms. Their outer wings shone gold, while the inner gossamer wings flashed green lace. What Matt called a little incandescence I saw as a tiny flame carried safe in a mica-like transparent belly. And M'ma, under the cover of the cleaners, reflected the sky and the grasses and the sun like stained glass. After his transforming molt he'd be breathtaking, and very much alive.

If we kept him safe long enough.

Matt believed me when I said we had to hide the scene in the ditch, without understanding how serious a problem it was, of course. His reasons were different from mine.

He knew a hundred scientists could be here by morning, doing biopsies and gathering specimens and slides.

They couldn't help the dying animal but could add to the poor creature's suffering. "I'd suggest we call in the marine rescue people from Riverhead, but they'd be too late. I doubt it could swim in that condition even if they managed to open the ditch to the bay. It couldn't survive transport to their facility. They'd have no idea how to euthanize it, either, besides needing permission from the endangered species people."

"Euthanize? He'll be fine."

"Fine, with its flesh falling off, out of the water, not breathing that I could see, smelling as if its insides were rotting too?"

"He'll be fine."

"How can you be so sure?"

Because M'ma told me? Because beings from Unity might be eternal? "Because we are going to make certain no one bothers them until they are strong enough to take care of themselves."

"Them? You are worried about the maggots and the beetles as well as the deformed, dying dolphinoid?"

"They are all together." One life, One heart, like my pendant said, even if they didn't have the same kind of hearts we did. "They need each other."

"Okay, I can see that. That's how symbiosis works. Except sometimes it's a fine line between cannibalism and partnership."

Even though Matt wasn't convinced, he started shoveling dirt while I gathered seaweed and driftwood to pile in front of where the ditch opening should be. We found a thick tree trunk—silver with sun and saltwater—to pull on top of the pile. Then we scattered sand and loose dirt to cover our footprints as best we could. We had to trust the incoming tide to cover some of our boat's skid marks, and pray no one did a flyover.

When we were done, Matt lifted me into the narrow outboard without asking. I might have taken offense at being manhandled, but it felt good, especially when my chest rubbed against his as he set me down and I inhaled his scent of sweat and swamp and something spicy. My nipples hardened, and not from the cool breeze kicking up.

Whoa. This was not the time, the place, nor the man to be stirring senses that had no business feeling anything but worry about M'ma. Matt's quick intake of breath told me he'd felt that touch, that stirring too, which made me think about whether he was attracted to me or not. Which mightn't help M'ma and the luminaries any, but did get my mind off the dark, choppy waves keeping the boat jittering and jouncing. Then I remembered what Piet said about sex and adrenaline, how danger made men horny. I still didn't think it worked for women. Most females I knew wanted to curl up after a crisis, not curl into a hard, naked, aroused body. Besides, there was no danger to me or Matt. Did nausea count? Dread? How about the euphoria of actually communicating with an alien being?

No matter, the thought of Piet brushed aside any lustful notions. So did those waves. I couldn't get sick; my stomach was empty. But I could panic at how many people I spotted out on Rick's boat and the Bay Constable's. The Coast Guard cutter from Montauk cruised by, too.

Sexy feelings, when we had to sink an armada? No way.

Piet was furious I'd gone searching without him. I wanted to think he was jealous, and he was, but not of Matt. I got to see Mama and he didn't. I'd seen more of the forbidden otherworld beings than anyone since Unity and our Earth were connected—and he'd never seen one. My reminder that the fireflies were not of our universe did not appease him.

"They're bugs. I can see bugs any time I want. Granted

not ones that start fires, but they are still bugs. Further-more, your actions were dangerous and irresponsible, showing an Other to a nonsensitive."

"You had your own duties and I could not wait. I thought Matt's veterinary knowledge could come in handy. Besides, he is a good man who considers Pauma-nok Harbor his home. He wants to help keep it safe. Most of all, he has no idea he is seeing magical, mystical creatures with incredible powers."

Piet scowled and rubbed at the scar on his jaw. He didn't think I was brave or clever or super-gifted to hear M'ma in my mind, which aggravated me. I knew the gift was M'ma's, not mine, but he chose me, didn't he? I changed the subject.

"Did you find Roy? What about the fire at the camp?"

He told me they'd never seen Roy, but the fire looked like insect-assisted arson, not that the East Hampton fire police had an inkling of that. The last was said with a drop of sarcasm; he wouldn't point out an aberrant creature to an ordinary person.

There'd been no electric wires to short out, no light-ning, no accelerants. They did find a cigarette butt and sent it away for fingerprint and possible DNA matching. That took time, though, so they couldn't immediately prove Roy had anything to do with the blaze. They had a manhunt going for him anyway.

And Barry had shown up there, flashing a press pass and claiming freedom of information. The police kept him behind the yellow tape. He'd come along with Mar-tin and Ellen and scores of other ambulance chasers and fire fanatics. He tried to shout out rumors that weird in-sects were involved. Some of the spectators laughed.

"You said the beetles *were* involved."

He took two out of his shirt pocket. Alive.

For a minute I thought how foolish he'd been to carry them close to his skin, until I remembered how he had nothing to worry about from these two. They couldn't ignite anything in Piet's presence. And their kind weren't easy for ordinary people to see with their fires out, thank goodness.

Piet handed them to me. "I scooped them up before anyone noticed their size or oddity."

Anyone like Martin or Barry.

They almost filled my palm, feeling cool. Their wings fluttered against my fingers in what I sensed as distress. I sympathized. Any creature would hate being without its defenses, but Piet's magic had saved them from discovery. "Shh," I whispered to them, and tried to transmit peace and security. "It's Willow, your friend."

Was that relief I felt or was I inserting my own emotions? I couldn't tell. "It's okay, you're back where you belong. Now go find M'ma. Your fires will come back way before you get there. Tell him I am working on keeping him safe. See if a bunch of you guys can flap your wings fast enough to get the air moving, to waft the smell away." I pictured wings moving so rapidly they blurred, and then I puffed my cheeks and blew out.

The two Lucifers flew away. Piet shook his head. "Do you really think they understood? Those were complicated instructions considering your buddies can't understand English."

"They understood. M'ma does, anyway. But go back to the fires. Were any others, um, mutilated?"

He took one out of the other shirt pocket. Dead. It had no wings and a blackened body. "Oh, my God, how could someone do that?"

"People don't look at bugs the way you do. They sure as hell don't hold conversations with them." Once again, he sounded jealous, or maybe resentful that I could do something he couldn't. "I'd like to go see Mama for myself."

"It's M'ma, I think, and he needs to rest. Maybe it's

part of the process of his rejuvenation. We need to make calls first."

We decided Piet should phone his contacts at DUE before anyone else, to get them to call off the environmental people and the Coast Guard, whose presence could only muck up the situation worse. DUE had influence at the highest levels, including the White House.

While Piet waited for the call to go through the encrypted, password-protected channels, he asked, "You're sure they'll all go home after the metamorphosis?"

"I can't be positive of anything. I do know the beetles will not go before then, not leaving their babies and their host mother. M'ma cannot fly or swim."

I wandered around while he was on the phone. Little Red was upstairs on my bed, sulking that he'd been left alone so much. I missed Elladaire. My arms felt empty. The house felt cold.

So I called my father. He warned me about fire, finally. Except he thought he'd seen Saks go up in flames. He'd also seen his friend Leila's car get wrecked.

"Did you warn her, Dad?" I could see the end of that relationship if he started forecasting doom.

"No time. The diaper truck skidded straight for us."

"You mean that was real, not a vision? Are you all right? What about what's her name? Was her car really wrecked?"

"Diapers all over the street, but we were fine. Better than Saks."

I checked the Internet. Saks was still intact everywhere.

Then I called the police station and asked for Chief Haversmith. I told Uncle Henry about M'ma and begged him to fend off any local investigations of the nesting area, like they did for the piping plovers. And maybe see what the weather people could do about dissipating the smell.

The chief listened, grunted a couple of times, then told me his news, which was worse than that the fireflies were here for awhile.

That fire at Rick's? One burning boat sank at its slip, but Rick's dock hands towed two others out of the harbor to protect the rest of the marina, where the harbor's fire boat could pump more water at them. The problem was one of the boats, a big trawler, sank before they reached open water. The Coast Guard sent down divers, who reported the trawler was breaking up, which meant the full fuel tanks and oil reserves would leak out soon. The mix would come ashore in a day or two, depending on the weather and the current and if there were storms in the area.

"Your guys can keep storms away! We can call in skimmer boats, booms, anything. Maybe the Coast Guard can siphon off the gas before it gets in the water. Keep it away from the marshes!"

"It's a federal case now, cleaning up a coast. They won't listen to us. By the time they decide what to do, it'll be too late."

Images of the Gulf of Mexico and those pelicans covered in oil almost made me sick again. I know our situation was nowhere near the calamity in the Gulf, but we also depended on clean beaches for tourism and clean water for the fishing industry. "Where do they think the spill is headed?"

I knew what he was going to say before I heard it. That's how my luck went.

"Depending on storms and full moon tides, it'll reach the salt marsh soonest, and worst environmentally. The vegetation won't survive, nor the clams and mussels and fish eggs that need the grasses, then the sea life and shorebirds that feed on the bottom rung of the food chain."

And M'ma.

"Can't you manipulate the winds to keep everything offshore?"

"Sure, the bunch of us could. But not with the boys from Washington watching. It's not a huge amount. There won't be permanent damage."

Except to M'ma, maybe.

"Fishing and clamming will be shut down, but it's almost the end of the season anyway. The scallops and the lobsters are in harm's way, but we can reseed them and replant the eelgrass they need. The area will recover, we hope."

Hope wasn't good enough.

A couple of days ago, all I had to worry about were Roy and Barry and Martin, the fireflies and their mother, the baby and my intentions not to get my heart broken. And my creativity, or lack thereof. Those were traumatizing enough to keep me rattled for months. The only thing I had going, until ten minutes ago, was that I didn't have a boil on my ass.

Now I did, kind of.

I had oil in the grass.

Good try, Dad.

I won't go to Saks.

CHAPTER 32

WE TOOK ATVS THIS TIME: absolutely terrifying velociraptors also known as all-terrain vehicles. They were open and fast and bumpy and noisy, especially in the numbers we had coming through the salt marsh toward the shore. The chief had called in a lot of equipment, on land and in the bay, with an esper in every seat, except for Matt. Everyone was unhappy to have him, except for me. I insisted we required his medical and veterinary skills. The chief made him ride with Mayor Applebaum, in case he saw too much.

The mayor forgot where they were going and would have been lost if Matt hadn't corrected their direction, to my satisfaction.

"See?" I shouted to Piet as I clung to the side bar of the golf cart on steroids. "He is useful."

I couldn't hear Piet's mutters over the engine noises as we raced toward the water, but I thought it had something to do with frogs and bicycles. Good thing I didn't hear it all, or I might have accused him of being paranoid in addition to jealous. Matt was trustworthy. I knew it.

The air smelled better, too. Maybe the beetles had understood my orders to stir up a breeze to dissipate the stench, or maybe M'ma was closer to being free of the rotten flesh. Either way, we could breathe without face masks, without getting nauseous.

When we got to the narrow strip of sandy muck that passed for a beach, everyone lined up their vehicles, turned off the engines, removed their helmets, and unloaded their gear. As few people as possible were going to walk back to M'ma's position—which Matt would point out to them, I pointed out—to defend him, or get a good look at what we were lying to dozens of government agencies about. The rest of our army of police, firemen, weather wizards, water dowsers, and telekinetics were going to deal with the oil spill from the shore.

Before Uncle Henry started to issue hushed assignments, we saw a faint light on the water, where no boat was supposed to be. The Coast Guard, after a bit of subliminal persuasion, had agreed to stand back until morning and close the entire area to water craft. Whatever vessel was out there had most of its lights off, which was suspicious in itself.

The chief held up one hand and we all listened: voices and laughter came from down the beach, so the trespassers had already landed in smaller boats. The voices sounded young, high-pitched, excited. Kids, we all decided, out for the thrill of forbidden danger. Most likely they'd taken out one of their parents' boats without permission, too.

We waited. The chief prepared to put the fear of God into the youngsters and send them on their way before we got down to the serious business of saving alien species. Only they weren't all kids.

When they got close enough for us to see their flashlights, one of the firemen turned on a portable floodlight.

"Oops." The feminine voice ended in a giggle. "Busted. Hello, Dad."

Her fireman father let out a string of curses from his days in the Marine Corps. Then he went after the man who led the pack of three kids, all with flashlights and butterfly nets. Two of his fire department friends held him back before he could bury Martin Armbruster in the sand.

"You brought your students here, when it was strictly forbidden, Armbruster?" the chief of police demanded.

"These aren't my students. They are former students, now in the high school science honors program. It's not an official school outing."

"You still broke the law. These are posted lands, with signs everywhere."

Martin blustered, although he kept his distance from the firemen. "No one can read signs in the dark."

"You knew damn well this was a closed area, possibly toxic, probably dangerous, yet you brought the kids anyway, teaching them to break the laws? For what, so you could catch a firefly?"

"Barry says they're a new weapon, maybe escaped from Plum Island."

"That man hasn't spoken a true word yet," Uncle Henry swore, popping a Tums in his mouth in memory. "Now take the kids and get out of here before I have to arrest you again."

But Martin could not lose face in front of his former students. He scuffed at the sand, like a bull about to charge. Then he caught sight of me and went totally apeshit, his control over his temper as thin as his hair.

"She can be here, but I can't?" he shouted, pointing a finger at me and kicking sand in my direction. "Who'd you fuck this time, bitch, to get preference?"

The girl in her father's arms giggled again, more nervously this time. Her father pulled her behind him, as if that could keep her from hearing.

Martin wasn't finished. "First the Brit with a title,

then the rhinestone cowboy, now you're screwing the scarface jerkoff who plays with fire? He using his hose on you good, Willow?"

I couldn't decide whether to be mad that he'd called me a bitch and Piet a scarface, or yell back that I wasn't sleeping with him, only thinking about it.

Piet settled it. "I'm no jerkoff, I take fires real serious, and Willow is no bitch. You are a dickhead, though."

I knew I liked him for a reason.

Martin didn't. He charged, head down. I screamed, so did the girls.

Next thing I saw was Martin on the ground, Piet on top, and no one trying to stop the punches he was throwing. I was ready to give Martin a kick in the ass myself when I saw two more kids appear out of the tall marsh reeds.

The girl stayed back, but the acne-faced boy asked, "You okay, Mr. Armbruster?"

How okay could he be, flat on his back with blood pouring from his nose and five more strong men—and me—ready to hit him if he tried to get up? If this was the caliber of our best science students, we'd never solve the problems of global warming or renewable energy.

The new girl laughed so hard she started swaying.

"Damn," Bill from the hardware store yelled, "that's my brother's kid, and she looks drunk." He smelled her breath and her clothing. "Or stoned."

The boy tried to toss a beer can into the weeds, along with a joint, which had gone out this close to Piet.

The chief of police went over to Martin, pushed Piet aside, and pulled the teacher to his feet. "You brought children here against all warnings, and provided underage minors alcohol and illegal drugs? You are in such deep shit, you'll never teach again, when you get out of jail."

Someone handed Martin a towel to hold on his broken nose. We could barely make out his words around it, but we heard enough to know he'd lost his bravado along with his job. "I...nothing to do...beer...or dope. Ask the reporter." He pointed his bloody towel back the way they had come.

Bill bellowed, "Jensen, you son-of-a-bitch drug pusher, get out here now."

Barry staggered out of the tall grass, zipping his fly with one hand, and holding up another teenage girl with his other. She giggled. He pushed her away. No one claimed to be her uncle or father, so she sat down in the sand.

Martin pointed at Barry now. Without the towel, we understood him perfectly: "He brought the filled cooler and offered them joints. I told him not to mess with the kids, but he said they all do it anyway."

"Shit, dude, it was only a joint," the pimply boy tried to say. "He wouldn't share the good stuff."

Now the girl in the sand snickered. "He would for a price. You know, a little blow for a little blow job."

The chief kneeled next to her. "How old are you, miss?"

"Seventeen, but I'll be eighteen in November."

"She said she was eighteen!" Barry yelled.

"Gee, other people lie, too? She's not lying now." Uncle Henry used his walkie-talkie to get police from the roadblocks to come in and get Martin and Barry out of his sight. "Cuff them and read them their rights," he told his men on the beach.

Barry held up his press pass. "What about my story and freedom of the press? I know you're trying to cover something up. It's the people's right to know what."

The chief held up his badge. "Trumped. Nothing entitles you to rape a child or contribute to the delinquency of a minor. To say nothing of possession of controlled substances. And trespassing, of course. Maybe threatening an endangered species."

Barry swung at Baitfish when the young policeman tried to put cuffs on him.

"Add resisting arrest," the chief told his men. To Barry, he said, "You can write lots of stories about the conditions in prison. A good-looking guy like you ought to have enough material for five to ten years. At least. And the label of child molester. That doesn't go over so big with the inmates, I hear."

Barry screamed obscenities into the night.

"Oh, and you'll have to register as a sexual predator. Good thing your father owns the scandal sheets. He's the only one who'll hire a pig like you."

Before one of the younger cops clipped Martin's handcuff to an ATV, the chief told the former teacher they were confiscating his boat to get the kids home. Martin could face their parents tomorrow. "As for you," he addressed the teenagers, who were not giggling anymore at all, "maybe this is a lesson. Maybe not. Maybe spending the night in our cozy little police station will drum some sense into those empty heads of yours. You ought to have known better. I'll be talking to your parents, too, and your school principal."

The girls started crying, clinging to each other. One of the boys wailed something about his college applications while the other male wiped his nose on his arm.

"Now get this mess out of here," Chief Haversmith ordered his men. "They're littering the beach."

The rest of us waited until we couldn't hear the ATVs or the boat's engine anymore, then about ten of us followed Matt to the path we'd made to M'ma. We didn't really need him as guide, because as soon as we pulled the driftwood tree trunk aside, we could see light up ahead, like a giant sunset though the marsh grasses. The maggoty glow worms were still blanketing their breakfast. The fireflies guarded their young.

Better than the parents who let their kids go off with two jackass adults.

On the way I tried to project an image to M'ma of help coming, of the oil on the water, of the special people I was bringing. I got no response back, which was worse than the blood and the curses and the frightened kids.

As soon as we got within Piet's range, the lights ahead of us went off. Matt did not say anything, he simply adjusted his flashlight.

Some of the men were breathing hard when we finally reached M'ma. They still gasped when they saw the huge mass of decay covered in writhing grubs with hummingbird-sized beetles hovering nearby. I was happy to see one of the firemen throw up in the grasses, proof that I wasn't the only one affected by the sight.

No one spoke, including M'ma. Damn.

Matt did what he'd done that afternoon, brushing some of the maggots aside so we could see the firm skin beneath, and the faint movement of the creature's own body.

"See? It's alive."

"Doesn't look alive to me," Mac, the fire captain, said. "That's the tide coming in, moving the sand." He gulped. "Or the maggots."

"He's alive," I insisted. "Just resting."

Everyone looked to Chief Haversmith, who always recognized the truth. He nodded. "Willy says it's a male, it's a male. She says it's alive, it's alive. So I guess we better go keep the oil from killing it."

Most of our small troop headed back to the others on the shore. Piet had to stay behind to guard M'ma and the beach grasses from the fire we were going to set to burn off the oil in the water. We couldn't light a match with him nearby, of course, but no one wanted to admit that in front of Matt. Or that the firefighting canister he held was filled with nothing.

I stayed behind to talk to the beetles. Matt wasn't leaving my side, no matter how many glares Piet sent his way.

I tried to explain to M'ma and his minions what we had to do, without using any words. Matt didn't need to know about the mindspeak either.

I fixed pictures in my head, pushing my brain to transmit the information, sending my emotions to emphasize the danger. Who knew if any of them understood about chemicals and their potential side effects?

I did not feel any of the usual inner warmth from the lightning bugs, just the cool, dank air with its permeating dampness, the kind of half-fog, half-mist that made you hate to put your head on a clammy pillowcase.

"Don't be angry," I whispered.

Matt must have thought I was talking to Piet, because he stepped away, giving us privacy. Piet ignored me. He was still angry that I'd brought a nonsensitive along, forcing everyone to maintain the pretense of normalcy. Now he was mad because he had to stay away from the real action.

I left him with one of the cops and hurried after Matt so I wouldn't have to pick my way through the wetlands by myself.

The plan was for the Bay Constable to set reflector markers in the oil slick, then get himself and every other boat out of the area. When Mac received the all-clear, he'd set off a rocket over the water to ignite the oil and gas leak. Just in case, I gathered half a dozen beetles in my baseball hat before I left M'ma. On the way back to the bay I sent mind picture after mind picture of what was necessary to keep M'ma safe. When we got far enough from Piet, their lights came back on. So did the good feeling they usually spread. They understood.

Mac set off his rocket. I set off mine. *Fly, friends, get rid of the poison. Save the big guy.*

Mac's first flare sputtered out before it hit the water. My lightning bolt didn't. Soon the bay was on fire in streamers, with an acrid odor that overpowered the lingering smell of decay. Good. By tomorrow morning the officials wouldn't find any toxins in the water, and no miasma on shore.

"Come back, come back. Don't get burned," I yelled across the water, fear for the Lucifers making me forget to keep my thoughts unspoken.

They landed on my arms and shoulders. I saw the tiny flames, but had no fear of being burned. Not from these creatures. "Good job, my brilliant beauties. Good work."

Uncle Henry stood next to Matt and the mayor. "You didn't see that, Doc. Or hear it."

"No, sir. I definitely did not see Willow Tate send out a flare and then call it back onto her shoulder."

Uncle Henry patted the mayor on the back. "Good job, Applebaum."

Matt winked at me and mouthed, "Good job, Willow."

CHAPTER 33

PIET WAS PISSED. He'd missed the good part, again. It was like every birthday party he wasn't invited to because the candles went out, every backyard barbeque he had to leave before anyone could eat. The disappointment covered him like . . . well, like the maggots on M'ma.

"But you got to see the alien being."

"I saw a lump of rotting flesh."

No, he'd seen a potential fire god. "Who knows what he'll look like when he grows up? Now he'll have the chance, thanks to you and everyone else."

That wasn't enough for Piet. "All I've been is an effing babysitter. Even the damn vet got to do more."

And Matt got to drive me home while Piet made certain all the fires were out. I tired to soothe his jealous ego. "Look, we cleaned up the spill, so no one will be sniffing around the salt marsh. We got rid of Barry Jensen and Martin Armbruster. You should be happy."

"Your pet bugs are still potential firebombs. And Roy Ruskin is still out there using them."

I understood his frustration, I really did. Piet was a man of few words but a lot of action. He was used to being set down in the middle of a blaze, not trying to prevent one. "How can I make the situation better for you?"

He brightened up instantly. "How about coming to bed?"

I knew he meant his bed, or the couch or the carpet. I also knew part of me wanted to take him up on the offer. He was sprawled on the living room sofa, Little Red in his lap, his blue chambray shirt open. He looked like Mr. August on a fireman's calendar: hot. And the look in his eyes could steam the stamp off an envelope. He wanted me. He deserved a reward for all he'd done. And yet . . .

Maybe it was the worry over M'ma and the others. Maybe it was Matt, or Piet's bad mood. Or maybe that fire had simply gone out. I did kiss his cheek when I went by on the way to the kitchen, leaving the hypothetical door open. "I know what'll cheer you up. I'll make s'mores in the toaster oven. You said you never had one."

At least that wouldn't burn the house down, not with him nearby.

While I gathered what I'd need, Janie called. Elladaire had no burning problems, and her grandmother, Mary's mother and Jane's sister, had come to take care for her. Best of all, Mary was out of danger.

Janie and Joe the plumber decided to stay over near the hospital and the baby, do a bunch of shopping at the malls and the warehouse clubs tomorrow for the benefit dinner next week.

Mary wasn't the only one benefitting, then. I felt good about pushing Jane and Joe together after his accident. He'd needed someone to look after him, and Janie was a natural-born caregiver with too much time on her hands. Maybe they'd find the kind of happiness that lasted, not that I had much faith in forevers. No matter, they were adults. They could find satisfaction with careers, friends, even casual sex if that's what they wanted. I would *not* turn into my matchmaking mother. I wished them a good time shopping, and promised to get out more posters for the benefit dinner.

As if I'd conjured her up, my mother called. She sounded worried. One of my father's neighbors had called to tell her the old goat had been in an accident. Was he all right? Should she go back to West Palm?

"He's fine. I spoke to him after the accident."

"So how come he couldn't see that trouble coming before it hit him? Heaven knows he sees every other bit of doom and gloom."

"I guess he didn't care enough about the woman in the car. You know he only sees danger for those he loves. Or he may have dreamed about hockey pucks instead of diaper trucks. You know how his talent goes. He can't always figure it out."

Mom gave one of her sniffs that passed for an audible sneer. "What's the old clunker good for, then?"

Dad was only three years older than my mother, and his many lady friends had to think he was good for something besides oraclelike prognostications. It was always better not to mention the ladies to Mom, though. "Go ahead, admit it. You were concerned because you do care for him."

She sniffed again. "Is that a crime? Just because I don't want to live the rest of my life with him? What should I do, take up golf or mah-jongg? Can you see me waiting in line for an early-bird dinner? Besides, you can't trust him."

I wasn't getting into that. I trusted my father and his wacky premonitions, but Mom wasn't talking about his unreliable talent. She always believed he cheated, no matter what he said, or the fact that she didn't have the truth-detecting trait. They loved each other, but better at a distance, and with reservations. Kind of like me and Piet. "No, Mom, it's not a crime to care about him."

Susan bounded in, so I had an excuse to say good-bye and get back to laying graham crackers on a tinfoil lined tray. My cousin talked a mile a minute in her excitement, when her mouth wasn't full of the marshmallows I needed.

Everyone in town heard about the oil spill and the effort to get rid of it, she explained, breaking up the chocolate for me and eating half of that, too. As a result, half the Harbor's population—the ones who were not on the beach or in patrol boats—came to the restaurant where she cooked. The Breakaway sat on one of the highest hills, facing the bay. A lot of times people came for cocktails at sunset. Tonight they came for the amazing sight of the water east of Paumanok Harbor on fire.

"No one ever saw such a sight before!"

Piet grumbled, "I didn't get to see it. The animal doctor did."

"But I am making Piet s'mores, so don't eat any more of the ingredients."

Susan's eyes got big. "The animal doctor?"

I shoved an uncooked marshmallow into her mouth.

When she was done chewing, she decided to make coffee frappes, with a dash of Kahlua, to accompany the gooey snacks. She gathered her ingredients, pushing mine aside. I almost ignored her taking over my kitchen until she said she was glad I had a part in the blaze. Maybe now she could stop having to defend me from all the gossip and finger-pointing. Maybe people would forgive me for bringing the whole mess down on the Harbor, once they saw I was fixing it.

"I didn't bring . . ." I needed a marshmallow myself.

Before I could eat the whole bag, Piet snatched it out of my hand. "Hey, you're eating all the goodies!" He had one, too, then twisted his lips. "That's what I've been

missing all these years? Rubber cement dipped in pow-
dered sugar?"

"You haven't tasted the finished product yet." I
changed the topic by asking my cousin what she was
cooking for the benefit dinner. And had a tiny sip of the
Kahlua, which didn't give me headaches, like wine did.

Susan had more news, though, which interested Piet
way more than gallons of clam chowder and buckets of
brownies.

Someone at the restaurant thought they'd seen a man
on the Paumanok trail, a hiking path cut through woods
and nature preserves and a few side streets throughout
the east end. The man had a shaved head, which was not
unusual, but he also wore long sleeves and a jacket,
which were unnecessary on such a nice September
morning. He carried a large shopping bag in one hand,
beside the backpack over his shoulders. He held his
other hand close to his body, as if it were injured, and
put his head down when he passed the other man, not
speaking, not looking him in the eye. The hiker reported
him to the police, he said, when he heard they were
looking for Roy Ruskin. The man he'd seen fit the de-
scription.

Someone else heard that police were out on the path,
but Big Eddie and his K9 search dog hadn't turned up
anything yet. The path crisscrossed roads, even had
bridges over streams where a determined fugitive could
wade to hide his scent. There were abandoned cabins,
old foundations, and a few leftover munitions bunkers
from when the Navy had a base during World War II.
Roy could be hiding anywhere.

Susan and I hoped he was gone for good.

Piet didn't think so. The man had shown too much
thirst for revenge. Now he'd be like a wounded animal,
twice as dangerous, with more reason to get even. Piet

decided to join the hunt, as soon as he had his first Boy
Scout experience.

Not enough pieces for the three of us could fit on the
toaster-oven tray at once. I set half aside and had to slap
Susan's hand to keep them safe.

"Oh, yeah," she said. "I forgot to say how sorry I am
that I sicced Barry Jensen or whoever he is on you. He
seemed nice and I thought he'd help your career. I guess
I'm no judge of character."

I remembered the men she'd paraded through the
door in the past couple of months. "You think?"

"Hey, I apologized for Barry, didn't I?"

Just then Ellen walked in the back door. "And I need
to apologize for Martin. You were right. He's a first-class
ass. I didn't realize how obsessive he was, how determined to advance his own career and reputation, no
matter the consequences."

One look at her and Piet pulled her out a chair. I
handed her an uncooked s'more, and Susan poured her
a tumbler of Kahlua and cream over ice, with a scoop of
coffee ice cream. Her hands shook, but she took both.

"Can you imagine? I spent another hour in your jail.
I've never so much as gotten a traffic ticket, and now I'm
involved with actual criminals." She started to cry.

Piet decided to leave. The hero didn't do well with
women's tears, it seemed. "But you'll miss dessert."

He pulled me aside. "It sounds like I won't be getting
any sweet stuff later, either, not with the hen party going
on. I might as well be useful out there. I'll set up a search
zone and patrol the neighborhoods."

"Be careful."

His good-bye kiss was almost scorching enough for
me to tell him to come back in an hour or two, until I
heard Ellen ask Susan if she thought it would be okay
for her to sleep here.

I was *not* going to add more kindling to the gossip bonfire. "I'll leave the door open for you. Ellen can sleep in my room."

He sighed and left, taking another uncooked s'more with him.

Ellen wanted to know why we weren't using the outdoor grill, or the oven to melt the marshmallows and chocolate.

"Good idea," I said. "I should have thought of that. So what happened out there?"

Ellen never went ashore that night. She'd stayed with the boat, already disapproving of Martin's plan to get into the prohibited area. She only came onboard because of the kids. She tried to get them to stay away from the shore, too, but they wouldn't listen.

She swore she never saw any drugs or booze. "They must have had it in the cooler they took with them in the dinghy and the life raft. I thought it was filled with specimen bottles for the lightning bugs."

Martin told her to turn the boat's lights off as soon as they were away, and she was so afraid of being caught that she did it. Then the youngsters came back, with police and other men who commandeered the boat and took it back to the harbor.

They took her to the police station along with the kids and almost arrested her, too. "How could I explain that to my school's director?"

Luckily, someone believed Ellen when she swore she had nothing to do with Martin and Barry's crimes. I figure the someone must have been the chief or Kelvin from the garage or one of the other truth-detectors in town. So they let her go, but state troopers were searching Martin's house and wouldn't let her in, not even to retrieve her car keys.

"They most likely wanted to search your car, too, for

illegal substances," Susan guessed, sending Ellen into another panic.

"What if they plant something there? I've heard how cops do that, to make a case look better."

"This one looks fine without you." I tried to reassure her. "We'll straighten it out in the morning. Don't worry."

By now the first batch of s'mores was done, stuck to the tinfoil, melted into one sticky mass. So we got out knives and forks. Susan poured a little more Kahlua into the blender with the coffee and ice cream and crushed ice.

An hour later, Ellen was still weepy, still afraid for her job, and still apologizing. "I'm so sorry, Willow, for trusting him. He seemed so intelligent and interesting. I never meant to hurt anyone, I just wanted to know what the insects were and you wouldn't tell me."

So that was my fault, too?

I said I forgave her and told her to go on to bed. I needed to walk the dogs. She didn't offer to come, and I was glad.

I forgave her in a way, but I no longer trusted her. She was upset by Martin's involving the children—not by his plan to study, subjugate, and slaughter the fireflies. I felt I hardly knew this person I'd roomed with for three years. Our lives had taken such different paths; I didn't see how we could be more than Christmas card friends.

The dogs forgave me for ignoring them. They didn't lie or cheat or take up with sleazy strangers—unless the strangers had hot dogs. I felt my heartbeat finally return to normal and a sense of calm spread through my body and mind. Then I realized what I sensed was the fireflies in my backyard.

Only ten appeared this time, staying up in the trees, away from the dogs.

Where are the rest of you? I asked, picturing the swarm of them from before.

Soon, I got back, with the same picture.

Hurry, guys. Help the babies fix M'ma if you can. Too many people know about you, and it's dangerous. Piet is angry, I lost my old friend, and the town still blames me.

Soon.

A rainbow of peace washed over me. Everything would be all right. Soon.

CHAPTER 34

PAUMANOK HARBOR RELAXED. You could almost hear the huge sigh of relief like a Macy's parade balloon deflating. Sure Roy Ruskin was still at large, but there'd been no more fires, few lightning bug sightings, and the kids were all right.

Best of all, they'd gotten rid of the reporter. Now people could gather at the deli or the post office or the barbershop and discuss events without fear of being overheard. They used circumspection, of course, around nonsensitives, but that was a habit, not a fear-driven silence.

They'd come up with a good story to explain why the salt flats were cordoned off with high fences, a police guard at the land side, a marine patrol boat in the bay: A number of large wayward sea lion females had beached themselves to give birth, lumbering inland. Both mothers and infants died. Localized noxious gases and godawful smells resulted, along with a glow from the microscopic deep-water parasites that had driven the group to shore, then killed them. The officials were waiting for the full moon high tide at the end of next week to flood the channel and flush the unfortunate creatures out to sea where nature's recycling center could take care of the disposal problem.

Quite a few of the Harbor residents had a strange virus after telling the story. Some had rashes, some had stomach problems or eye twitches or runny noses. They'd breathed the bad air near the mama seals, they said, discouraging the curious. In truth, the lies made them sick, but everyone considered it worth the effort. With a little help from the Department of Unexplained Events, who sent a scary enforcer, people left us alone.

The tourists went home—as usual after the summer season—and many of the stores and restaurants closed except for weekends, Main Street had empty parking spaces, the beaches didn't smell of suntan lotion or sound like a rock band studio. The glitch was having to find a new science teacher after the start of the school year. On the other hand, the village now had a bunch of high schoolers owing a lot of hours of community service. Free labor never went unwelcome.

Best of all, the year-rounders had a party to plan and look forward to. Helping one of their own was as important to these people as keeping their secrets.

Ellen left.

Piet wanted to. Forest fires burned in the west, brush fires in the north, oil wells in the south. He was needed other places.

"You can't go till after the party. You're the guest of honor."

"I thought Edie's mother was."

"Yes, but she can't come. Too much danger of infection. Everyone knows what you did, taking care of Elladaire and curing her, so they're planning the meal for you."

He shifted from foot to foot in embarrassment. Piet didn't blow his own horn; he didn't want to hear it tooted at a small town gathering, either. "I'll eat anything."

"It's not about the food. It's about how they're cooking it in advance, then keeping it warm at the firehouse on electric hot plates they're borrowing from caterers in Amagansett. No candles, no open grills. No using the gas stoves or ovens."

Susan, who appeared to have moved back in with me, uninvited as usual, added her two cents: "We're going with clam chowder, cold fried chicken, raw clams on the half shell, cold crab cakes, lots of salads and ice cream and brownie sundaes for dessert. The only thing needing cooking there is the corn on the cob. We'll manage with electric heating coils. No problemo. There'll be a cash bar, lots of door prizes, a fifty-fifty raffle, and dancing later. It'll be great. Save me a dance."

No one said no to Susan.

Piet agreed to stay, but he couldn't just sit around waiting. He joined in the search for Roy and went on every fire call between Montauk and Southampton. The other fire departments were thrilled to help test out his new chemical extinguisher. They all wanted to order cases of the stuff as soon as it hit the market, it worked so well. In between, he put out a lot of those deck chimineas, a couple of romantically lit fireplace settings, every charcoal briquette in his drive-by vicinity. He did more to help people quit smoking than all the government ad campaigns combined. Susan's presence kept us from acting on impulse, which, I suspected, was her intention.

I wanted to leave the Harbor, too. I had deadlines, friends in the city, dry cleaning waiting to be picked up, a jade plant, and a notice from my dentist that I was due for a cleaning. Okay, nothing was crucial, but the east side apartment was home. Paumanok Harbor was a summer place, and summer was over. Mostly, I was getting too little work done on my new book, too much time spent thinking about sex and men and sexy men. And bugs, of course.

I decided to get back to the fire wizard story and

leave the one about the sea god for my next project. Maybe by then I'd figure out if the mythic tale I'd made up to explain M'ma was true or merely my imagination. I'd ask M'ma if he knew which, when he woke up.

Which was another reason I had to stay. No one was throwing me a party, or even happy to see me remain in town, but I had to be here. I couldn't leave M'ma and the Lucifers. Everyone else felt like Piet: they cared more about getting rid of the otherworld creatures than they cared about their welfare. I heard whispers about explosives, napalm, and bulldozers.

No way, I shouted back to anyone who'd listen. These were sentient, sensitive beings, I told every psychic I knew. They were intelligent and loving and beautiful. Killing them could bring down the wrath of far more dangerous beings. And they'd be gone soon, I swore, and hoped it was so. The nights were getting cooler, the police force was stretched too thin, hurricanes spawned in the tropics, and outsiders were bound to question the story about the seals.

The local espers accepted my arguments, then they appointed me the expert on the unmentionable in the wetlands.

Should they dig out the channel? Should they erect an awning to keep the sun off? What about food and water? How soon would the blasted bugs be gone?

I went to ask.

A committee came with me when I visited M'ma. They said it was too dangerous for me on my own. I believed they wanted to see him for themselves.

They'd be disappointed, if past experience meant anything. So far no one but me and Piet, slightly, had seen the glorious colors of the lightning bugs or felt their mantle of peace and goodwill. Matt described M'ma as a lump of grayish decaying flesh, but he didn't have any special powers. Piet, though, who was pure magic himself, saw the same thing. Nobody on the visiting committee was a Visualizer. Only I was, which did not make me feel special, only more responsible.

We walked a recently cleared path from the nearest parking spot to a gate in the hastily erected fence that kept M'ma's region private. Charlie, the Town Hall attorney, manned the gate along with Vinnie the barber. Only people on their lists could enter the proscribed area, which aggravated me. If I was in charge, why hadn't anyone consulted me about who could bother M'ma? He wasn't a damned sideshow freak, or a science experiment like Martin believed.

I demanded to see the lists and wanted to know who wrote them without asking me, but Vinnie waved a hand in a circle around his head, and then I remembered: he could detect auras of paranormals. No ordinary citizen could get past him. Charlie pointed to his heart, and I recalled that he could sense evil intentions. I wish airport security had a thousand Charlies, instead of a thousand rules and regulations. M'ma was safe under their watch.

Everyone with me passed their tests.

I had Lou from DUE (the ominous old guy who had a sometime thing going with my grandmother. Talk about unmentionable!)

Two water wizards.

Three telepaths.

Four healers.

Five truth-seers.

And a partridge in a pear tree.

Well, maybe the partridge was an exaggeration, but someone brought kelp and baitfish in case M'ma was hungry, and someone else carried in an olive branch, a Russian olive that grew wild around here, in case M'ma recognized the symbol.

He didn't talk, not to me, not to the telepaths. Then

again, I didn't hear anything from them, either. Maybe they chatted among themselves, but I had no way of knowing.

The healers had no idea how he had survived this long, how he could improve, or what could hurry the process.

The water dowsers didn't think they could make the ditch flow again, and the human lie detectors now believed what I'd said. Lou just shook his head.

"That's no whale or dolphin."

"No seal either."

"No fish."

"No insect."

"No nothing anyone's ever seen."

The truth people agreed.

I watched their expressions and saw repulsion, curiosity, fear, and pity. None of the serenity and peacefulness M'ma and the beetles usually exuded. They saw a huge expanse of bloated, dead flesh and misshapen appendages, with eyes, ears, and mouth, if such existed, buried beneath the mud. I saw M'ma's brilliance shining through more cleared patches. In my head I saw what he could be.

They saw a problem.

I saw a miracle.

We all had so many questions, so few answers. Even the beetles seemed to have gone into hiding rather than communicate with the specialists or me. I wanted them to show their nonthreatening nature, if not one of their artistic flight patterns, but none replied to my mental callings. I wondered if they expired when the new batch hatched, their job of propagating the next generation completed. We had no way of knowing, because no one was talking, out loud or across minds.

Discouraged, the Paumanok Harbor group started back to the gate. I stayed behind a minute for a last try to make contact. "I know you are resting," I said, and pictured a slumbering giant. "And that's fine. It's a big step you and the young ones are taking." I visualized a tadpole turning into a frog, a butterfly emerging from a chrysalis. Then I tried to send my curiosity, my need to know.

I got nothing back, so I gave up, too. I just wasn't good at that. I could draw it, but without eyes, how could M'ma see?

Before I joined the others, though, I made a quick circle around M'ma's bulk, for a fast estimate. Many less maggots worked their way down to the new shape beneath the decay. Where did they go? Maybe they went somewhere to make a cocoon, if that's what they did. Grubs couldn't fly, so they had to be near. I searched, trying to get an idea of the progress. I was careful where I walked, but I couldn't find anything that could house an infant firefly. I knew some beetles spent their entire lives underground so maybe the larvae burrowed alongside M'ma to complete their growth and transformation. But I didn't see any holes in the soft dirt, either.

What I saw, in my head, was a picture of a rainbow-colored seahorse.

"A pretty picture, that's what you send me when I need to know how to help you? I need more."

This time I saw a crocodile, or maybe an alligator. I never could remember which was which. This one gleamed lavender.

"A seahorse and a crocodile? That's supposed to make sense to me? You're as bad as my father."

Father, yes.

Oh, boy. I waited for more explanation but none came, so I left.

Lou waited at the gate. "Any progress?"

"Nothing that's any help in getting him out of here."

"Keep trying."

I heard the unspoken "or else" and shivered.

* * *

I checked in with my father, in case he had better advice, or if he'd dreamed about seahorses or alligators. He had a stiff neck, maybe a lawsuit. His lady friend had a sore knee and three frantic, overprotective daughters. My mother was a pain in the butt, as usual.

In other words, no help at all.

"Seahorses and purple crocodiles?" Piet swore. "What's next with you, fiddler crabs playing 'The Flight of the Bumblebee'? This is real, not some kiddie story."

I knew how real it was without his frustration bubbling over on me. I might invent a million plot lines, draw a million pictures, but I could not hurry M'ma along, or understand him better.

"Come with me and see if you can do any better," I snapped. Things were not going well in the personal relationship department, either. Kiddie story? Our partnership took another turn for the worse when he refused to come visit the salt marsh with me the next day.

He didn't want to see the ugly sight, he said, not when he could be putting out fires, rescuing people, saving property. Important stuff.

As if what I did was less valuable.

So I asked Matt to go with me.

I had to argue with Charlie at the gate, but he let the veterinarian through. Matt mightn't have any supernatural powers, but he did not have any malice in him either.

He listened to what could possibly be heart sounds again. "It's stronger, whatever it is."

"Do you feel anything?"

"Damp." The weather had turned raw and dank, the mud where he knelt sopping through his pant legs.

"No, I mean do you feel anything inside?"

"Hungry?"

I handed him one of the apples I'd brought along. "Not a physical sensation. More an emotion."

He smiled at me. "Does that include attraction?"

Hmm. "I mean do you sense any calm, restfulness, welcome?"

"Here? In a swampy place with a dying beast? Not likely. Is that what you feel toward this poor animal?"

"Not recently. Sometimes, when the fireflies are up." They had not been around for three days. I still couldn't find a dead one or anything like a birthing nest for lightning bugs. I wasn't getting any vibes from M'ma either. I hadn't really expected Matt to, although I'd hoped his affinity for dogs and cats might help.

He couldn't see the brilliant colors or the graceful shape coming clearer every day. Matt still thought the beached creature was a dolphin or a small whale. He thought he spotted a blowhole, but no eyes or mouth.

I knew M'ma's eyes were shut. I knew they'd be azure blue and emerald green and gold, all at once. That's how I'd drawn them.

"It's a wonder this thing is still alive. I still think someone ought to consider putting it down. I am upset that the marine rescue people haven't come, or the Humane Society."

Lou and his agents had called them off.

Matt had no malice, but empathy gone awry could be equally as dangerous. He didn't understand, and I couldn't explain. I turned him back toward the path, away from M'ma. "Killing him is not an option. But tell me, do you know of any connection between seahorses and crocodiles?"

"Is this a riddle? I've never really studied either one. They're not related, scientifically."

"There has to be some common thread."

He mightn't have magic, but he found it. Seahorse fathers kept their babies safe in a pouch. Crocodiles were thought to carry their infants in their mouths to protect them from predators, like other crocodiles.

I rushed back and knelt by what I took to be M'ma's head. "Is that it? You've got the babies in your mouth? That's where they've gone?"

I felt a smile, inside out. *Soon.*

So I hugged Matt.

He didn't understand that any more than he understood about M'ma. I didn't care. "He's almost ready."

Which meant I couldn't bring Matt back here again. I could not chance him seeing something so far beyond belief that he'd be a threat to all of Paumanok Harbor. Telling him that hurt his feelings, and mine.

We stopped at the gate. Charlie looked relieved I was leaving with the nonsensitive. "He won't be coming back," I told him and Vinnie, so Matt got the message.

"But you have no marine scientist here."

"No. We don't need one."

"This is wrong! Who will care for it?"

"Could you?" I hated to hurt him worse, but there was nothing any of us could do to help M'ma.

"At least I'd make an effort to see about getting it back into the water."

I wasn't sure M'ma swam. "We'll have help when the time comes."

He looked back at the lawyer and the barber, and then at me, a writer and illustrator. "I see."

CHAPTER 35

MY DRAWINGS LOOKED LIKE SHIT. My words sounded like they'd stepped in it. Sadness could do that to a writer. I missed the joy I usually felt in creating something.

My partner acted distant, as if the lack of sex meant a loss of friendship and goodwill, which was plain wrong and beneath his intellect, if not mine. We both knew he'd be gone at the end of the week, so neither of us was pushing for anything but to see Paumanok Harbor in the rearview mirror. I missed his solid strength and quiet confidence.

Matt turned unapproachable. He'd been scorned by his friends and neighbors, shut out again by the town he called home. His neighbors trusted him with their pets, not with their secrets. Now his snippy receptionist said he was in surgery; he'd call back. He never did. I missed his calm acceptance and steadfast decency.

I did not miss my cousin Susan's snide remarks about my love life, or lack of it. How many unsuitable men could I fall for, she wanted to know. I wanted to know if she'd been sent by my mother. Why was it that Susan could sleep with half the men on Long Island, but I was supposed to be looking for that happily ever after with a man of magic? I wasn't that much older than she was.

We stopped talking.

My two closest companions seemed to be a cranky Pomeranian and a sleeping leviathan. Little Red would be cranky tomorrow. Heaven only knew what M'ma would be when Rip Van Whalish finally decided to wake up: insect, sea creature, merman, or god? Maybe all four.

I took Little Red with me the next morning. He latched onto my ankle whenever I tried to leave the house, and peed on my shoes when I got home if I didn't take him. And I needed the company, too. He'd be safe from fireflies because most had disappeared.

Someone new was at the gate today, a friend of Lou's, it turned out, but not half as surly or intimidating. I did not know his talent, but he looked formidable with tattoos, muscles, and dreadlocks. Either he was a mind reader of some sort, or he'd been given an actual list this time. He gave Little Red an uncertain look, but he instantly opened the gate for me.

I carried the dog most of the way, then spread a thick blanket on the ground near M'ma. We sat, Little Red didn't growl, M'ma didn't send any messages. I felt better about things, though. Maybe M'ma sent his particular warmth my way, or maybe my spirits rose to see the otherworlder looking better and brighter. I still couldn't figure out if the appendages stuck in the mud were arms and legs, fins or wings, but I knew he'd be beautiful.

We stayed for a couple of hours, simply keeping each other company. That felt right also, as if none of us had a better place to be or any urgent tasks like putting out fires or transmuting into gods or writing books. I wasn't afraid out here, alone with an alien being and the ticks in the grass. I wasn't lonely or depressed or feeling inadequate to meet the town's expectations.

Even Little Red relaxed and went to sleep in my lap

until I rustled the bag of potato chips I'd brought. Then dark clouds covering the sun and sky meant it was time to go. I might be braver than ever before, but those black clouds meant thunder and lightning. "I won't be back tomorrow," I told M'ma. "There's a big party." I made mental pictures of people gathered together, eating, laughing, dancing. "I have to help set up. It would have been nice if your friends could put on a fireworks display, but I guess they're all too busy. I'll come back the next day to see how you're doing. Should I bring anything?" The idea of bringing fried chicken and a beer out to this lump of decay was ludicrous, but I still had manners.

I got no response until I picked up the blanket and the dog.

Careful. Hurry. Soon.

"Careful of the storm, or some other danger? Come back soon, or you'll be leaving soon?"

Careful. Hurry. Soon.

"Yeah, I got it."

I ran home before it rained.

The storm raged all night. I huddled under the covers, feigning a headache. I didn't want Piet or Susan to see how unnerved I was, not when I was supposed to be in charge of countering an alien invasion. Some heroine I was, clutching my dog every time thunder boomed.

The storm had blown out—or been blown out by the weather wizards—the next morning, the day of the benefit for Mary Brown. All that remained of the gale were some fallen branches, a couple of puddles, and some high clouds that looked like quotation marks around a lovely mid-September day.

The organizers decided to move half the party outdoors, onto the village green. That way more people could hear the live music in the band shell, and bring kids and blankets to picnic on the grass after fetching their meals from in front of the firehouse, half a block away. The firehouse got cleared of trucks for dancing later, a cash bar throughout, and an auction of donated goods and services.

Almost everyone in town donated something. Besides the gifts and baskets of cheer and tote bags filled with delicacies from the deli, Janie'd given a wash and blow-dry, the bowling alley donated free games for after the repairs, the restaurants provided gift certificates, and I put up naming rights to a lead character in my next book after Susan promised to make a bid on it. That way I wouldn't be embarrassed when no one wanted the only thing I had to offer except the quick cartoon sketches I volunteered to do for anyone who paid twenty bucks.

We worked all day wiping down tables, laying out dishes and plastic silverware, hanging balloons and streamers. Just before the opening time, I set up an easel on the corner between the firehouse and the grassy area, near where they were selling tickets. I did a quick portrait of Elladaire from memory to show people what I could do. Right after that, she came with her grandmother, but toddled over to me, grinning. I scooped her up and twirled her around before she could call me mama.

"I missed you, pumpkin," I told her, but she was already gone as soon as her pink mary janes hit the ground, squealing with happiness and shouting, "Pipi! Pipi!"

The man of the hour had arrived.

Janie wanted him to donate a dinner date for the auction, but he couldn't promise his time. Or else he used that as a damn good excuse.

"How about a dance, then?"

He still held Elladaire. He pulled her closer. "Mine are all promised to my best girl."

"Hey, you promised me one, too," Susan reminded him.

Janie added, "And the baby's going home after dinner. You'll have plenty of dances left."

I swear the man blushed. He looked toward me for help. "You can spare one dance, hotshot. I'll bid ten dollars."

"Fifteen," came from someone putting serving spoons in the cole slaw and potato salad, "if it's a slow dance."

"Twenty," from one of the high school girls who'd been with Martin and Barry on the beach. She now wore a hairnet and rubber gloves to ladle out the clam chowder, to her dismay.

With the back of his neck still red, Piet allowed them to put his name on the list of auction items.

I grabbed a piece of fried chicken, swearing to be a vegetarian tomorrow, and hurried out to my easel on the sidewalk to start making money for Mary.

My first customer was Lou. He wanted a picture of my grandmother. She snorted at his nonsense, but smiled and sat on the posing chair. I did not put her in a pointed hat with a wart on her nose since this was a charitable event, after all, but set her in her garden, surrounded with flowers. I even put in that seldom-seen smile.

Lou loved it and shoved an extra twenty in the jar. After that I did kids and couples and whatever anyone else wanted, including a Harley, the nearby library for Mrs. Terwilliger, and a tiny Yorkie a woman had in her pocketbook. Someone handed me another piece of chicken and a paper cup of chowder. Susan brought me a crab cake. I kept sketching, having a great time basking in the compliments that flowed. I got fan mail for my books, but this was more personal and immediate. Maybe if my book ideas dried up, I could start a new career as a street artist, or do kids' birthday parties. Then a six year old dropped his ice cream cone on my foot. Nix that idea.

My pregnant friend Louisa and her husband Dante came by with their two kids and asked for a group portrait.

"That'll be extra."

We all laughed when the dot com genius and real estate magnate said he thought he could afford it and stuffed two hundred dollar bills in the nearly full jar. I switched from the quick-sketch magic markers back to charcoals and tried my best to show the love that enveloped this little family, not just the handsome faces.

Louisa cried. "It's the hormones, from the baby," she apologized through tears. "But I love it. It's better than anything that hangs at the arts center."

She had one of the finest collections of contemporary American paintings in that gallery, thanks to a bequest from a famous art critic. "That's bull, but I love you anyway. I'll do another one next year, with the new baby."

We hugged and they went home, now that they'd eaten and helped pay Mary's bills. I put away my supplies. It was too dark to keep drawing and my jar was full. My stomach wasn't. I wanted to get to the brownies before they were all gone.

Then Piet brought me one on a napkin. "How are you doing?"

"Great." I showed him the jar. "What about you?"

"Trying to remember half the people I got introduced to. Nice folks. Trying to recover from all the food people kept bringing me. Good food. They took Edie away, so I was defenseless. I needed you by my side."

Funny, I hadn't missed him at all.

He carried my easel and paint box while I took the pad and the cash jar.

The PA system announced coffee and the auction, before a dance band took over in the firehouse. Most of the people on the grass either left or went inside.

I handed my earnings to Janie at the ticket table and

asked how we were doing. "Fantastic. And the auction will bring in more. I never expected such a turnout, or such generosity. God, I love this place."

For tonight I did, too. Until I went inside and saw Matt sitting with an older couple I did not know, which meant they were ordinary, nonsensitives. I'd seen how people shared blankets and picnic tables not by age or color or religion, but by talent. That bothered me, but I could understand wanting to be with people who understood your interests, who could not betray you without betraying themselves and their families.

Matt looked good in a long-sleeved, light blue pullover and jeans. His brown hair was curling in the damp night air, making him more boyish, but he seemed serious, keeping apart from the merriment and camaraderie. His demeanor grew cooler when we walked in and the announcer reminded people there'd be no smoking, then everyone looked in Piet's direction and laughed at the not-so-private joke. A third of the audience didn't get it.

Damn, I'd felt like an outsider here half my life, but I thought it was because I was a summer resident, not a real local. This struck me as worse.

Nothing could be done about it then, as the bidding started. The restaurant dinners went first and fast, then the baskets and gift certificates for haircuts and gas fill-ups. Piet's slow dance won a lot of laughs, and fifty dollars.

Susan started the bidding on naming a character in my book at twenty dollars, raised by my uncle, then by the mayor. Piet bid fifty dollars. People nodded. Matt bid five hundred. People gasped. I felt the heat in my cheeks and knew I looked like a tomato from my toes to my nose.

Piet turned to look at him, then me. He smiled but shook his head no. He wouldn't outbid the veterinarian.

The gavel banged. "Sold for five hundred dollars for Mary's bills to our good doctor. Make it a good character, Willy. A real hero."

Everyone laughed and applauded and threw out suggestions for what kind of hero I could name Matt Spenser. I tried to hide behind the coffee urn. That was too short. I fled to the ladies' room.

Until I heard the screams.

CHAPTER 36

SIX MONTHS AGO I would have run in the opposite direction. No, six months ago I would have cowered in the ladies' room, behind the stall door, standing on top of the toilet so no one could see my feet and know I was there.

Now the screams and shouts and breaking glass noises got louder. I got braver. These were my people: my relatives, my friends, my neighbors. I crashed out of the bathroom and ran toward the hall.

And came to a screeching halt behind Roy Ruskin, who held a pistol in one hand and two burlap bags in the other, the kind potatoes used to come in. Potato *sacks*, in fact. Not Saks.

A sinking feeling in my stomach told me what was in those sacks: the fires my father warned of, my fireflies, in the firehouse, where at least fifty people waited to dance. "Oh, shit."

I hadn't meant to screech out loud, but Roy heard me. He spun around, keeping the pistol on the crowd that dropped under tables, ran for the exits, stood still in shock. Two policemen had their hands on their weapons, but I knew they couldn't shoot with so many innocent bystanders in their way. Roy knew it, too.

"You," he yelled, pointing one sack at me. "Give me my daughter. She's mine and I want her. No one can touch me if I've got the kid."

I couldn't see around him to find Piet or Chief Haversmith. I did get a better look at Roy. His face and shaved head showed burn blisters—yup, he had the fireflies. The hand holding the sacks was bleeding; the one still waving the pistol had a filthy bandage around it. His ripped pant legs were dirty and charred in places. His eyes were way too bright for anyone in his right mind.

Reasoning with a crazed gunman on meth or something didn't make a lot of sense, but what choice did I have? "I don't have your baby, Roy. Mary's mother came up from North Carolina to care for her. I don't know where they are staying."

Three voices from the crowd yelled out: "She's telling the truth, Roy."

"They left a little while ago."

"Willow's not lying."

"See? So you're frightening all of us for nothing. Why don't you put the gun down, and the bags, and then we can find where Elladaire is. You can go visit her to see she is in good hands."

Everyone knew that was a lie. He was going to jail, no matter what. I heard one truth-seer groan. Uncle Henry belched. Roy knew my words for a lie, too. He wasn't getting out of here so easily. He kept shifting his glittery eyes from me to the others, moving to keep his back to a wall and the gun a continuous threat.

I tried to find Piet in the crowd again, to make sure he knew what was in the bags and was ready, but I still didn't see him, only a lot of frightened people and some determined cops.

Roy snarled. "You and this frigging town will keep her away from me. You took everything else. You'll make her into one of you freaks, besides. First you'll pay, you especially, bitch."

He set one of the sacks down and started to swing the other against the wall. "No!" I screamed. They couldn't start fires, not in Piet's range, but they'd be hurt and angry. M'ma wouldn't trust us anymore. "Don't do it!"

Roy gave me an evil grin, showing a missing tooth and a swollen tongue. "You want me to do this one instead?" He picked up the other bag, which bulged and twitched and barked.

Barked? I recognized that high-pitched yelp. I screamed: "Not my dog!" The bastard had been at my house to gather more fireflies. He'd broken in; that's why his pants were torn and his hand was bloody. God, what if he'd set it on fire? The old dogs—my mother would kill me!—and Grandma's house—but Little Red!

"He didn't do anything to you!"

That same truth-seer groaned again. Oh, yeah, the blood, the likely tooth marks on Roy's ankle.

"Okay, but he was defending himself. Roy, there's no reason to hurt the dog." I held my hands out, begging, trying to make my voice heard over the sob in my throat. "Please, please give him back to me."

Roy laughed. He started to swing the bag back. He was going to smash my poor little abused dog against the concrete wall. I couldn't look. I had to look.

What I saw was Matt launching himself over a table and snagging the burlap bag before it hit the wall.

Roy gave a bloodcurdling howl, let go of the sack, and fired wildly at Matt. Everyone screamed. A ceiling light shattered, raining glass down on the crowd. "Get down, get down," I heard Chief Haversmith order.

I got down, trying to reach the other sack before Roy did. He kicked me in the head, knocking me into Matt, who held Little Red under his body, protecting him.

I felt blood running down my face, into my eyes to mix with the tears, but I still fought to reach the bag of beetles. The bag was smoking. Where the hell was Piet?

Roy grabbed the sack away and ripped it open, then he threw it to the ground and raised one foot to step on it . . . not to put out the flames shooting out.

"No!" I screamed and grabbed his leg before it touched the ground. He aimed the gun at me. I tried to apologize for all my sins and failures in the half second I had left to live, but a shot fired out. Not at me. Roy jerked away and lurched toward the door.

"Don't let the bastard get away!" the chief bellowed. "But only shoot again if you've got a clear target, Shaw."

I'd forgotten about Robin Shaw, the best marksman or -woman in the county. She'd saved my life. But she kicked the burlap bag out of her way when she raced after Ruskin.

If there was panic before, there was bedlam now. The beetles were hurt and angry and frightened and sending sparks everywhere in the enclosed space. People were trampling each other to get away, batting at their hair and clothes.

"Where the hell is Piet?"

Someone shouted that he'd carried Elladaire to her grandmother's car.

"Call him!"

Someone else ran for a fire extinguisher. This was the firehouse, after all.

By now the big American flag over the door was in flames. So was a coatrack filled with jackets and sweaters. A small fire burned in the garbage pail, and a table-cloth under the auction items ignited. Women cried, men swore, everyone reached for water to throw at the flames, and for ladles and towels to swat at the bugs. Some got burned.

"No, don't hurt them!" I cried. "That will make things worse."

I didn't know if I shouted to the people or the bugs. It worked both ways. No one listened to me.

Matt handed me the shivering dog. I was shivering, too, too hard to say anything but "You saved my dog."

"Great. Now what should I do?"

He was right. We weren't done yet. "Get them to stop trying to hurt the luminaries. Tell the people to be quiet so I can talk to the beetles."

He whistled—the loudest whistle I'd ever heard. "Stop. Stand still. The fireflies won't bother you if you leave them alone. Willow needs quiet."

The Paumanok Harborites who knew what was going on—the sensitives—hushed the others. Healers took the hands of those most hurt or frightened. Aunt Jasmine took Little Red from me.

I closed my eyes. *Come to me, guys. Come to Willow. I'll take you to M'ma.* I flashed pictures of him, the way I'd last seen him, then the way I'd first seen his image, like a sky dolphin in lights. *I am so sorry one of us hurt you. Come, I won't let anyone else do so.* I held my hands out again, begging again.

Tiny flames started toward me, then went out.

"What the f—" Piet yelled, then went around making sure all the other fires were out.

The firemen and -women started herding the crowd out, setting up a triage station for the EMTs and the healers and the empaths to work in the parking lot. Matt handed me the now empty brownie tray, with three beetles on it. I plucked two more unlighted fireflies from my hair, one off my shoulder. "There you go, guys. Safe. Call your friends."

Then I called directions to the people who were leaving, those checking on the fires, the few espers who were gingerly trying to gather the bugs, now that they weren't small torches. "Be careful where you step. Hold them carefully."

Big firemen, little old ladies, two community-service teenagers, and the blind postman cautiously handed me beetles. They all smiled. Some could see the pretty colors; some could sense the relief and the gratitude. Others were simply glad they got to touch a once-in-a-lifetime creature.

I prayed it was once-in-a-lifetime! I doubted I could live through another encounter.

Susan pressed a wad of napkins against my scalp to stop the bleeding. "You've really gone and done it now," she said, but she dabbed at my face to wipe the blood and tears away. Janie held a glass of water to my parched lips. Someone else tucked a sweater around my shoulders.

Now I could see that some of the beetles were injured, a few barely moving. All I could do was try to send encouraging thoughts to them. I hoped M'ma could fix them.

No one could fix Roy Ruskin, I heard.

When Piet returned from the parking lot, he had seen Roy running from the firehouse. Officer Shaw shouted at Piet to get down, then fired, but guns were another thing that didn't work around Piet. So Piet tackled Roy, then the other police piled on, with a plumber and an accountant adding their weight and their fury.

Shaw's first shot had been aimed to stop Roy, not kill him. It struck a thigh artery, though. The ambulance corps tried to put a tourniquet on the wound, but they were too late. No one mourned his passing except Robin, who fainted.

They covered Roy with one of the singed tablecloths, then stationed cops to guard his body until the medical examiner could be sent out from up island, hours away.

Mayor Applebaum went around talking to nonsensitive villagers, reassuring them that everything was under control and the madman with the matches couldn't start any more fires.

I waved him away from Matt, who had his vet bag out to examine Little Red. I watched, holding the brownie tray and my breath until he declared the Pom okay but in shock, which is how Matt could handle him at all. Little Red had blood on his ear and his snout, but there was no telling whose blood it was. He might have a broken rib, so Matt was going to take him back to the clinic for X-rays as soon as he knew I'd be all right, too.

The EMTs mopped up the gash on my temple from Roy's boot and declared it minor, just a scalp wound that bled a lot. No stitches, thank goodness. I might have a headache, they said, so I should go home and rest.

With a tray full of traumatized beetles in my lap? "I promised to take them to M'ma."

Hurry. Soon.

A couple of the telepaths must have picked up the urgency if not the words. They ran to get cars and help.

Piet nodded to Mac, the fire captain, who called out to Uncle Henry. They both sent signals out to all their men and women. Matt said he'd meet us at the salt marsh after taking care of Little Red. No one argued with him. Susan brought me a carton to lay the brownie tray in, to make it safer for the beetles that couldn't fly. I sent her home to check on the house and Grandma Eve, who'd left with Lou before the auction.

Everyone else piled on the fire trucks parked outside or got in the cop cars and unneeded ambulances. Piet and I and the beetles rode in Mac's SUV.

I wasn't sure M'ma would like all the tumult and the crowd, but the *Hurry. Soon.* kept getting more intense. The beetles in the box started to stir and show agitation. A couple of the strongest ones flew out the car window, headed in the same direction we were.

"Tell him we're coming," I called after them.

Heaven knew what we'd find.

Hurry. Now.

Now?

"Put on the sirens, Mac."

CHAPTER 37

THE HEADACHE THEY SAID I might get? I got
it. The flashing lights, the piercing sirens, the speed,
the bumpy roads, the urgency. And I think one of the
beetles died on the way. The color faded, and it blinked
out of sight. Or I was concussed and hallucinating.

Mac jounced the chief's car through the gate and
right down that widened path to a few hundred feet
from M'ma's glow. The others had to leave the big rigs
up by the parking area and carry equipment and floodlights down the path or wait for the ATVs to arrive.

Mac, Piet, and I, still holding the carton as if it were
a heart ready for transfer, walked closer. The glow
went out.

Mac and Piet had flashlights, and the full moon was
out. We had no trouble finding the mass that was M'ma.
No maggots crawled over his smooth, sleek outline. A
few faded-looking Coleoptera hovered over him. Several of the ones on my tray rose to join them. The others
disappeared into the night or the ether.

I knelt by M'ma and put one hand on his skin. It felt
warm, alive. Suddenly my headache disappeared, and
the shivering, too. "Is it time?" I asked, picturing him in
the sky, not stuck in the mud on earth.

The same picture came back to me, in colors I could never duplicate, with the sound Matt must have heard when he listened to a heartbeat. "What can we do to help?"

He smiled, in my head. It was such a strange feeling, but not threatening, not intrusive. Just a friend sharing a joke, as if we puny humans could hardly assist a being from Unity, but thanks for the offer.

As the others arrived, they must have asked the same question, and I wondered if M'ma answered or conversed with people far more attuned to communication across ordinary boundaries. No one said anything. They all filed past, each laying a reverent hand on his side, then they started to dig out the channel around him, using shovels or just their hands. Bill, from the hardware store, used his telekinesis to move the mud faster, but everyone helped. I stayed kneeling beside M'ma, waiting for a sign that he was ready, or growing annoyed at our silly efforts.

"Do you see the colors?" I asked Piet, who studied the large form.

"A little, I think, if I squint."

"He's beautiful. All technicolor with changing highlights."

"Maybe you're seeing stars after getting kicked in the head."

"I don't think so."

They had the channel almost cleared all the way to the water, where the full moon tide nearly obliterated the narrow beach.

"Should we bring the water into the ditch?" a couple of the weather mavens asked. In tandem with the water wizards and Bill, they could move a current anywhere they needed. I asked M'ma. Those were easy pictures, water flowing around him, over him, so he floated.

You cannot breathe water. The picture I saw had people floundering, falling, maybe drowning.

"We can move back."

Stay. Friends.

Okay, no water. I gave the order, and everyone stood around, waiting. I took the opportunity to ask where the missing fireflies were. "Did they die? I know some burned in Roy's fires, but not all." I had no mental picture except a beetle on its back, feet in the air, wings not moving.

Home.

Ah. His peaceful acceptance made me feel better, that and knowing my fiery friends weren't as short-lived as ordinary, earthly insects. They lived on in their home world.

Then Matt arrived with a flashlight and knelt beside me. I could feel the disapproval of those around me, but they didn't dare comment or try to get rid of the un-psi vet. I didn't care if he was a plain, ordinary man. He'd saved my dog. He'd stood by me to visit M'ma. "Red?"

"Red will be fine. He is sleeping off a sedative. I'll check on him later and bring him home to you."

I touched his hand. "Thank you. For everything."

Embarrassed, he said, "The creature looks better."

"Do you see colors?"

"Try squinting," Piet suggested, from my other side.

Matt shone his flashlight directly at M'ma. "Just gray, but shinier."

Piet seemed pleased that the interloper didn't see as much as he had. Then Matt took out his stethoscope and listened. "The odd sounds are a lot stronger."

He handed the stethoscope to me. I heard the surf breaking on the shore, a breeze through an aspen tree, snow falling, rocks tumbling, birds singing, a baby's laughter, a rabbit's heartbeat, a butterfly's wings beating, rain, humpback whale songs, and a hundred, no a thousand more sounds. Stunned, I passed the instrument to Piet.

He didn't say anything, but he let someone else take the stethoscope. Phyllis the clairvoyant listened, then whispered, "It's the music of the spheres. Shakespeare wrote about it." Her eyes glistened with tears.

Earth. Life.

"Yes. Thank you."

Everyone took a turn. Some heard the music, some just random noises. They each said thank you. To M'ma? Me? Matt? I didn't know, but I was grateful to have heard it, too.

Then we waited. Nothing happened, no movement, no words, no lights, no images. Some of the Harborites looked disappointed. A few walked back to the parking area. They'd seen enough and the night had grown cold.

I sat in the dirt and let my mind float, waiting for whatever was going to happen. I couldn't control it, couldn't stop it, couldn't speed it along, couldn't understand it. That felt right, too.

Restless, Piet started pacing around. The others clustered in groups, talking quietly among themselves. Matt stayed by my side. After an hour of waiting with nothing changing, I asked why in the world he'd bid so much to name a character in my book.

He shrugged. "It was for a good cause."

"So do you want to be the hero in the book?"

"Not really. I, ah, want to be a hero in your eyes."

That had to be one of the nicest things anyone had ever said to me. I started to reply, but M'ma shifted and raised his front half. People jumped farther away.

Now I could see he did resemble a huge dolphin, although not perfectly. His eyes were closed, but he opened a cavernous mouth. Thousands of glistening fireflies flew out, all 3,549 of them. They hovered an inch or so above their host. We all held our breaths.

An hour later, M'ma shook out those six appendages and brought two to his back, where wings might be positioned. Two more surely looked like fins at his sides, and the last two might have been legs, or a split tail.

Another hour went by before M'ma opened his eyes. I heard the gasps of wonder around me when people saw orbs as big as car tires, all swirling gold and blue and green, like the music of the heavens if a master artist tried to paint it.

"What?" Matt wanted to know. "Why is everyone's mouth hanging open?"

He didn't see it and I had no way to describe it. I should have brought my pad and charcoals, but I knew I'd never be able to duplicate eyes full of such coruscating colors, but also wisdom and benevolence. M'ma gazed around at all of us and liked what he saw. I knew that the same as I knew my name. A few others seemed to also. They smiled.

More time went by, but M'ma did not rise; the newborn beetles lost their sparkle.

Someone asked "What should we do?"

I remembered M'ma telling me that they got here, they could get out, but my neighbors went back to excavating the area around him, careful of the flying juveniles, but determined to help this amazing creature complete his journey.

I sensed M'ma's appreciation for their efforts, tinged with amusement. Then his amusement turned to concern. Something wasn't working.

"What's wrong?" I demanded.

All I saw in my mind was a raging blaze. In his incredible knowing eyes I saw flames, orange and red and yellow, hot and reaching higher.

"He needs the fire." I looked at Piet. "You have to go."

"What, not see something no man has ever seen? After all this? Not on your life."

"Then control your fire-damping. Turn it off."

"Damn it, you know it doesn't work that way."

Damn it, all right. I dragged him by his shirt a little bit away from the others. Then I shrugged off my sweater, grabbed the hem of my black lace-trimmed camisole top, and pulled it up. For king and country and all that.

His eyes opened wider, and the night grew brighter behind me. People murmured, at the sudden lights or my flashing Piet. Unfortunately, the glow grabbed his attention far more than my less-than-lush bra-less boobs could. That ship had sailed. The lights went out again.

I told him to go back to the highway. He'd be able to see the fireworks I expected from there. He nodded. I started weeping again. Both of us knew he would not be coming back.

He brushed a tear off my cheek. "I almost loved you, Willow Tate."

"Me, too, almost."

"It wasn't meant to be."

"No, no matter what the people at Royce thought."

He held me close. "We are too different. Our lives are too different."

I wrapped my arms around him. "And we're not puppets, with them pulling the strings."

"We showed them, didn't we?"

"Yup. Our lives can't be foreordained, right?"

He shook his head. "I don't believe in it."

"You do believe we did something good here, though?" I waved one hand back toward M'ma and the villagers.

"I believe in you, Willow. I hope you find what you're looking for."

"You, too, Piet Doorn."

He stepped back, leaving my arms empty and my heart sore. "Me? All I'm looking for is the next fire."

"Be careful."

"And you stay out of trouble."

"I'll try," I said to his back as he strode away, back up the path. With every step he took, the lights grew brighter until he was out of sight and the whole sky filled with three thousand plus lightning bugs, each a living, dancing, joyous flame. They made circles and waterfalls and bursting chrysanthemums. They made bouquets and hearts and leaping fish and flying birds.

Grucci, eat your heart out.

Then M'ma rose. No one made a sound. The fireflies landed on him, so he was an entire wall of fire, somewhat dolphin shaped, but in the sky, with wide wings ablaze.

Farewell, my friend.

"Wait! Can you tell me why you came?"

To meet you, of course.

Now I hoped no one else heard him. "Me?"

I caught images of the elf king and the stallion. *You see.*

"But others saw H'ro and J'omree."

Now the images pictured the halfling Nicky and his troll half brother, and the little lost colt, H'tah. *You see with your heart.*

Ah. While he was answering questions, I tried to think of everything I wanted to know. "How often must you do this . . . this metamorphosis?"

Centuries by your time.

"But why come here? Surely your own world would be a better birthplace for the beetles, a better locale for your transformation."

It is a time of grave danger and vulnerability, for us all. An old enemy rises.

"For us, too? Did you come to warn us? Help us?" But he was high overhead now.

Matt stood beside me, looking up. "Where did the creature go, Willy? Did it blow up in the fireworks?"

I wished Matt could see M'ma, that he could be part of the magic.

For an instant M'ma seemed to change into a winged human form, outlined in fire. His laughter rumbled across the sky. *Love is the only magic that matters.*

I heard Matt's *ooh* of awe.

"You can see it!"

"Great gods, I cannot believe what I am looking at."

"Believe it. He's only a minor god, though, I believe."

"And I am not going crazy?"

I laughed. "No, but you are going to be a bigger part of Paumanok Harbor, though."

"You did that, for me."

I laughed. "No, M'ma did it. In gratitude."

Matt took my hand while we watched the flaming god turn back into a sea creature and dive with his brilliant companions into the bay water. The starburst disappeared beneath the waves.

I knew right then that's how I was going to tell my next story, with the sea god changing forms to look after his people, his children. He'd keep them safe against every danger, dragon, and ancient evil. He'd sing the music of the world as their lullaby until they were grown, then let them fly away in a blaze of joy. I'll call it LIFE GUARDS IN THE HAMPTONS.

Matt Spenser'd make a good hero.

1/12